TEMPTED BY HER OUTCAST VIKING

Lucy Morris

MILLS & BOON

First published in Great Britain 2022
by Mills & Boon, an imprint of HarperCollins*Publishers* Ltd,
1 London Bridge Street, London, SE1 9GF

www.harpercollins.co.uk

HarperCollins*Publishers*
1st Floor, Watermarque Building,
Ringsend Road, Dublin 4, Ireland

Tempted by Her Outcast Viking © 2022 Lucy Morris

ISBN: 978-0-263-30193-9

09/22

MIX
Paper from
responsible sources
FSC™ C007454

This book is produced from independently certified FSC™ paper
to ensure responsible forest management.
For more information visit www.harpercollins.co.uk/green.

Printed and Bound in Spain using 100% Renewable Electricity
at CPI Black Print, Barcelona

Lucy Morris lives in Essex, UK, with her husband, two young children and two cats. She has a massively sweet tooth and loves gin, bubbly and Irn-Bru. She's a member of the UK Romantic Novelists' Association, and was delighted when Mills & Boon accepted her manuscript after she'd submitted her story to the Warriors Wanted! blitz for Viking, Medieval and Highlander romances. Writing for Mills & Boon Historical is a dream come true for her, and she hopes you enjoy her books!

Also by Lucy Morris

The Viking Chief's Marriage Alliance
A Nun for the Viking Warrior

Shieldmaiden Sisters miniseries

The Viking She Would Have Married
Tempted by Her Outcast Viking

And look out for the next book, coming soon!

Discover more at millsandboon.co.uk.

For Alma, my little shieldmaiden,
who also loves animals and bread.

Chapter One

Autumn AD *913—Jorvik River Dock*

Valda had fallen—not in battle, as was a shield-maiden's privilege, but into marriage—a fate far worse in Brynhild's mind. However, an unexpected bitterness squeezed her throat at seeing her sister so happy and she couldn't understand it. She was jealous and it made no sense to her why she should be.

Needing a distraction, Brynhild helped untie the ropes anchoring Valda and Halfdan's longship to the jetty. Once released, the magnificent dragon drifted out into the river, catching the current with ease, the rhythmic splashing of oars their last goodbye as they sailed out and into their new life together.

Brynhild firmly wrestled her envy into submission.

She was pleased for Valda, *truly she was*! It wasn't as if Brynhild wanted a rich merchant like Halfdan for herself. She didn't particularly enjoy the sea, or men for that matter, and had always known she would never marry. The fortune rune she'd picked had proven it, there was no reason to begrudge Valda her joy.

But the idea of jumping on to the nearest ship and sailing to distant lands certainly appealed to her at this moment. Of course, Brynhild could never do such a thing. Who would care for her mother and youngest sister if she did?

No one.

Being left behind to care for her family felt like a millstone around her neck. Her resentment towards them burrowed deeper within her chest like a worm and she feared she would never be free of it, the guilt of such unkind thoughts adding to her shame.

Oblivious to Brynhild's inner turmoil, Helga, her youngest sister, and Porunn, their mother, continued to wave goodbye even as Halfdan's longship followed the curving river out of sight.

'I am going to miss her so much,' sighed Porunn and Helga sniffed back tears in agreement. 'But the life of a merchant with Halfdan will suit her well. She did always love to travel…'

Yes, she did. It was why Brynhild had always stayed behind.

At least now Valda wouldn't be alone. Halfdan, the love of her life, was with her, a kindred spirit. They would explore the world together and as she was already pregnant with their first child, they would do so as their own little family. It was a life that suited Valda even if she hadn't realised it until recently.

Brynhild wasn't adventurous, she was the dependable, eldest sister who would always provide for them, no matter what. Protectively she draped her strong arms over each of their shoulders, as if they were a set of trading scales and she the central pin. They leaned into her embrace and she felt the invisible chains that tethered them to her tighten.

How much longer could she carry them?

Not often, but sometimes, she longed to be free of them.

Her gaze flickered to Halfdan's brother, Erik, and then quickly skittered away in alarm. He was staring at her again, ruining her day with his mere presence.

Of course he was!

Silently judging her in that knowing way of

his. As if those dark eyes could see into her head and see the ugly thoughts within.

Maybe that's why she was so foul tempered? Because he was here…*staring* at her.

She looked at her muddy boots quickly, the shame twisting up her insides, until she felt tied up in knots.

Did he know? How her family duty some-times felt like a burden?

When she looked up again, the dragon ship was gone, the early autumn sky bright and clear, reflecting ripples of gold in the river beneath. The dock began to bustle with noise and people, signalling the start of another day of busy trade.

Helga smiled up at the sky. 'A beautiful wedding, followed by a glorious dawn. An auspicious start for Valda and Halfdan's life together. I am so happy for her, she deserves it, she was always so lonely before…even when she was with us.'

Helga's insight startled Brynhild out of her own self-pity and she squeezed her youngest sister's shoulder in silent agreement.

No, she would never jump on a ship and sail away.

It was just the ale and tiredness making her feel glum.

Brynhild sighed and squinted against the sun. The light was beginning to hurt her eyes and her head was beginning to pound terribly. The excess of the wedding ale, combined with her lack of sleep from an entire night spent feasting, had begun to take its full vengeance on her body. Unwrapping herself from her mother and sister, she took a long drink of water from the flask at her side.

Usually, she didn't mind the responsibility, *preferred* it in some ways, taking pride in providing for them. Porunn was too old to sell her sword and Helga, too...

Brynhild looked down at her sister. She barely reached her elbow despite being a full-grown woman of one and twenty winters. In comparison Brynhild had seen eight and twenty winters, as well as battle—and she felt ancient for it. They were as different as night and day.

Helga was pretty and delicate. Her eyes shone with delight, happy as a child after their first taste of honey. Valda's love match had only added to Helga's usually cheerful and optimistic mood.

The wedding ceremony aboard Halfdan's extravagant ship, followed by the magnificent feast, would have thrilled Helga. She loved passionate declarations and all things romantic. She'd even insisted on putting a crown of flowers in Valda's hair and had sighed dreamily over her Byzantine silk bridal gown.

'It was so…*wonderful!*' sighed Helga, smiling wistfully as she wrapped her willowy arms around herself.

Brynhild smothered a groan.

Helga would be chattering about this until Ragnarök—the end of the world and possibly the start of the next. Her romantic heart would be invincible against all sense and reason. They would be tripping over love potions and runes for years to come. If it were for Helga alone, then Brynhild wouldn't have minded. But, no, Helga was convinced a great love was destined for each of them and Valda's marriage only confirmed her beliefs.

All because of a silly dream and a rune game they'd played in their youth.

The idea was ridiculous, but she didn't wish to remind her sister of the harsh realities of life. It would be like squashing a butterfly or whipping a horse. Cruel and pointless. Better to let her keep her dreams and the small happiness it gave her.

Helga was everything Brynhild was not. Soft, gentle and feminine.

Weak.

As soon as the thought pierced Brynhild's mind, she pushed it aside, guilt twisting her stomach in knots once more. It was wrong to think of her like that, she was different, not weak.

Fresh remorse washed through her, making the blood in her ears pound faster.

Her sister was not a burden and neither was her mother! she reminded herself.

They looked after each other, in their own ways. Yes, Brynhild tended to earn the most silver as a mercenary, but they each had their parts to play. Her mother hunted and Helga looked after the home. They worked as a team, she reminded herself firmly—like a shield wall, together they stood strong.

Unable to help herself, she looked back at Erik, pleased that he was the first to look away this time. He stood slightly away from them on the dock, part of the remaining wedding guests, but not standing with them as kinsman...even though that was now what they were. But that was Erik's way, always an outsider, even in his own family. A dark lonely shadow in the morning light.

For some reason that irritated Brynhild, although she couldn't think why. It wasn't as if she wanted him to join them. Erik had never liked her—*not really.* Why should she care that he still avoided them? Or if he hated her?

His rejection no longer hurt her like it had as a young woman, because she was used to men's stupid insults by now. Usually, they were made by men intimidated by her, which made them even more pathetic in her mind.

Erik was a powerful warrior and had faced some adversities she couldn't even imagine. For him to be as narrow minded as those other useless men was so...disappointing.

She'd avoided him like a pestilence throughout the celebrations. By his grim countenance, his opinion of her had not changed in nine winters and she had no wish to drag up the past. They had both behaved badly. Been too young and hot-headed to see the errors in their judgement. He'd been cruel and she'd lashed out. Still, she didn't regret it enough to apologise.

Best not to dwell on it. If he wished to be childish and hold on to an old and ridiculous feud, so be it.

It was a time she would rather forget anyway.

She stared pointedly at the bobbing ships along the dock and tried to ignore the shiver of awareness his presence caused her. Annoyingly, she found him as attractive now as she had then, if not more so. Back then, her desire for him had been so intense and bright that his rejection had dimmed something inside of her. For years she'd brushed it aside, blaming her intense desires on her tender age at the time. But seeing him now... He was still *obscenely* attractive and it was infuriating that her body would continue to betray her!

Especially as he'd been tasked by his brother to secure a farm for her mother from another Jarl. Even Halfdan's man, Tostig, who was staying behind with Erik, had left them on some personal errand almost immediately after the celebrations had ended.

Which meant Erik now stood alone, *awkwardly.*

'I suppose you're going to need somewhere to stay...since your father disowned you?' she called out.

She'd not meant it to be unkind, only to speak the truth—so that he wouldn't have the embarrassment of having to explain himself. However, it was clear she'd failed, by her mother's and sister's horrified expressions.

Maybe she shouldn't have mentioned it?

Anyway, what did she care if he had nowhere to stay?

Erik's head rose at her tart words and she braced herself against those penetrating eyes as they locked on hers. Rich dark brown eyes, hooded by full black lashes. His gaze swept over her body and she felt dizzy, as if she were falling.

She rolled her shoulders and looked a little over his head to distract herself. 'Our hut is small, but you are welcome to sleep in Valda's space until we leave.'

She prayed to all the Gods that he would refuse.

'Yes, you are more than welcome to join us,' said Porunn with a significantly warmer tone, adding, 'We are grateful for your help...with the farm.'

He shook his raven head, his thick hair loose around his shoulders. 'I already have a place to stay. But I will walk with you to your home.'

'We can protect ourselves!' retorted Brynhild sharply.

Erik ignored her arrow and spoke respectfully to Porunn instead. 'I must know where to find you...regarding your farm.'

'Of course, and thank you, Erik,' Porunn replied. 'I think I will go hunting, get something for the pot.'

Helga smiled with her usual cheerful manner and tapped the purse at her waist. 'I will get us some fresh bread...and honey cakes! From the market as a treat. We have enough silver, thanks to Valda, and we should celebrate their marriage a little while longer. Yes?'

Porunn nodded and limped her way towards the city gate in the opposite direction while the rest of them walked further into the city towards the hut they currently called home.

Brynhild could understand why Erik needed to know where they lived, but she grew more tense with every step. The hut was embarrassing and only showed how far they'd fallen. After Valda had left with so little warning, Jarl Gunnar had halved Brynhild's silver out of spite. If it hadn't been for Halfdan's regular deliveries of food they would have certainly starved, or at least would have been forced to leave Jorvik. As it was, they'd received enough supplies to survive and had tried their best to save as much silver as possible to ensure the buying of produce and tools for their new life. Sometimes it had meant selling the food they'd received from Halfdan, but they'd managed regardless.

She had always been proud of their hard work and fortitude through difficult times. At least until Helga had given away how dire their circumstances were in front of Erik. By speaking of the fresh bread and honey cakes as a 'treat', she'd revealed their poverty to the one man she could not bear to be pitied by.

Brynhild's face was already hot with embarrassment. She regretted her unnecessary outburst straight away.

Of course he needed to know where they lived! Why did he always bring out the worst in her?

She almost considered apologising, but then remembered the cruel things he'd said all those years ago, and she'd be damned if she ever apologised to Erik Ulfsson!

Instead, she ignored him and strode forward to join Helga. But as usual she found herself struggling to slow her pace. Helga always walked everywhere as if she were in a pleasant dream. Unlike Brynhild, who—according to Valda—walked everywhere as if the ground had insulted her.

Brynhild sighed—maybe that was why she was so irritable? She already missed Valda terribly. She made her laugh.

As if reading her thoughts, Helga said, 'It will not be long until we see her again. Spring will come round in no time at all, you'll see.'

'She only returned to us a few days ago and already she's gone again.' But that was the way with Valda, always following her own path and leaving Brynhild behind.

'Don't worry.' Helga smiled thoughtfully. 'We will have plenty of distractions this winter to keep us busy.'

'I suppose so,' replied Brynhild without much enthusiasm. 'We have enough silver now to bribe a Jarl—not Gunnar, of course, I have cut ties with him, but another Jarl. A man not averse to allowing three unmarried women farm land for him.'

'And, once we have it, there will be plenty to do. We will need to build or repair the farm, plant crops and tend to our animals.'

Brynhild nodded. It would be hard work… and most tasks would be completed by her own sweat and labour. But she didn't mind that so much, she liked physical work and would gladly do it, especially if it meant a happier future for them all.

They entered the square of one of the little markets. Helga stopped at a stall selling bread and cakes and began to speak with the owner. Erik joined her and Brynhild stepped back a little, surprised that he'd been closer to them than she'd realised, a disturbing thought for any warrior. He had an annoying habit of sneaking up on her. She'd noticed it a few times at the wedding feast, but had quickly moved away whenever he'd got uncomfortably close. She was sure Valda and Halfdan would not have appreciated an argument during their celebration.

'Brynhild, may I speak with you?' Erik asked quietly, moving to her side.

She stared at him in silent shock for a moment.

He wanted to speak with her. Why? Was he determined to goad her into a fight?

She hoped not, something told her she would behave just as badly as she had then…if provoked.

She groaned, her eyes locking with his. He was *ridiculously* handsome, except for the slight bump to his nose. Satisfaction warmed her blood at the sight of it—she'd been the one to break it. Her pleasure soured when she realised it suited him in a strange way, adding a rough twist to his handsomeness.

Unlike his brother Halfdan—who was all golden and bright in his appealing looks—Erik was all darkness, his skin a darker shade, inherited from his Persian mother, as well as the raven hair and dark brown eyes.

Maybe if he'd looked a little more like his younger brother he'd have been treated better by his father? Although she doubted it. Brynhild loathed Ulf far more than even Erik, because Ulf was where Erik had learned his cruelty first hand.

Sucking in a deep breath she tried to appear unshaken, despite feeling lightheaded and jittery in his presence. She shrugged. 'Speak then.'

He glanced at Helga, who was still busy paying for her purchases. With a nod of his head, he suggested they walk further on, creating some distance between them and Helga. Brynhild followed, knowing that her sister would be able to catch up easily, as she was already gathering up her produce. They walked together for a while side by side.

'I wanted…to apologise…to you, Brynhild.'

His words were quiet and uncharacteristically hesitant.

'What?'

She stumbled a little in the muddy earth and his hand snapped around her forearm to steady her. The hairs on her arm rose as if in expectation of a storm and she shrugged it off quickly.

Well, she'd not expected that!

If he'd admonished her for making assumptions earlier, or worse, offered his aid, she could have believed it.

But to say he was sorry?

He frowned at the way she'd shrugged off his touch. As if she'd insulted him.

When she had every right to do so!

'I've been meaning to say it since we met again yesterday, but I never seemed to find the opportunity.'

She turned and strode forward, flustered and unsure of how to respond. Then she stopped for a moment and stared at the ground. He'd seemed sincere—hadn't she already thought their previous feud childish? His shadow fell across hers, their shapes on the floor merging into one.

'There is nothing to apologise for,' she said and to her surprise she meant it. She hated him for what he'd done, that much was true, but she'd also been unkind and had humiliated him…in her own way.

She moved forward, hoping he would leave it at that. But, of course, he didn't.

'I think there is.' His long stride matched her own and she felt an odd excitement rush through her veins. They were forced closer together as the twisting path between the buildings became suddenly narrower. 'I was young and still trying to prove myself to my father. A waste of time, as I later learned… But, regardless, I shouldn't have treated you as I did. I was wrong.'

How many times had she dreamt of him saying such words?

She'd always imagined them meeting again… but on the battlefield with weapons in hand, not on the muddy paths of Jorvik.

In her fantasy he'd fallen beneath her axe, after a long and epic fight. It would have been a hard-won but satisfying victory and with his dying breath he would have wheezed out those three wonderful words… *I was wrong.*

Somehow this did not feel as satisfying. It felt awkward and humiliating instead. As if she were his victim and not his equal.

Anger raced through her like lightning, burning away all reason.

She grabbed him by his broad shoulders and thrust him against the nearest wall. His hands in response locked around her biceps to steady himself, his grip firm, but not painful, and the heat that radiated from his fingers only angered her further, because of the effect it had on her. It caused her body to warm and her breath to catch in her throat, shivers of longing twisted in her gut and she thrust him back a second time, the plaster on the little house cracking and crumbling with the force.

'I don't like you!' she snarled, 'I've never liked you! So, let's make this very clear. I do not *care* if you are sorry or not! Just do as you've promised and get my mother a *damn* farm!'

They stared at one another, their breathing heavy and the tension between them thick in the silence. Their big bodies filled the space of the alley, making the wattle and daub buildings seem even more fragile and small, neither of them willing to back down, their bodies held in a tight balance of frustration and stubborn pride.

The dark pools of his eyes locked with hers and then dropped ever so slowly to her mouth. 'There was a time when you liked me…'

Her face burned and she almost shoved him for a third time against the wall, not that it seemed to affect the big ox…which only irritated her further.

But then he frowned and looked away from her as if a sudden thought had distracted him. 'Where is your sister?'

Brynhild stepped away, dropping his arms as his question drew her back to the present. 'She was just behind us,' she muttered, stumbling back down the path in a confused daze. But there was no sign of her sister.

Helga wasn't a natural fighter, although she'd been trained far more than most women. A prick of awareness shivered down Brynhild's spine and she hurried out of one alley and straight into the next, fear chasing quickly at her heels.

How had she got so distracted? Been so stupid?

Helga wore a heavy purse of silver now and therefore was more vulnerable to thieves, and if she were outnumbered…

Brynhild began to run, the heavy boots of Erik following close behind. As the path twisted, she jerked to a halt with a gasp. The air was ripped from her lungs as her vision narrowed at the sight in front of her and all else was forgotten in that terrible moment.

'*No,*' she whispered.

Dimly she heard Erik skidding behind her. He grabbed the walls of the narrow alley at either side of her head, to stop himself from knocking straight into her. She had never been paralyzed by fear in battle, but she was now, terror locking her muscles as she stood on the precipice of disaster, unable to take another step forward until her mind could accept the awful truth.

'What is it?' he gasped, looking over her shoulder to see what had caused her to stop dead in her tracks.

On the ground was Helga's basket, fresh bread and honey cakes scattered in the mud. But most disturbingly of all was her sister's dagger thrust through a scrap of linen and into the loaf of bread. Drawn in charcoal on the material was the image of a dragon. The air was sucked from her lungs as she realised her sister's prophecy had come true.

Someone had taken Helga.

Chapter Two

Erik stared at the fallen basket as cold dread washed through him. Helga wasn't lost or distracted; she was gone. He watched the emotions ripple across Brynhild's face: confusion, disbelief, horror and, worse of all, guilt.

Brynhild felt the responsibility of her family keenly—he could only imagine the pain she must be feeling at this moment. Imagine, and curse himself for his part in causing it. He had hoped to reconcile with her, to remedy his past mistakes. Instead, he had caused more harm and for what? Because he'd been too proud to apologise in front of Helga? If only he'd waited until they were back at their home to apologise…

She would never forgive him, or herself, if Helga was harmed.

But who would take Helga?

When terrible things happened, his first thought was always, *Ulf.*

Could this be Ulf's revenge against Halfdan for defying him and marrying Valda? Would he steal her away? But to what end? Surely, if it were purely revenge, he would have killed Helga without a second thought? Slit her throat while she slept, or attack all of the shieldmaiden family with force? But to just take her? That didn't seem right.

And yet, who else would kidnap her?

Walking around the paralyzed Brynhild, he went to the scattered belongings and removed the dagger from the bread. The strange charcoal drawing was still attached to the blade and he pulled it off.

A dragon.

He knew of only one man that called himself the dragon. His spirit sank in his chest like a cold stone. His instinct had been right after all. Ulf was responsible...indirectly.

Brynhild stumbled past him, her face ashen. They were at a crossroads and her wild eyes darted down each of the four paths, as she tried to make sense of what had happened.

'Helga!' she shouted, the sound reverberating against weak walls and hitting only silence. 'Helga!'

She ran from alley to alley, searching the mud for tracks. The earth was so churned from the autumn rain that it was difficult to see anything in the sludge. The city, usually clamouring with noise and people, seemed oddly empty.

There was no sense in deciphering tracks in the filth beneath their feet. Erik looked at the walls, paying close attention to the areas that would have been within Helga's reach.

'Brynhild!' he shouted, pointing at a section of the wattle and daub wall at the entrance of an alley. It looked as if a small hand had raked through the woven wood and clay, desperately trying to cling on as the person was dragged away.

Without a word they both began to run down the path. Up ahead at a fork in the road several children were playing with wooden swords.

'Have you seen a woman brought through here? Small and fair. Which way was she taken?' barked Brynhild, and several children stared up at her with slack jaws.

'They went that way!' said one of the older boys, pointing ahead with his sword.

Again, Erik and Brynhild ran, winding quickly

through the narrow walkways. But he was losing hope with each passing step. Especially when he realised the path led straight back to the little market square.

Brynhild darted from one stallholder to another, asking questions. But no one had seen Helga since she'd bought her bread and cakes.

Had the children sent them down the wrong path?

Even if they hadn't lied, there were several homes and workshops Helga could have been hidden in along the way.

Running around in circles was getting them nowhere.

'Brynhild,' he said, but she was already marching towards another stallholder.

'Brynhild!' he repeated, this time gripping her arm and turning her to face him, forcing her to focus on his next words. 'Do you know anyone who might have taken her?' He only asked because he wished there were another possibility.

She stopped and stared at him, her beautiful sapphire eyes wide with despair and shock. 'No one, no one would take Helga... She's so... *good*...' He winced at the way her voice cracked on the word *good*. To see her lost and tormented like this caused his protective instincts to surge forward in his blood like a tide.

'We will find her,' he said immediately, hoping to reassure her. But then guilt pricked at his nerves. He should never have offered such a false promise.

'They cannot have got far. Helga would fight back. She's not the best at it, but she knows what to do…she will not make it easy for them.' As she spoke her face became paler and he knew that her thoughts were only making her worry worse.

'Ulf may know…something. I will go to him.'

Her head jerked up like a wolf smelling blood. She was too quick-witted not to notice his suspicions. 'Why him?'

'He may have heard something…'

She grabbed his arm in a pinching grip. '*Why?* Do *you* know something?'

'No.'

Her eyes searched his face and he found he could not lie to her, so with a grim sigh he said, 'At least… I hope not. Ulf was very angry when Halfdan walked away from the marriage he'd arranged for him…'

'And, what? He's taken his revenge out on… *Helga? Why?*'

'I do not know.'

'If he's hurt her, I'll skin him alive!' she snarled, looking at him with such fury he almost pitied his father.

'I think it is more than that. But if he *has* taken her, then I will hold him down while you sharpen your knife,' he said firmly.

She blinked with surprise, the strength of her anger suddenly lost to her. 'You would?'

'The man means nothing to me.'

Her head tilted slightly, her eyes as clear as the ocean and just as deep. So deep, in fact, that a man could drown within them if he wasn't careful. 'I don't think that's true,' she said softly.

'I despise him!' he said, his stomach lurching with revulsion.

'Then he is not *nothing*, is he?' she said perceptively, but before he could react to that cutting statement, she strode forward towards the path that led to the Jarls' Square. 'I will see what your father has to say about it myself.'

Erik followed; he didn't need to lead the way. Brynhild knew this city better than he, having spent almost a year here already, whereas he barely knew it from only a handful of trading visits.

The lack of people within the city streets became more apparent as they approached the central square, the place where the Jarls of the city lived. It looked as if every Jorvik warrior was there this morning. Erik's stomach churned with growing apprehension.

As the path widened and they weaved through the mingling crowd, Brynhild suddenly stopped, her head slowly turning to focus on a row of closed-up workshops opposite them. Abandoned and beyond repair, they looked like squat drunken men leaning against each other for balance.

Erik moved to stand beside her, trying to see what held her gaze. 'Should we search them?'

Brynhild shifted slightly and, within the blink of an eye, her axe was in her hand. Without a word he unsheathed his own sword. Although he could not see what had alerted her, he did not question her instincts. In his experience, women had always had the ability to see the unseen.

She took a single step forward and a rooster flew out from one of the holes in the workshop's wall, screeching angrily in a spray of feathers. Followed quickly by another hen. They pecked at each other in a flurry before settling down to scratch in the mud. The tension in his spine dropped, and he glanced at Brynhild who was still staring at the birds with narrowed eyes, even as she sheathed her axe, slotting its curved blade into the leather pouch at her belt and tightening the strap tie with a sharp tug.

More people hurried past them on the way towards the square and she focused her attention back on the crowds.

'I think Ulf is leaving...' he muttered in disbelief, when he saw the horses and a horde of warriors gathering outside Ulf's Hall. He'd said it more to himself than to Brynhild, shocked at his sudden departure.

Was his father going to war and was this all connected with Helga's disappearance?

He had an uneasy feeling it was.

Would he never be free of this evil man?

'Then we should hurry,' she growled, breaking out into a sprint towards the Hall.

Maybe Brynhild was right and that hating his father was a strange kind of caring?

To be truly free, he should be indifferent towards him. Walk away and never look back. But he'd promised Halfdan that he would look after Valda's family, and besides, he owed Brynhild his loyalty, so he rushed to join her.

Warriors were everywhere, all heavily armed, and packing horses with even more weapons and supplies. She pushed through until she was within sight of Ulf.

'Are you going to war, Jarl Ulf?' called out Brynhild as she slowed to a standstill outside Ulf's Hall, her breath tight in her chest, not from fear or exhaustion, but from anger.

By Odin, she would have answers!

He was surrounded by a personal guard. She recognised some of the men from Gunnar's retinue, as well as several mercenaries she'd had previous dealings with. Some were decent men—the majority, however, were led by coin rather than by honour.

Ulf moved from a heavily laden wagon of silver to meet her, his expression as hard as iron. He was an older, more bitter version of Half-dan. Blond, slightly greying hair, cut short with a long fringe at the front just visible around the helm he wore. Clean shaven, scarred and weathered. He might have been called handsome once, but the permanent sneer of disapproval on his face twisted his features into something predatory and cruel.

'I am abandoning this foul pit. Jorvik has been a great disappointment,' Ulf replied, his eyes sliding over Erik with disgust.

She ignored the shiver down her spine and stepped forward. 'My sister, Helga, is missing.'

Ulf laughed, the sound dry and mocking. 'And what has that to do with me?'

'We are kin now.'

His eyes flashed with disgust. 'Not in my mind. You shieldmaidens are nothing to me. Halfdan is gone and I no longer have a son.'

'But do you know anything about it?' asked Erik, his voice a deep rumble of thunder beside her.

Ulf stared with narrow eyes at the son he refused to acknowledge. 'I know Halfdan caused many problems, and not only with me, when he left with that *whore.*' He smiled slowly when he saw Brynhild stiffen. He walked forward, until he was almost eye to eye with her—not many men were. In fact, Ulf, Halfdan and Erik were some of the few men who could match her in height. He stared at her, his face creased with disgust and his sour breath hot on her skin causing her stomach to churn.

She refused to show weakness by moving away. Even though he spoke to Erik his full attention remained on Brynhild, his spittle hitting her face. 'If I were you, Erik, I would avoid these *unnatural* women at all costs. However, I doubt a beast such as this one could tempt any man, even a beggar like you…'

The men around them became still, quietly watching the exchange with anticipation. If she argued there would be bloodshed and Brynhild cared more about Helga's well-being than petty insults.

She smiled slowly, watching with satisfaction as Ulf's eyes narrowed with pent-up rage. 'So… Who else has a grievance against my brother-in-law besides you, *old man*?'

Anger flared to life in his ice-blue eyes and she felt a hand grab her arm and drag her backwards. Not expecting an attack from behind, she stumbled a little as Erik pushed his body between hers and Ulf's.

'Just tell us what you know!' Erik shouted into his father's face, grabbing the man's attention from her with a swiftness she was sure was deliberate on his part. She wasn't sure who she wanted to kill first, Ulf or Erik for doubting her strength.

'Why should I, *runt?*' retorted Ulf, his hand flying to the hilt of his sword.

'What has happened?' The voice that interrupted them was quiet and calm. Cutting through the tension like a blade. Brynhild herself was already reaching for her weapon and she saw that several men already had theirs in hand.

They all turned towards the commanding voice.

Tostig, Halfdan's man, stood a few feet away. Kinsman to Halfdan's dead mother, he had always seemed harmless to Brynhild, yet Ulf took a step back when he saw him. Tostig's head was tilted, his stance relaxed. She would have thought him oblivious to the tension except for the sharpness in his eyes. A stout man with a bald head, his long white beard braided to a thin taper at his waist. He'd struck Brynhild as a mild-mannered sort—if a little dour.

'Nothing!' snapped Ulf, before spitting on the ground at Erik's feet and turning away to mount his horse. His voice was hard and dismissive when he spoke again. 'I don't know anything about the little *halfwit*! There is no alliance, therefore I have been forced to take action. Lord Rhys has done the same. His sister and representative have also gone missing—no doubt after Halfdan's encouragement.'

'Does Lord Rhys think you have them? Is that why he took Helga?' asked Erik and her stomach flipped.

'He wants a hostage exchange?' It made sense. If Lord Rhys thought Ulf held his sister captive, then it would be natural for him to take a member of Ulf's family in return. Family bonds meant everything to most Norsemen. He wasn't to know that Ulf was not *normal*.

Halfdan had left with Valda and Erik was known to be an illegitimate outcast, which only left kin bound by marriage, like Valda's sisters. Stealing Helga would have been easy, especially if they'd heard about the recent wedding and had seen them at the docks. The only flaw to the Lord's plan was that he'd misjudged the kinship between Ulf and his son's new family.

Ulf sneered at her as if she were stupid. 'The man refuses to accept that his sister defied his orders and left of her own accord. This morning he demanded I return her to his fortress within a month—as if I had lied to him about her escape! If he thinks to force my hand by taking your sister, then the man is an idiot!'

Tostig glared at Ulf and strode forward. 'How did you leave it with the Welsh Lord?'

Ulf gestured to the army around him in triumph. 'Look around you, Tostig! How do you think I left it? I am going to war. I have plenty of silver now, nothing can stop me. He dares to threaten me?' He laughed. 'I had gathered my own hostages well before the breakdown of this proposed alliance. I will order their deaths as soon as I arrive at my fort in the west.' He looked meaningfully at Brynhild. 'Within a month, I will have amassed an army that will crush this *Black Dragon Lord* into the dirt. I will rule the Western mountains.' His eyes were still fixed on Brynhild and a slow smile passed across his face, freezing the blood in her veins. 'Should I find your sister among the rubble… I will send her bones to you for burial.'

Chapter Three

$\sim\!\!\infty\!\!\sim$

The three of them watched Ulf leave in grim silence.

What more could be said?

Ulf was not a man to be reasoned with. Her sister's life now depended solely on their ability to negotiate with the Welsh Lord. A man Brynhild had never met and who thought nothing of kidnapping an innocent young woman.

She shivered, chilled to the bone as Ulf's impressive force left the square. How had things turned so sour in only a few hours? This morning she'd been waving goodbye to one sister and now both of them were gone.

She took a moment to assess the long procession of warriors. Some were on horseback, others on foot, all heavily armed. Large carts rattled through the muck with them, piled high with supplies and Ulf's silver. A formidable force, but at least he had no boats. It would make his travel over land slow and tiresome with such an army.

That would give them *some* time at least.

'Where is your mother?' asked Tostig with a frown of concern and Brynhild felt another wave of dread wash through her, a little like the foreboding she'd felt when she'd passed by those workshops earlier. Somehow telling her mother would make everything that had happened seem terribly real.

'She went hunting, but by now she will be back…*home.*' Brynhild's voice stumbled over the last word. For once not because she was embarrassed by it, but because it made a ball of grief swell in her throat and tears burn the backs of her eyes.

Helga had made it their home.

She cleared her throat and raised her head, pushing her emotions deep down where they belonged. She needed to focus on helping Helga, not mourning her loss.

She's not dead yet, stupid! she reprimanded herself sharply. 'I must go to Porunn and explain everything that has happened.'

Tostig nodded thoughtfully. 'I will ask around

here. See if there is any more information regarding this Welsh Lord and his demands. I will speak with the Jarls, ask them to search all those leaving the city.' He paused, before asking gently. 'I am sorry to ask this… But are you certain she was taken? Could she not have got lost, or visited a friend instead?'

Brynhild shook her head. 'My sister is a daydreamer, that much is true. But she would not drop her basket and leave us without saying a word. There was also a symbol left behind by her captor, a black dragon.'

'The Welsh Lord's symbol,' added Erik and Brynhild felt a rise of irritation.

'Yes, *obviously*,' she retorted.

Tostig interrupted her murderous glaring at Erik with a pragmatic question. 'Where is your home? I will come to you before nightfall— hopefully with better tidings.'

Brynhild quickly gave directions, hating how easily Erik's presence distracted her. 'We live near the tanners, so ask any of them about us and they will guide you to our plot.'

Tostig nodded and headed towards one of the nearest Halls. Brynhild began to walk briskly back towards her home, but cursed under her breath when Erik fell into step beside her.

'I will come with you to see your mother,' he said.

'There is no need.' Her jaw ached as she ground out the words.

For the love of all the gods would he just leave her alone?

'Your sister went missing under my protection. I am duty bound to—'

She turned on him. 'She went missing under *my* protection!' Brynhild shouted, banging her chest with her fist. *'Mine!'* A passing trader gave a surprised yelp at her sudden movement and danced away from them in alarm. She tempered her voice, but kept a biting threat behind her words as she stepped nearer to him. 'She is my responsibility, *not yours!* Your family has caused enough trouble as it is!'

He stepped forward, closing the space between them. So close that she could feel his breath on her lips and a warm, disconcerting sensation fluttered through her body. 'You will need all the help you can get to release your sister. Would you risk Helga's future to save your pride? I thought you wiser than that...'

Cursing, because she knew he was right, she strode away from him, his dark shadow matching her pace easily with his long legs.

They walked in silence, her mind constantly churning with guilt and worry.

How was she going to tell her mother what had happened? How could she tell her that she'd failed them both?

Still irritated and looking for a distraction, she said bitterly, 'There was no need for you to protect me against Ulf either. I am capable of defending myself, especially against men like him!'

Erik sighed. 'I know…' It was a quiet acknowledgement that tempered some of her fury with him.

Why could she never stay angry with him?

'I just couldn't stand it. To watch him insult and bully you like that…'

She rolled her eyes. 'I do not care what he thinks of me. I would never seek the approval of a man like him.'

Erik was silent and she looked over at him curiously as they turned down yet another narrow alley together. His jaw was clenched tight, a frown on his brow that hinted at a deeper conflict within.

'And neither should you,' she added.

His eyes flickered to her in surprise, then he

gave one light nod of acceptance before returning to stare at the muddy path ahead.

Their sides brushed lightly against one another as they awkwardly navigated the cramped thoroughfares. They were both so large that they had to squeeze around one another to fit through some of the smaller paths.

In one particularly tight spot, he braced his hand against a wall as he allowed her to pass.

It was his scarred hand, she realised. The one she'd tended to, all those years ago, when they'd first met.

A lot had happened that year.

In the spring they'd picked the runes foretelling their fates. Brynhild had picked the rune that meant 'warrior's sacrifice'. She'd known immediately what that had meant. That she would sacrifice her life to fulfil her dream and become a great warrior. Helga had argued it meant she would marry a warrior. Which was ridiculous and foretold nothing—most men and some women called themselves warriors. The runes might as well have said 'you will marry a person'—they'd laughed about it. Helga had been adamant that it had a greater meaning, while Brynhild remained convinced that she would find more meaning staring into a pile of horse dung.

Then they'd spent the summer in Gotland, for their cousin's wedding. Staying at Ulf's settlement, as the groom had been one of his warriors.

Gotland had changed everything for them. Arriving as naive girls, they'd left as hardened women.

Valda had fallen for Halfdan. An all-consuming, passionate love that Brynhild had been jealous of at first. But then she'd watched as Valda's heart had been broken and she'd felt no envy for her sister then, only pity. Valda had never been the same after, her heart cleaved in two and her spirit badly bruised from the disappointment.

Valda had pulled away from all of them and Brynhild had mourned her loss. It was as if her sister had closed a door between herself and the rest of the world. She talked, ate and fought with them. But she was always remote, slightly apart from them. As Brynhild had not felt such passion in her own life, she could never offer the comfort, or find the right words of solace for her sister, and so a wall had formed between them.

Valda's heartbreak hadn't been the only thing to happen that summer. Poor Helga, who'd always struggled to learn fighting skills, had finally stood up to their mother and refused to follow the path of a shieldmaiden. Porunn had struggled to accept it at first, but Helga had held firm and eventually she'd relented. Eventually accepting that she would never have all three daughters beside her on the battlefield.

And Brynhild? She'd also learned a valuable lesson that summer. One she would never forget.

A wounded animal was the most dangerous kind of beast—even if you were only trying to help it. Without warning, like the monstrous wolf, Fenrir, it could turn on you and bite the hand that fed it.

It had been a summer of disappointment and bitter lessons for the whole family.

At least Valda and Halfdan had finally been reunited and were now happily married. Her sister had finally freed herself from the cage she'd locked herself in.

Brynhild only wished she could do the same.

Erik's hand flexed against the crumbling plaster of the wall and she realised she'd been staring. Embarrassed, she looked away, only to be caught in the dark embrace of his gaze.

'If your mother isn't at home, do you know where she goes hunting?'

She frowned for a moment, wondering the reason for his question, and then laughed coldly. 'My mother would not have allowed herself to be taken. There is a reason he took Helga instead of one of us. The coward saw her as an easy target. You think some man would try to snatch one of us off the street? Ha! And, believe me, although my mother may be past her prime...*any* man would still struggle to steal her from us.' Guilt suddenly washed through her. 'I should have paid better attention to protecting Helga. I knew she was more vulnerable, yet I treated her the same as I would my mother...'

'It happened so quickly, there was nothing you could have done,' he said kindly with infuriating compassion.

'I could have waited for her. I could have *not* been arguing with you!' She strode forward without a backwards glance, determined not to fall for his charm a second time.

Erik's voice was calm and reasonable behind her. 'I wasn't arguing with you. I was apologising.'

Brynhild sucked in what she hoped would be a calming breath, but nearly choked when the stench of the tanning yards hit her throat.

She was home.

* * *

Erik tried to mask his shock when he saw the tiny hut Brynhild and her family had been living in. It was little more than a squalid shelter, held together with sticks and mud. Around the small plot was a low hazel fence, marking out their tiny vegetable garden. He suspected it had been Helga who had taken the time and effort to ensure it looked tidy and welcoming, but despite her care it was still a poor hovel and nothing could hide that fact. Erik wouldn't have kept swine in it, let alone four women.

It even made his barn back in Gotland seem like a shining Hall in comparison.

The doorway was open, small tendrils of smoke threading out into the crisp autumn air. Porunn had her back to them as she bent over the fire. 'Where have you two been?' she said as the squelch of their boots on the muddy path announced their arrival.

'Mother… Something…has happened,' Brynhild said quietly, her voice raw with pain. Porunn's back stiffened before she turned around to face them.

'Where's Helga?' she asked, her face pale as she took in the sight of her eldest, racked with guilt.

Brynhild's pain overwhelmed him, filling him with a desperate need to protect and comfort her. She might act tough, but he had seen the true heart of her once. The sweetness behind the warrior's armour, the girl who cared for animals, and had treated him with a kindness he'd thrown straight back in her face.

Erik stepped forward. *Better to say it all at once.* 'She has been taken. By a Welsh warlord, called Rhys Draig ddu Gwynedd—the Black Dragon of Gwynedd. Partly out of revenge for Halfdan and Valda's marriage and partly as a ransom to ensure his sister's safe return. The man who took her doesn't realise that our connection with Ulf is meaningless and that his sister ran away of her own accord. But... I promise we *will* get Helga back.'

Porunn gripped the edge of the doorway, her knucklebones white against the wood.

Brynhild stepped forward. 'I'm sorry, I should have been looking after her... She stopped for bread and we only walked ahead for a little while...and then...and then she was gone.'

'Who must we return...his sister?' Porunn asked, her voice quiet, as if her mind were already planning several steps ahead.

'Yes,' said Erik, 'Her name is Lady Alswn of Gwynedd. She was due to marry Halfdan on his return to Jorvik. But she ran away with the man who brought her here. I believe they were lovers, or will be by now…'

'And you know where they went?' asked Porunn hopefully.

He shook his head. 'No, but I know what they both look like. They were here when we arrived, so they could not have got far in only a day or two.'

'Where is Helga being held?'

'We don't know for certain. But it's likely she will be taken back to the Black Dragon's fortress in Wales.'

Porunn smothered the flames with a ladle of water. 'Then she might still be in the city. We must search for her—someone must know something!'

'I doubt that she's still here. The Welsh warlord arrived yesterday for his sister's wedding and I believe left straight away with his entire retinue when he discovered the wedding was cancelled and his sister missing. At the time, I presumed he left to find her. However, with Ulf waging war against him, he will need to return to his lands quickly. He must have left a small party behind to capture Helga, but there is no way of knowing if they are still here, or if they travelled with her by boat or horse. Tostig is petitioning the Jarls to search all who leave the city, but to be honest…she is probably already on her way to the Black Dragon's kingdom—he would not risk keeping her here for long.'

Porunn's voice was quiet and haunted. 'Is he really called the Black Dragon?'

He nodded. 'Yes, that's what they call him in his homeland. Why do you ask?'

Porunn's face drained of colour.

'It was just a dream,' Brynhild said, although her face was also pale.

'Helga's dreams have a habit of coming true,' said Porunn grimly.

Confused, Erik asked, 'What are you talking about?'

Brynhild sighed. 'As a child, Helga dreamt repeatedly of a black dragon. She became obsessed with it and drew it everywhere. On rocks, and…runes…but she has not had those dreams for years.'

'A black dragon? Like the Welsh Lord's symbol left in the basket?'

Brynhild nodded miserably. 'Exactly like that.'

Erik wanted to wrap her in his arms and assure her that all would be well, but he couldn't do that. It would be a lie and she wouldn't care for his comfort anyway. He would do everything he could to make up for his past mistakes, but he could not rush her forgiveness.

Brynhild visibly shook off the depressing thoughts that plagued her, like a dog coming out of the rain. It was impressive. 'Only time will reveal its meaning. I only came to tell you, Mother, before I begin my search of the city. I swear, if they are still here, I will find them... even if I have to break down every door in Jorvik.'

Porunn grabbed her bow and quiver of arrows. 'I will join you.'

Erik couldn't help but admire them, but he also knew that searching for Helga would be fruitless. 'Maybe one of you should remain? For Tostig... He said he will come here at nightfall, after speaking with the Jarls.'

Brynhild turned on him like a striking serpent. 'I would rather search for my sister in what light remains than cower by the fire waiting for news of her. Stay here if you wish. But I have to at least *try* to find her!'

Porunn raised an eyebrow at her daughter's

outburst and Brynhild took a deep breath as if to steady herself.

He had not meant to enrage her, but that was all he seemed able to do in her presence. But he knew it was because she didn't trust him and that she blamed herself for her sister's kidnapping, so he ignored it.

'I will search the area surrounding the docks, and will be back here before nightfall,' he said and the pulse in her jaw jumped. He stared at it in fascination, his palms itched to touch her, to smooth away the tension in her face.

There were only two people alive in this world that he would, without question, do anything for. Halfdan, who was his brother in blood and spirit, and Brynhild. What would she think about such a confession? She wouldn't understand it, that much was certain. Would probably think that he was mocking her again in some strange way. But Brynhild had shown him friendship when no one else had, she'd held him when he'd been vulnerable and at his lowest. Saved his life, and his sanity.

A rosy colour flushed her cheeks, whether from irritation or embarrassment he couldn't tell. 'Thank you,' she said, unable to meet his eyes. 'It is…appreciated. We will cover more ground that way.'

Bowing respectfully to each of them, Erik left. He might not have her forgiveness, but at least she was willing to accept his help.

Chapter Four

Brynhild stared at her clasped hands. The knuckles were raw from pounding on doors all day. Endless blank faces, indifferent shrugs and a soul-destroying lack of hope had plagued her through the streets of Jorvik. She'd never felt so helpless, or so exhausted. Battle was nothing compared to this despair.

Night blanketed the city and smothered their attempts to find out anything more useful about Helga's disappearance. Miserable drizzle rolled in with the mist and with heavy hearts they waited for Tostig's arrival back at their hut, praying that he would have had better luck with the Jarls and city elders.

Erik handed her a bowl of pottage, but she barely tasted it, focusing more on filling her stomach than enjoying her meal. She had no appetite and only ate to feed her strength for to-morrow. Her head throbbed with pain—the ear-lier soreness having only got worse after hours searching the city. No one had seen or heard anything of note, or at least that's what they had told her.

It was as if Helga had been plucked from the earth by an evil spirit.

Erik had learned that several ships had come in and out of the city since that morning, but no one had seen a woman like Helga leaving. But, as Erik had said, 'A man could bundle her small frame in a sack and carry her aboard without much notice.'

Porunn sat quietly by the fire, refusing food and brooding into the flames. Her sister's ab-sence was marked on every surface and stick of furniture in their home like a stain. The blanket she usually wrapped around her body at night, the leather shoes she'd been trying to repair, the bundle of herbs hung in the ceiling to dry out. All were reminders of what was now painfully absent in their home.

'*Heill!*' came a weary shout from the garden and all three of them turned towards the sound with eager anticipation.

As Tostig dipped his head to enter the tiny

shelter, they all stared at him expectantly. Wet with rain, his cap looked like a soggy mushroom on his weathered scalp. Meeting Porunn's eyes first, he shook his head solemnly and Brynhild felt as if the pottage she'd eaten had been made with ash and pebbles.

Tostig sat down beside Erik, took off his cap and wrung it out through the doorway. An easy enough task considering the cramped space available. Brynhild sat with her mother on one side of the fire, while Erik loomed on the other, taking up most of the opposite pallet. He looked as if he were sat in a child's den rather than a family home.

'Well…it is as we suspected,' said Tostig with a sigh. 'Whoever has taken her has already fled the city. I found the messenger who delivered the ultimatum to Ulf—one of the city's children paid with a scrap of silver. They were instructed to deliver the message to Ulf not long before you spoke with him.'

Brynhild glanced at Erik before shaking her head. 'There was something strange about that workshop…'

Erik nodded, accepting her words without question. 'I wonder if he or one of his men were in there watching for our reaction?'

Brynhild released a long and frustrated breath. 'I should have checked!'

Tostig huffed. 'No point in cursing the "should haves" of this world. I should have left with Half-dan, but it is clear the gods needed me here. We all have our thread in the tapestry of fate. I am certain Odin will protect your sister. When I asked the child to repeat the message they gave to Ulf, they did say that he would not harm Helga—as long as his sister was returned within a month. We still have time to set things right.'

'Thank you, Tostig, we appreciate your help,' Porunn answered, not looking up from the flames.

'I also learned that he did despatch at least one man to search for his sister. However, that man was asking for information about all of Ulf's old settlements and alliances before he left the city—I suspect he will be looking in the wrong place for his sister, as Ulf was right—she did leave of her own accord, I know because Halfdan arranged horses for them. So, I would not rely on that man being of any help to our cause. One thing I did discover, however, was regarding Lord Rhys's warriors. They are con-siderably further ahead of Ulf's army. It will be a race to see who will reach his lands first.'

Brynhild and Porunn exchanged a look. 'So, whoever has Helga is travelling alone, or in a small group, and left *after* Lord Rhys's men...'

'We should leave tonight—try to catch up with them!' Brynhild said—it was the first glimmer of hope she'd felt all day and it made her blood sing with the need for action. Even if it were dangerous to ride in the dark, she would rather be doing that than sitting here doing nothing.

Tostig shook his head. 'I think Helga will be taken part of the way via the south-westerly rivers. It's quicker than crossing land if you're a small party. I expect they will be able to catch up with the rest of their warriors within only a day or two—perhaps even less. I do not think rescuing her on the road will be an option... Do not look so glum! At least with his men ahead of Ulf's there is little chance of the warlord being defeated before he returns to his fortress.

'I asked around. He lives in Gwynedd, high in the western mountains and close to the Irish sea. The Saxons call the land Wales and it is an old Brythonic Kingdom. Ulf has a settlement in the borderlands. There have been petty grievances between them for months, raids and retributions. It was why Halfdan was set to marry the warlord's sister—'

Porunn interrupted him, 'Tell me more about this feud and the relevance it has to both my daughters.'

'Ulf had lost his influence in Jorvik—even before he broke from Erik and Halfdan. Saxons have retaken his land in the south and he is no longer considered as one of the great Jarls. In fact, his connection with Halfdan might have been the only thing keeping his seat among the city's leaders. They would not risk insulting him when his son flooded their markets with the finest silk and silver. Ulf knew this and sought to regain control. He still has one small settlement on the Welsh borders, not on Lord Rhys's land, but in the Dane-controlled area. Nothing much, little more than a farm, but last year he sent men there to create a fort. When it was complete, they plagued the area with raids and bloodshed.

'Lord Rhys retaliated in kind, but could not risk a war with Danelaw by trespassing on their lands. Hostages were taken on either side and negotiations begun. That's when Halfdan's marriage alliance with the Lord's sister, Lady Alswn, was arranged. Their marriage would seal a trading alliance between Ulf in Jorvik and the Welsh Kingdom. I believe Ulf thought to create a trading network, controlled by himself, that would reach from Ireland to Miklagard. He did not truly care for his small settlement, he only used it as a means to create an alliance that would regain him power in Jorvik.'

'But then Halfdan and Valda were reunited...' said Brynhild, her mind churning with worry for both her sisters.

'Yes.' Tostig nodded. 'Your family needed silver and Valda joined us on a trading voyage to Miklagard. Halfdan had told Ulf it was to be his last voyage before marriage tied him down.' Tostig snorted with amusement. 'But I suspected he would never go through with it even then. It was clear he still loved Valda. What man finishes one journey only to immediately begin another—one almost impossible in the time available? The stupid boy thought to impress her, of course, anyone with eyes could see it. Nothing could have kept them apart— except maybe their own stubborn stupidity... Thankfully, the gods helped them see reason in the end.'

Porunn gave a light chuckle of agreement, and Tostig smiled at her warmly. It was the first time Brynhild had heard her mother laugh since Helga was taken. She wasn't sure how she felt about it. Glad that her mother could find some relief from the worry, but also a little confused that of all people it would be the dour Tostig who would make her laugh.

'But…' continued Tostig, '…that left Ulf without an alliance. I'm sure he planned to marry the girl himself and force the alliance regardless, but Halfdan warned the Lady's guard and gave them horses to escape with.'

Tostig sighed miserably. 'Halfdan is reckless at times, but only because he wishes to do the right thing by all. Sadly, that's not always possible. I'm sure he thought that by buying Erik's freedom and cutting ties with his father that the alliance would crumble. With the Lady Alswn's escape, I am sure he thought no one would be harmed by his marrying Valda and that Ulf would be forced to make other plans…'

'He did make *other* plans!' cried Brynhild. 'He's waging war with the silver that Halfdan paid him and my youngest sister is suffering because of it!'

'Yes,' came Erik's sombre voice from across the fire. 'The silver we gave him has made Ulf too powerful. We should never have bought my freedom from him.'

Brynhild choked on her anger. 'That is not what I meant!' Then she frowned because she wasn't sure what she'd meant. To blame anyone but herself, probably, which wasn't fair.

After a heavy silence Tostig continued, 'Well… Ulf now thinks to take Lord Rhys's land for himself. It is an ambitious plan and he will need a mighty army to achieve it. For all Ulf's posturing, he has always struggled to hold the loyalty of men. After a long march across land, he will need more than silver before he can attack. He will need a strategy. Supplies for a siege and to fortify his own defences first.

'If he is wise, he will try to tempt Lord Rhys out of his stronghold first and meet him out on the open field, rather than attack the fortress directly. All of this will take months of planning. We can still help Helga.'

'But she will remain his captive throughout…' Brynhild's heart dropped in her chest as she realised how long freeing her sister could take. Months, not days! 'What if he lied about treating her well…? What if he *hurts* her?'

Tostig reached across and patted her knee kindly. 'Let us hope for the best…that this is a simple exchange of hostages—like the ones Jarls make regularly with the Saxons—and that no harm will come to her in the meantime. One thing that reassures me of Helga's treatment is that this Lord has never been on good terms with Ulf… As strange as that may seem—that bodes well.'

Erik looked at Porunn, his eyes warm with kind reassurance. 'That is true. Ulf has many enemies and all with good cause. The ones that hate him the most are *usually* honourable men.'

Tostig nodded in agreement. 'I have also heard that the Welsh lady and her protector—the representative who brought her to Jorvik and escaped with her—left through the Northern Gate. I met one of the guards who saw them out and he said he overheard the man mention they were heading towards the land of the Picts high up in the north-east. If that's the case, they will take the usual route up to the old wall and beyond. Hopefully, you can find their trail along the way… Erik is a good tracker…' A silent exchange passed between the two men, and Erik nodded firmly.

'So…you think we should do as he says and find his sister? Bring her back to him?'

'Yes. It is the only way of guaranteeing your own sister's safety. Or I suppose you could go to him, plead for her release? Explain that you have nothing to do with Ulf…'

They all frowned at that option.

Would a man who had snatched an unarmed woman from the streets of her home, and dragged her back to his fortress, ever be willing to let go of his advantage so easily?

He obviously had continuing threats to his own land from Ulf's raiders to deal with, otherwise, surely, he would be searching for his own sister and not forcing others to do his bidding for him? The fact that his own man was searching Ulf's old lands suggested that he thought Ulf held Lady Alswn captive. Therefore, he must have hoped that by taking Helga he would ensure his own sister's safe return, believing that Halfdan and Valda's family would have some influence over Ulf eventually, regardless of what he'd said to the Lord. Either way, there were very few options available to them.

'I know what they look like and can track them easily. I will go north to search for them,' said Erik.

For some reason his offer didn't surprise her, but she found herself questioning him anyway. 'Halfdan only asked you to help us find a farm. There's no need for you to do this.'

'There is every need. Halfdan caused this, even if he did so unintentionally. My brother's schemes have borne fruit and your family is now suffering because of them. He suggested the lady should run away before the wedding, he even provided them with horses! He may not have meant for this to happen, but he did set the wheel in motion. As his brother, I am honour-bound to help you.'

For some reason his answer disappointed her, although she couldn't think why. It wasn't as if his earlier apology had meant anything more… or that his feelings towards her had changed. He did this for his brother, not for her sisters or mother, and certainly not for her.

'It will be a difficult task to find a runaway bride in an unfamiliar land. What will happen if we fail to find them within a month? We must have another option,' said Brynhild and she looked pointedly at Porunn.

Her mother nodded gravely and then looked into the flames. 'I will go to Helga's father. He acknowledged her as his kin and always said to come to him if we ever needed help.'

'You never have before…' Brynhild said resentfully, thinking of the time when they'd lost everything to one of Porunn's ex-lovers and had been forced to begin again here in Jorvik. The months of hardship they'd faced and the sacrifices they'd made. To think they could have just asked for help at any time—it was infuriating and typical of her mother.

Porunn sighed. 'I was too proud before... I will not make that mistake again.' She turned to Tostig. 'You have already done so much for us, Tostig, and I barely know you. But can we impose on you once more? Helga's father is Jarl Sihtric. He won control of Waterford in Ireland this year. Can you help me find a ship to get there? If I can speak with Sihtric then he might help us, he could give us warriors to aid in Helga's return—either during the exchange, or, if there is war, to help get her out. I know it's a lot to ask, as you are Halfdan's kinsman and not ours...but...we have silver...' she finished saying weakly.

Tostig gave a snort of disgust. '*Odin's teeth, woman!* Do not offer me silver! Of course I will help you.' He waved a reprimanding finger at her. 'I do this not because of your kinship to Halfdan—that boy causes trouble wherever he goes—but because you are *Valda's* family. I would do anything for that stupid girl and will happily take you to Helga's father. The best way for us...' he said, thoughtfully scratching his snowy-white chin, '...would be to go south-west via the rivers, then take a boat from the coast to

Ireland. I have a friend here who regularly sails the Irish trade routes. I'm sure he will help us.'

'Thank you, Tostig. What would we have done without you?' Porunn gave Tostig a warm smile. It lit up her entire face in the firelight, illuminating the beauty still there beneath the scars and adversity of the last few years. Brynhild was surprised to see it.

Tostig seemed surprised, too. He blinked as if blinded by the smoke, before giving a grunt of acknowledgement and an embarrassed shrug. 'It is nothing.'

Porunn clapped her hands. 'So, Tostig and I will go to Ireland while you and Erik search for the missing Lady?'

'Yes, Mother.' Brynhild could tell by the way Erik sucked in a deep breath that he was considering arguing the point, so she glared at him, daring him to argue.

Brynhild knew she needed him—after all, he knew what the couple looked like—but with her sister's life at stake she could trust no one but herself to this task. Whatever his feelings towards her, he could not argue it with Porunn.

As Helga's mother, her decision was final.

Chapter Five

Tostig and Erik arrived as dawn poured its milky light over Jorvik. They'd not stayed in the women's hut the previous night. There'd been barely enough room to sit around the fire let alone sleep. It made him wonder how the four women had managed in it for so long. Instead, they'd slept in the hall of one of Tostig's kin. It seemed as if the man had family everywhere.

They looked at each other in surprise as a shovel of earth came flying through the doorway, followed quickly by another. Erik jumped to the side to avoid muddy earth hitting his tunic.

To think Erik had worried this morning about disturbing them so early from their much-needed rest. It seemed that Brynhild and her mother had already been awake for some time and were furiously digging up the floor of their home.

Their two straw pallets, the only pieces of furniture the women owned, were tossed haphazardly out of the front door, and were quickly becoming covered in earth. A neat pile of cooking equipment, blankets and weapons were placed by the water barrel out of reach of the steady spray of soil.

'Got it!' cried Porunn triumphantly as she started to back out of the hut, tugging at a sack, as if she were pulling up a very large and stubborn turnip. The light clang of silver, the only indication of the treasure inside.

Suddenly, their behaviour made sense.

They were digging up their hoard. The silver Valda had left for them—of course they'd buried it. Where else was safe enough to keep it within the city walls?

With a grunt and a clatter of metal, Porunn fell backwards out of the doorway, still clutching the sack tightly to her as she toppled out of her home and into the light of a new day. She squinted up at Erik and Tostig with a wry smile. '*Heill*, friends!'

Erik offered her his hand and she took it, swinging to her feet with a speed and strength that surprised him. Brynhild walked out shortly afterwards, dark circles under her eyes, as if she'd barely slept.

As usual she was both an intimidating and beautiful sight.

Her pale blonde hair was tied up high, sweeping down her back like a waterfall of sunshine. She wore a padded leather byrnie over a dark red tunic, brown inexpensive slim-fitting trousers, bound around the calf with warm woollen leg wraps. They were manly clothes that on her tall, curved frame, still managed to look incredibly attractive and fiercely feminine.

Erik's mouth became dry. She was glorious, always had been. But now as a woman—rather than the youth he'd known—she was breathtaking. A true shieldmaiden, with the heart of a warrior and the body of a goddess.

He lowered his gaze out of habit and by chance met Porunn's. She'd missed nothing and her eyes pierced him for a moment, the same sapphire shade as her daughter's. He'd never noticed the similarity between them until now—her eyebrows lifted with wry humour and then she looked away.

Brynhild moved closer to him. 'You look tired,' he said, unsure of what else to say and more than a little embarrassed by his wayward thoughts, and Porunn's perceptive eyes.

Brynhild glanced at him, a dry smile curving her lips. 'Thank you.'

He felt like an idiot. 'Sorry... I only meant, are you well enough to travel?'

'Of course I am,' she said with an unbothered shrug, before she began to put on the weapons that lay at his feet.

There were two axes, the smaller of which attached to her hip, while the large battleaxe had to be strapped to her back, followed by her shield, neither of which she needed help donning. A seax was placed at her other hip, its short blade sheathed in a leather holster, followed by several throwing knives concealed throughout her clothing, including her boots. Finally, she threw a cloak around her shoulders.

'Here, take this,' Porunn said, passing a small bag to Brynhild. By the delicate shiver of sound from within he would guess there were silver coins inside. 'Use these for horses and supplies. I'll take the rest. If all fails, then I will offer it to Lord Rhys and pray to the gods for Helga's safe return.'

Erik watched the exchange with grim understanding. These women had worked so hard and had made many sacrifices to accumulate this kind of wealth. It was their future, piled up in a dirty sack. With it they would have left Jorvik and run their own farm. But now all of it might be given away to save Helga, who had been captured through no fault of her own.

Life is unfair, Erik thought grimly. *Especially to those without power.*

At least when Halfdan returned in the spring, he would recompense the women for their sacrifice. His brother could be reckless at times, but his heart was ruled by a deep sense of honour and justice…without it, Erik would never have been freed from his father's enslavement.

'We've sent a messenger, as we discussed last night,' Tostig said, 'directly to the Welsh Lord's fortress. Informing him that, regardless of Ulf's actions, we will do our best to find his sister and return her to him.'

Porunn nodded. 'Thank you. I agree it's a risk…' She paused, as if remembering their debate last night around the fire. 'But even if Ulf does intercept it, he cannot blame us for trying to help Helga. Lord Rhys must know that we are not connected with Ulf in the way that he believes. Halfdan made no deals with him and we are not responsible for his missing sister. She left freely. If Ulf does go to war before we arrive, at least he will know the truth from both of us, as well as from Helga. For surely Helga will have told him this as well. Whether he believes it or not…only time will tell.'

Brynhild nodded in agreement, then took one last look at the hut. 'I guess this will no longer be ours by the time we return.'

Porunn squeezed her arm. 'Probably not, some other family will take it. I hope it brings them fortune.' Stepping forward, she opened up the hut door, so that anyone passing would see it had been abandoned.

'I hope the next people look after her garden,' Brynhild said softly and he felt an unexpected tightness in his chest as he looked at the pretty plot of autumn vegetables and herbs growing there. Soon, winter would strip it of its beauty, but today it looked full of life. A rare splash of colour in an otherwise dull patch of the city, Helga's gentle touch clear on every flourishing plant.

'Brynhild,' Porunn said firmly, causing her to turn and face her mother more fully. 'Our Helga is strong. Stronger than either you or Valda have ever given her credit for. She *will* survive this!

We will all do our part to help her... But she will triumph in the end. I am certain of it.'

'How can you say that?' Brynhild whispered, her face full of torment. 'She can barely swing a sword! She always stayed back with the other children when we fought in battle. She knows nothing of the hardships of life, or of how cruel men can be—'

Porunn interrupted her, gripping her strong arms tightly and staring up into blue eyes that reflected her own. 'I believe in her. She is not like you or Valda and it took me a long time to see that. But when I finally did, I realised she was gifted in her own way. Look at this garden! The earth was hard and poisoned when we first arrived—now it is thriving! I am convinced that wherever Helga walks, she will nurture life and bring harmony wherever she goes. She only stayed behind with the children because she could not stomach to take life. Instead, she knew she would always rather protect it.

'She has a fierce spirit and is strong in her own way. She might not be a fighter like you or I, but she has the heart of a shieldmaiden all the same. We will not know what she has or has not suffered until we are together again. Focus on what we can do to help her now. And try not to worry about what we cannot control.' Porunn embraced her, wrapping her arms tightly around her daughter's shoulders. 'We will get her back, sweetling. Try not to worry.'

They parted from Porunn and Tostig then, waving farewell to them as they headed towards the river dock. Brynhild and Erik headed through the city towards the Northern Gate.

After buying horses and supplies, they headed towards the stone archway, which was already bustling with a flood of people heading in towards the markets, and they fought like salmon against the current.

Tostig had given them the name of the guard he'd spoken to and, after a quick conversation with the man, he suggested they might want to try stopping at the settlement of Njal Bjornsson on their journey north. It was the first known stopping point for many travellers heading up towards the land of the Picts.

As they packed their animals with their supplies, Brynhild hesitated before getting up on her horse. She ran an arm up and down the animal's front flank as if measuring it. Erik wondered if she suspected an injury and was nervous about mounting it.

'Do you need help?' Erik offered, unable to

help himself. He already knew the answer by the sudden scowl on her face.

'Don't be ridiculous!' replied Brynhild sharply, before adding in a much more soothing voice, which was obviously aimed at the horse and not him, 'We are introducing ourselves, aren't we, *my darling*?'

He watched in fascination, as she wandered around the beast, offering gentle pats and more loving words that did strange things to him. Finally, she pulled herself up into the saddle with an easy swing of her long legs. Another wave of desire rushed down his neck, as raw lust surged into his groin at seeing her straddle the horse so confidently.

She looked down at him with a cocked eyebrow slightly darker than the rest of the hair on her head. 'Come, we haven't got all day. My sister is being held prisoner...remember?'

This journey was going to be torturous!

'Of course, my apologies,' he said, before swinging up into his own saddle with a flourish done purely for her benefit. Brynhild was a woman of stark contradictions. Strong and fearless, but also gentle and sensitive.

'There would be no shame if you did need help,' he added. 'Yesterday must have been very hard for you and if you haven't slept well...' It was the second time he'd commented on her exhaustion and by the narrowed eyes that glared at him, it was most unwelcome. He cursed the stupidity of his own tongue. He'd never been very good at talking to women…to anyone really. He'd not had much practice. 'Understandable, of course.'

She frowned and he thought for a moment she might deny it, but then her expression softened with acceptance. 'I missed her,' she said quietly. 'I missed the weight of her against my back.' She laughed bitterly as if the admission surprised her. 'I've hated sharing that pallet with her all these months. Moaned about it incessantly. Now? I can't sleep without her—isn't that ridiculous?'

'No,' he said firmly. He'd only known her for a short time nine years ago, but she had left her mark on him all the same. He'd missed talking to her, had even repeated in his mind their conversations over and over, whenever he'd felt lonely, just to remind himself that he could—if he wanted—make a genuine connection with someone other than Halfdan. Brynhild always spoke to him honestly, she never lied or played cruel tricks. She was as clear as spring water and just as refreshing.

With a click of her tongue, she rode out of the

stable and into the sea of people. After passing under the stone gate, her horse was startled by a cart that was being driven far too fast. The boy cursed and jerked the reins of his mule to slow it. A handful of apples spilled from the cart and Brynhild's horse reared up, stomping down on the fruit rolling around beneath its hooves. But with a firm pressure on her reins and a soothing voice she quickly managed to get the animal back under her control.

Then she spat some foul curses at the youth driving the cart. He had the good sense to look ashamed and immediately apologised profusely for his lack of attention. However, Brynhild didn't linger to hear him. She rode onwards without a backward glance.

She treated beasts better than she treated most people.

Nine years ago, Erik had been one of her beasts...

'Do you sleep here every night?' she'd asked when she'd found him sleeping in his father's barn.

'Yes,' he'd snapped, already in a foul mood after being woken up by the radiant young woman at the door of his home. He recognised her as one of the visitors to the island, one of

the many guests who had no idea who he really was.

*'My sister says you are Ulf's son. Are you?'
she asked. She asked the question as if she already knew the answer, but couldn't quite believe it was true. Her long strong body leaned
against the side of the barn door and she
watched him with the direct and easy confidence of a free woman, one leg bent and pressed
up against the wood, showing the curve of her
thigh beneath the length of her tunic. He'd never
seen her in a dress, not even at the feasts, but
then again, he'd never seen her mother or Valda
wear one either.*

*They were shieldmaidens. Women who defied
men and lived the lives of Valkyries.*

*'Does she?' he had replied, not wishing to
confirm or deny it, because he didn't like to
acknowledge the truth, even to himself. Most
days he prayed for the man's death, so to call
him father felt wrong.*

*'We sleep in one of the barns too,' she said,
indicating with her head to the hay barn not far
from the main Hall. He almost laughed—was
she trying to sympathise with him? That because she also slept in a barn, and was deemed
unworthy in Ulf's eyes, they were in any way*

similar? Because they weren't—she was free to leave at any time, he wasn't.

'Shouldn't you be training with your mother?' he said, not wanting to talk about why he slept in the barn. The simple answer being that he was a thrall, a slave, and worth less than a pig. He'd never been allowed to sleep inside the Hall, not even on benches with the other thralls. Not since his mother's death.

'Yes,' she said with a sigh.

'Will your mother not be angry?' he asked, a little shocked, and he rubbed the sleep from his eyes to see her better. Brynhild usually seemed so dedicated to her weapons practice.

'I don't feel like training today,' she said with a dismissive shrug, but he saw the guilty glance she gave towards the direction of the beach.

He'd seen her there with her mother and sisters. On the beach, they trained every day without fail. From dawn until the sun reached the highest point in the sky and then they went their separate ways to enjoy the rest of their day. He hadn't been the only one to see them. Several of the island boys had gone down to watch. Some to admire them, like Halfdan. But others went to laugh in their sleeves, and trade new insults about the 'strange' women among themselves.

All by the same boys who could barely carry a sword and shield without fumbling.

He and Halfdan didn't laugh. They knew what true fighting looked like; they'd been pitted against each other for their father's entertainment for years. Erik had watched them with interest for tips and tricks and he'd learned a lot. Porunn gave expert training to her daughters and he wished he had the courage to ask her to teach him, too...in secret, of course. Maybe then he could challenge his father and end his misery.

Sune, one of the louder and more spiteful boys, had laughed heartily when he'd first seen Brynhild fight against Porunn. She'd been straining to match her mother's powerful blows and had gasped and grunted with the effort.

Now, because of him, the boys all grunted like pigs whenever they saw her.

'*Sune and his friends are all idiots. Just ignore them,*' he said quietly and her eyes widened with astonishment at his unexpected support.

'*I know,*' she replied, picking nervously at her calloused hands. '*It just...wears me down sometimes. I needed a rest...only for today, I—*' She stopped speaking as he stood up from his blanket in the straw. He wore nothing but his braies *to sleep in, preferring to wash them more often than his tunic. His tunic was hung on a hook by the door and he had to walk up and stand close to her to reach it. A flutter of movement caught his eye and he saw how her leg had dropped to the floor, her body straightening upright as if startled. She stared at him as he approached, her mouth slightly open.*

Immediately blood rushed to his groin. No one had ever stared at him like that, as if he were something to admire... Most people avoided him completely. He'd heard the whispers. That he was cursed. 'Don't get too close! Keep back or you'll feel Lord Ulf's wrath!' they'd laughed.

Only Halfdan had ever treated him differently. Until now.

A rosy blush flew up her face and neck, as she looked away, squinting into the morning light as if it were the most interesting thing in the world. Not because she was ashamed to be seen with him—which would have been perfectly reasonable—or because she feared he would curse her with an evil look. But... because...she desired him? Was that even possible?

'I'm Brynhild,' she said, her voice husky, her

eyes flicking back to his face, and then dropping once more. Her gaze betrayed her attraction to him. It wandered down his chest and back up again with significantly more heat. She was the same height as him and she spoke to him as if he were her equal. His head felt light and a strange pride filled his chest, something he'd not felt in a long time, if ever.

He stared at her, confused, and then looked down at his own body with a critical eye.

Thin, that's how he would have described himself. His bones taut with slim muscle, rather than the broad, burly strength of a well-fed warrior. And, his scars... Too many for a youth of his age to have, but he'd lost count of his injuries over the years. His skin was darker than hers by several shades. A light brown dusted with thick dark hair, while her complexion shone with a golden fragile light, like the inner colour of a seashell.

He had the dark colouring of his mother, the black hair, the nut-brown eyes. She'd been from the East, but he knew nothing else of her land, except the mother tongue she'd taught him, 'You are the seed I have sown, think well of me, when I am gone.'

The idea that this young woman, this proud

shieldmaiden, might find him even remotely attractive was...strange and exciting.

Maybe she hadn't seen his scars clearly, or hadn't realised they'd been made by a belt? He quickly pulled on his threadbare tunic and tattered boots, shame crawling across his skin. 'What are you doing here?' he said sharply, surprised at the sudden temper in his voice.

'I heard there were...' She paused, looking even more embarrassed than before, turning such a bright shade of pink he found he couldn't look away from her, so fascinating was every flush of her skin. 'Kittens...'

He blinked; he'd not expected that. 'Er... Yes...there are a few...'

Eager, bright sapphires pierced his heart. 'Can I see them?' she asked, her voice husky. Then she glanced around them, as if worried someone might overhear her next confession, 'I do love baby animals.'

Erik looked down at his hands as they followed the road out of Jorvik. Brown scarred knuckles clenched the reins tightly, one smoother than the other, but otherwise healthy and strong.

One apology? It wasn't enough.

Chapter Six

'Damn it, Brynhild! Slow down!' Erik complained, as he desperately tried to match his horse's stride with her own. When she ignored him, he said the only thing he could think of to stop her, 'You will lame the horses!'

'I will not!' she replied, but to his relief she pulled on her reins and eased down into a trot. It was the first time in hours since she'd allowed her horse any form of respite from the relentless pace she'd set.

'We have a month. There's plenty of time—'

A muscle jumped in her jaw. 'I am not leaving my sister imprisoned for a day longer than necessary!'

'I'm not saying that you should... But when and where will we exchange these horses for fresh ones? We do not know the land here, or what obstacles we may face, some caution would be wise. If we lame or exhaust them too soon—'

'Then we will have to walk on foot, I know that! I'm not stupid and I'm not overtaxing them, they can run for a while without straining themselves.' Brynhild patted her horse's sweaty mane, then slowed a little further into a walking gait. 'Shouldn't we at least try to close the gap between us and the Lady Alswn? They are already a day ahead of us. Not to mention their trail. How can we follow them if all clues to their whereabouts become stale and dead?'

He stared at her as her words rushed out of her mouth like the Dnieper rapids.

She sucked in another flustered breath. 'We need to hurry—if we do not, then we could lose them. I could lose—' The words suddenly died in her throat, and she looked pale as if she were about to be sick. Of course, he knew what she'd been about to say. *Helga.* She was afraid she would lose Helga. Her gaze drifted to the trees around them, unshed tears shining in her eyes. Stubbornly refusing to let them fall, or show any sign of weakness in front of him.

'We will not allow that to happen. We *will* free her,' he said reassuringly and he wished he could reach out and comfort her in some way, as she'd comforted him nine years ago with a gentle and innocent embrace. But he wasn't sure if she would accept anything more from him than words.

Brynhild's eyes snapped to his, filled with fury and pain. 'How can we know that? How can we even be sure she's alive and well? She could be—' Again, she couldn't finish her sentence and her eyes went back to the horizon.

'We can't,' he said gently, hoping that his honesty would work better than pandering words of consolation. 'We have to focus on what we can do.'

'And that's what I'm doing!'

'No, it's not,' he said and her spine stiffened with outrage at his tone. Before she could curse him and gallop away, he added in a more reasonable tone, 'You are putting yourself and Helga at risk by racing ahead. You want to find them quickly? Racing across the countryside will not help, you could potentially lame your horse, or miss clues regarding our quarry's whereabouts.'

'So, you expect me to treat this like some leisurely ride?'

'If that helps…'

She gasped, 'How dare you! I should split your head in two—'

'Sometimes,' he interrupted firmly, staring down at his hands as they gripped the reins, 'when things are at their worst, it is best to forget what *may* happen and concentrate on the next breath, the next step, the next part of your journey... Take yourself away from the pain—if you can. Ignore what you cannot control or the terrible things that may yet happen and focus only on what you can do in that moment, in that breath.' He looked at her then and saw the sympathetic understanding dawn across her face. She knew what he spoke of and now it was his turn to avoid her eyes, shame twisting his guts like a rusty knife.

'Is that what you did?' she asked gently, 'When you were under your father's control— when he...hurt you?'

Odin's blood! He hadn't meant for her to pity him!

Her horse moved closer to his and he felt the brush of her leg against his own. The warmth of her thigh was only there for a moment, but it bolstered his spirit. If confessing his past helped her in some way, then it had to be worth it. 'Yes, sometimes. Other times I would take myself fully away, in mind—if not body… But you do not need to do that. You only need to concentrate on the next steps ahead, like riding at a good pace to ensure the health and endurance of your ride. There is no need to punish yourself or feel guilty for not being able to do more.' Another thought occurred to him, one that thankfully moved away from talking about his past. 'Would you behave like that in battle?'

Brynhild sighed and he could see that she was beginning to accept his words. 'No. Fear and panic have no place on the battlefield. It only leads to a quick death for those who allow it to consume them.'

'Exactly—focus instead on the next goal. We were told we should stop at a settlement, were we not?'

She nodded.

'Then let us see what we learn there. That way we can ensure that each step we take is a good one.'

After a long pause, Brynhild gave a nod of agreement and a weak smile. 'You are right. I will try my best to do as you say.'

'Good. I cannot ask more of you than that.' He focused his attention back on the road ahead, allowing her time to digest his argument, while also trying not to obsess about how good the heat and firmness of her thigh had felt against his. They both rode on in silence, troubled by their own thoughts.

They reached Njal Bjornsson's settlement just before nightfall. Erik's muscles ached and when he saw Brynhild slump down off her saddle stiffly, he knew she felt the same. The first couple of days of riding were always the hardest. It took time for the body to get used to the constant motion and her earlier galloping hadn't helped matters. At least she'd taken to heart his words—the pace had been far more manageable after their talk.

A young lad by the stables looked at them curiously as they entered the village. 'We wish to speak to your Chief,' Erik said and the boy darted off up the hill to a large timber Hall. He didn't need to run for long, as Chief Bjornsson appeared from his Hall and walked down to meet with them, saying something to the boy before dismissing him.

Njal Bjornsson was a flat-faced man, with a large boil on one cheek. He had dark blond hair cropped short, with a tidy beard and an elaborately embroidered white tunic. Erik would guess him to be around ten years older than himself and Brynhild.

'Heill,' Njal said gruffly, looking at Erik with suspicion. A common occurrence that Erik didn't even bother to try to ease any more.

'Heill!' answered Brynhild, stepping forward with far more friendly enthusiasm than Erik was used to seeing from her. 'May we rest our horses here for a while? Possibly break some bread with you? We have a long journey ahead and had heard you were kind to weary travellers like ourselves. I am Brynhild Þorunndóttir, a shieldmaiden originally under Jarl Rollo's banner in Francia, before I came to England, and this is... Erik' She paused, suddenly at a loss for words. Njal frowned at him, obviously growing even more uneasy with his presence.

Erik knew why Brynhild had stumbled over his introduction. Thralls were not given last names, but he'd been freed by his father now—after a huge payment of silver by Half-dan. He could use his father's name—but he didn't want to, something Brynhild had instinctively known. He was no Ulfsson and had no wish to be, nor did he like the name his father had given him upon freeing him. But without anything better to call himself he said, 'I am

Erik the Black. I trade with Halfdan Ulfsson in the east—my mother's lands.'

'He's my brother-in-law,' Brynhild added.

Njal visibly relaxed, appeased by their lineage. It was a widely accepted custom for both Norse and Saxons to feed and shelter travellers. Understandably, most men preferred to know *who* they were opening their home to, if only to place a price on their heads if they proved untrustworthy. 'Welcome, Erik and Brynhild, I am Chief Njal Bjornsson. Come, rest by our fire, we have plenty of food to share with you.' He called to the stable boy who remained close by, 'Take care of their horses.'

'Thank you and what is the name of your Lady so I may thank her properly?' asked Brynhild as they followed the chieftain up the hill.

Njal smiled sadly. 'I have no Lady. My first wife died of a malady two winters past.'

'I'm sorry to hear that,' Brynhild said sympathetically.

Njal dismissed it with a light shrug. 'I have been meaning to remarry, but have been too busy to give it serious consideration.' Erik wondered how a man could be so dismissive of a partner's loss. Had he not cared for her? Then again, in his experience some men treated their wives no better than thralls.

'You have a fine settlement here,' Brynhild said with a broader smile than Erik was used to seeing from her. 'Good grazing land and rich soil. I'm sure your next bride will consider herself most fortunate.' Erik's foot slipped in the mud and he had to jump forward a step to regain his footing.

When he glanced back, he couldn't miss the way Njal eyed her with surprised interest. 'Thank you... Brynhild.'

Erik raised an eyebrow at her, as Njal walked into his Hall first, ordering his thralls to prepare a meal for his guests.

'What?' she whispered innocently, drawing close enough to him in the doorway that her shoulder brushed against his.

Erik stopped walking and held her back with the lightest of touches to her arm. 'Are you offering yourself to be his next bride?' he asked, in disbelief. Brynhild looked down at his hand, her expression blank. Perversely he brushed his thumb over the wool of her tunic—the area not covered by her thick byrnie between her elbow and wrist—before releasing her from his grip.

A light flush warmed her cheeks and she

rolled her shoulder, as if trying to shrug off the sensation of his touch. 'There's no harm in being friendly, and… I'd be glad to call a settlement like this my home…' She lowered her voice thoughtfully and he found himself leaning in to hear her better, as she reminded him, 'Besides, our quarry may have stopped here. We will catch them quicker if we appear the lamb and not the wolf. Didn't you say we should take our time here? To be sure we learn all that we can before choosing our next step? I am only doing as you suggested.'

'That does not mean you have to seduce the information from the man's bones!' he protested.

'Seduce?' She laughed, as if the idea were as likely as her growing wings. 'That is never going to happen with me, is it?'

Guilt twisted his stomach and, unable to help himself, he touched her arm again, this time lightly cupping her elbow. 'What I said…back then, I never meant it.'

She stared at him and then just as quickly shrugged off his touch with a jerk of her arm. Rather than walking away, she stepped closer, until her breath tickled his cheek and her breasts pressed against his chest. She'd meant it to intimidate him, he was sure of it, but all it did was fire his lust—which was definitely not the reaction she'd intended.

'And, what *I* felt back then?' Her eyes raked over him with cool disregard. 'I no longer feel. In fact, I care nothing for your opinion of me, past or present.'

'I'm glad,' he said gently and she blinked. 'It would be right for you to hate me—if you did… I was a coward.'

The ice in her gaze cracked. It was the strangest thing he'd ever seen. The mask of bluster and outrage suddenly fell away to shock.

To confess to cowardice was the worst thing a Norse man or woman could ever admit to. But he'd never felt Norse, not completely. It was as if he were straddling two worlds without secure footing in either.

Her gaze softened and she stepped back one pace. The cold fury in her eyes had gone, replaced by sympathy and begrudging acceptance. Then, as if unable to quite let go of her mistrust, she folded her arms across her chest and said, 'Fine. I forgive you, Erik. In truth… I also behaved badly. You are not solely to blame for how things ended between us. I was…' Her eyes drifted to his nose and then she laughed.

'My usual self, I suppose, aggressive. But you've apologised and we have much to do. We cannot keep raking through the ashes of the past.

'As you say, we have to focus on the task ahead. Let us agree that it is over and done with. I am grateful for your help now, *honestly*. You know what Lady Alswn and her guard look like and I would never be able to find them without your assistance... So, thank you, for your time and help...but *please*, for the love of Freya, can you stop bringing up the mistakes of our youth? It is...*humiliating!*'

He searched her face, trying to find the truth in her words. 'Are you certain we can begin again? Pretend our fight never happened?'

She forced a bright smile that didn't quite meet her eyes. '*What fight?* Come, he'll be wondering what is keeping us.'

She turned and strode into the Hall, her long hair swinging from side to side.

Her forgiveness didn't feel as comforting as he had hoped it would. He thought he'd be freed by it, but instead it sat like an ulcer in his mouth, sharp and ever-present.

A short time later they were sat beside the central fire on sturdy wide benches. Fragrant slabs of bread were topped with skewers of roasted pork and stuffed cabbage leaves filled with goat cheese. Njal sat in a large chair beside them as they gladly tucked into the delicious meal. A few families from the settlement were also dotted around on benches or talking in small groups around the hall. Lamp bowls suspended from the ceiling cast away all shadows, creating a bright and homely atmosphere.

'You said you had far to travel—what is your destination?' asked Njal conversationally.

Brynhild answered smoothly between tearing off bites of pork from her skewer, her voice remaining mild and cheerful. 'We have a message to deliver. A payment, in fact.' She tapped the silver at her belt and it made a delicate shiver of sound. 'Halfdan has trusted us with its delivery to Lady Alswn of Gwynedd—their betrothal ended abruptly when Lady Alswn decided not to go through with the ceremony. She did not realise that Halfdan had fallen in love with my sister and had already decided to break the alliance himself. Lady Alswn left with her guard before he could explain.

'Halfdan wishes to offer compensation for his broken word and the bad blood that now runs between their families... We believe she fears her brother's wrath and has run from him also. Halfdan hopes to now ease the path back into her brother's arms with silver…as is our custom.'

Njal appeared to think over her words before answering, staring into her face as if he were weighing up the truth of her statement. She smiled back at him, all innocence and warmth in her pretty blue eyes. A knot of jealousy tightened in Erik's chest as he watched them.

'What did she and her guard look like? They may have passed by here recently,' asked Njal.

Brynhild gasped with pleasure, elbowing Erik with a grin. 'See! I thought they might have! All being well, we can deliver our gift and be back in Jorvik before winter!' She leaned forward as if to confess a secret and Njal bent to meet her. 'Erik is bad tempered because he hoped to court a woman back in Jorvik. I do not mind, of course—I have no one waiting for me except my mother, so riding around the far north searching for a frightened bride and her guard, well, it is no hardship to me.

'*But,* if we could catch up with them, reassure the Lady that she has no reason to run from her brother, and that all is healed between our two families…well then! Erik can get back to pursuing his woman and I can have a comfortable winter beside my fire—'

Erik interrupted her, strangely annoyed that she would deliberately suggest she were free to be courted by Njal. 'The couple we seek are both young and attractive. The lady is small, with dark hair and green eyes. The man is of a slim build with dark hair and blue eyes. They are Britons from the west and speak with a heavy accent.'

Njal nodded. He'd obviously decided to accept their story. 'They stopped here late last night. Insisted on staying in the stable with their horses, so they could leave at first light. Although, come to think of it, they did seem nervous. They said they were heading northeast to Edinburgh and then possibly on to the Pict Kingdom of Alba in the far north... But...' he paused, then shrugged as if brushing away his concern '...when they spoke to each other in their own tongue... I heard them mention Rheged. That is to the north-west, an Old Briton Kingdom, now controlled by the Kingdom of Strathclyde. I can't be certain, but I suspect that was their true destination.'

'I think you are right! How perceptive of you, Chief Njal!' Brynhild beamed at the man and a flush rose up to meet the red-tipped boil on his cheek. 'They mentioned travelling to Edinburgh, back at Jorvik. I thought it strange that they would mention their destination to the gate-man... Maybe they hoped to trick anyone that might follow. Luckily for them, you realised the truth.'

'Glad to be of use to you, Brynhild. Do stop here on your return to Jorvik.' Njal held her gaze warmly as he spoke and Erik forced himself not to spit out the sudden bitter taste in his mouth. This strange flirtation was becoming unbearable to stomach.

She smiled. 'Oh, I will.'

'We should sleep in the stable tonight,' Erik snapped with a little more sharpness in his tone than he'd intended. 'So we can head out at first light...if not before... Cover as much ground as possible. Especially if you are wrong and they did indeed head to Edinburgh.'

Njal frowned and Brynhild shook her head. 'I'm sure the Chieftain is correct... But, yes, we should leave as early as possible tomorrow. Thank you, Njal, for your hospitality and counsel, it is greatly appreciated. Can I offer you anything in recompense?' she asked, tapping the heel of her hand against the silver purse at her side.

'No need!' replied Njal, staring a little too long at the curve of her hip for Erik's liking. 'It would be wrong not to give aid to a shield-maiden, especially one on such a noble quest.' His eyes trailed up the slope of her waist to her breasts. 'I look forward to speaking with you again on your return and I will have some supplies sent to you before the end of the evening.' He absently motioned to one of his thralls and they hurried off to prepare something for them.

Unable to stand another moment of their flirtation, or Njal's disrespectful looks, Erik stood up briskly, looking expectantly down at Brynhild. With a long-suffering sigh, she stuffed the last chunk of bread in her mouth. Turning to Erik, she grumbled with her mouth full, 'Fine! I'm ready!'

Then, she rolled her eyes good naturedly at Njal, who smiled back at her, although he appeared a little shocked by her manners.

Erik snorted. If Njal couldn't handle a woman with a healthy appetite, he would never make a decent match for Brynhild.

She ate like a horse.

Chapter Seven

Njal handed them a torch to light their way, as well as a sack of supplies and a flagon of mead. They wandered out into the fresh autumn night, a scatter of stars above their heads and a waning moon.

'Hopefully, the weather will not turn for the worse,' Brynhild said lightly, her face serene in the flickering light of the torch.

'Would you really consider him…a match?' asked Erik, unable to help himself.

'An unmarried chieftain of a prosperous settlement? He would make an impressive husband for any woman. It is not as if I have much to offer a man anyway. I have a mother and sister who are dependent on me. Potentially no silver to our name…if we have to use it to ransom Helga. I think it wise to keep an eye out for opportunities…whatever they may be.'

Her words enraged him and he glared at the moon. 'I *said* I would find you a farmstead. You do not need to sell yourself so cheaply.'

'Cheap?' Brynhild's laughter glittered like gold in the night, merry and bright. 'I'm eight and twenty, Erik. Meeting someone like that, a man not intimidated by my size and willing to see me as a potential mate? That's rare! For him to be an unmarried chieftain? Impossible! Do you think I get offered for very often? You know…' she said thoughtfully, as if remembering something amusing, 'before Valda married Halfdan, Jarl Ivar was willing to give us land, without any of us having to pay him a tribute, but *only* if one of us married a warrior of his choosing. His man immediately asked for Valda… Who could blame him? She is fierce *and* beautiful. Even when she told him she was carrying Halfdan's child, he was still willing to accept her.

'I saw that same man while I was out searching for Helga…he deliberately avoided me. I had to chase him down to check that he had not seen Helga! He was so afraid I would demand he marry me!' She laughed as if it were a hilarious jest, but Erik didn't think it funny and she sobered at his expression before adding

quietly, 'You are wrong Erik. Njal isn't cheap...
he's a rare pearl.'

'They are *both* not worthy of you,' Erik replied stubbornly, still angry that Brynhild would
consider either of them even half her match. She
deserved someone who would understand and
love her for who she was. Who would never let
her think she was *lucky* to have him!

Brynhild said nothing more as they walked
towards the stable, her silence a condemnation
of his own past behaviour.

He'd treated her far worse than that nameless
man. He had humiliated her and for what? To
protect her from his father—but that was only
partly true, because another part of him—and
he was ashamed to admit it—*had* been intimidated by her, although not for the reasons she
might have assumed.

Wanting her had terrified him.

Hoping to focus back on their task ahead, he
spoke quietly to her, being sure to check that no
one might overhear him first. 'Njal might not
be so pleased with us when we return, dragging Lady Alswn by a rope. He will know that
you lied.'

'If they are as far north-west as he suggests,
then we would do better to travel to Wales by

boat rather than over land. It will be quicker…
if we can find one.'

'True. But what a pity you will not see Njal
again.' The dry sarcasm in his voice wasn't lost
on Brynhild and she raised a cool eyebrow of
disdain at him that made him feel as worthless
as a maggot.

'Maybe after…' she teased, smiling smugly
to herself as if she knew how badly her admission would affect him. Jealousy rushed through
his veins. The idea of Njal, or *any* man, taking
Brynhild to his bed…irritated him.

They entered the stable and shook out their
bedding rolls in an empty stall. After they lit
the brazier with their torch, it sat near the door
casting only a little heat and light into the stalls.
She threw down her bedroll from their packs
that had been left by the door for them.

Erik quickly positioned his own next to hers
and laid down. 'I'll lie with my back against
yours…so you can sleep better,' he explained.

A flush crept up her neck and he wondered if
she would refuse, but then she nodded and settled down beside him, her back pressed lightly
against his. 'Thank you. I hope you don't snore!'

He looked down at his hands as they clutched

the blankets and tried to forget the feel of Brynhild's warm back against his. 'I don't.'

The scars on his left hand were faded, but still obvious, the skin tight and mottled on that side. It looked as if it were made from badly woven cloth, with its odd gathers and plucks of tissue.

Halfdan was the cause of his burns, as he'd been the cause of Helga's imprisonment.

No, that wasn't fair. Ulf was the man to blame.

Halfdan had just been trying to help, both then and now. It wasn't his fault that Ulf twisted even the smallest acts of kindness into something horrific.

Ulf had been angry with his blacksmith for something, he couldn't even remember what, something petty, no doubt. He had immediately ordered that the blacksmith and his family should be denied grain over the spring and summer. No one questioned it. No one would dare.

Except Halfdan, who had seen the withered children. He'd realised how close they were to starving to death, especially after their mother had taken ill, and he'd felt compelled to help.

In secret he'd given them a bag of grain. Just enough to keep them fed until the autumn, when Ulf's punishment would hopefully come to an end. But Ulf had grown suspicious of the family's sudden improvement in health and had decided to test his son's loyalties.

Halfdan's increased involvement with Valda had probably been their father's *real* cause for concern. Ulf had hoped to prove a point with his Erik, to remind Halfdan of his father's far-reaching and brutal power. Erik had just been a tool in his father's plan.

One night Ulf had told the brothers to come to him. One at a time he had asked them if they had helped the blacksmith's family in some way. They had both denied it.

Ulf had ordered Erik to fill a cauldron of water and set it on the fire in front of him. Erik and Halfdan had had to stand either side of him, watching in silence as the water slowly heated up to a rolling boil.

Then, Ulf had taken each of their forearms in a bruising grip. Even as young men they had been helpless to stop him. Erik was still a thrall and they had had no choice but to obey their Jarl.

'I shall ask you both again. Did either of you feed the blacksmith and his family?'

'No, my Lord, neither of us has,' Erik had replied first, letting Halfdan know that he will-

ingly took equal responsibility in protecting the family. If they admitted to feeding them now, the entire family would be slaughtered.

'No, Father,' Halfdan had whispered, his face pale, knowing that with his words he had condemned his brother with his act of kindness.

Erik still remembered the intense shock of pain he'd felt when his hand had been plunged into the water. How he'd tried to pull away, but Ulf's men had moved from the shadows and held him tight.

'If, after three days, your hand shows no sign of festering...then you are both innocent,' Ulf had declared, finally releasing him from the water after he'd finished speaking.

The agony had been blinding and Erik had fallen to his knees, clutching his throbbing hand to his chest.

He must have passed out, because the next thing he knew it was the morning, and he was lying in his barn, his hand screaming with pain. Halfdan had told him later that he'd been ordered not to see or speak with Erik until his three-day trial was complete.

He'd got word out, though.

Erik had been placed against the barn wall in a sitting position, a blanket over his legs, and someone had placed his scalded hand in a bucket of sea water. Bowls of fresh water and bandages were all within easy reach, beautiful iron bowls that could only have been made by the blacksmith himself.

Even though no one could be seen to be helping him, they'd done all they could to help him pass the trial.

Brynhild had found him struggling to wrap the wounds by himself.

'What happened to you?' She'd gasped, staring in horror at him from the doorway.

'Ulf,' he replied immediately and without thought, gritting his teeth against the agony even the slightest touch of the linen caused him.

She had rushed to his side then. 'Let me help you.' Gently taking the bandages from his trembling hands, she'd clucked sympathetically at the raw and blistered flesh. 'You poor thing, this looks awful!'

'I'm fine!' he'd snapped, but his teeth had chattered, as if he were cold, yet his hand still throbbed with heat as if it were still in the boiling water.

'I will get Helga, she's ever so good with injuries.'

He grabbed her tunic with his good hand

and dragged her close. 'No! Swear you will not tell them!' It was bad enough that Brynhild had seen him like this, he couldn't stomach anyone else. Sweat dripped in his eyes and he blinked rapidly to see better, but her face swam before him and he struggled to focus.

Gently she prised his fist from her tunic. 'I will not... But if you do not want it to fester, you will need some healing balms on it. I swear, I will get them and come straight back. Helga will not even question it, I promise!' Brynhild got up at his nod and ran out of the barn, the door banging shut behind her. The darkness closed in on him and he swallowed hard.

What choice did he have? If the wounds festered, he would be found guilty anyway.

Would that mean even more punishment for him...death? Probably.

He wanted to scream and howl over the unfairness of it all.

He was so close! So close to leaving with Halfdan on his voyage and never setting foot on this rotten island ever again. That was their plan. To work as merchants and earn enough silver to buy Erik's freedom from their father. Erik trusted Halfdan. Their scheme would work.

It had to.

It was the only thing stopping him from murdering his father in his bed. Which was probably why Ulf didn't allow Erik to sleep in his hall. He could see the bitter rage in his outcast son's eyes and knew that he dreamed of vengeance.

Now, even the hope for freedom seemed distant. Would his hand be able to work after this? He needed to be able to row and work the rigging of a ship. What if he couldn't do that? Would Halfdan leave without him?

Would he even survive this?

What if it poisoned his blood and he died of the fever?

He'd lived his life on a leaking ship, tossed up and down on the whims of his father's storms. He couldn't bear it any longer. At this point he wondered if death would be a mercy after all.

He only wished Brynhild hadn't left. He didn't want to be alone when it happened, but then... wasn't he always alone?

He lay down among the hay and curled up into a tight ball. Salty tears fell silently down his cheeks as waves of aching pain washed up his arm. He prayed in his mother's tongue and then in Norse.

Not for his life. He didn't want it. But for an-

other life, in a kinder land, whether it be in the east or in the afterlife.

When he woke again, it was the morning of a new day. He vaguely remembered Brynhild offering him sips of water throughout the night and tending to him, but he couldn't be sure if it was real or feverish imaginings.

No, they had to be real. His hand was properly bandaged now with clean linen. The skin blissfully numb beneath the well-packed layers. Brynhild lay against his back, her arm gently draped around his waist, her body curved around his spine. Her sword and shield within easy reach, as if she were protecting him even while they slept.

His brave and beautiful Valkyrie.

With his good hand, he picked hers up gently from his waist. He looked at it, dazed and confused. She didn't fear touching him or helping him.

She was his friend.

No one had ever been his friend before. Even Halfdan cared for him out of brotherly love and guilt, not because he liked him. But Brynhild had nursed him, and taken care of him, even staying with him throughout the night.

The warmth in his heart quickly cooled as fear washed through him.

What might his father do to her if he saw them together?

Before he had time to consider that terrible thought, a shadow covered them and he heard the sniggers of boys from the half-open doorway.

'Look who's tumbled the beastly Brynhild!' sneered Sune, from the doorway, followed closely by more boyish giggles and loud mocking grunts.

Chapter Eight

The weather was fair, which pleased Brynhild. The air had a little more frost in it than the day before. The ground firm but not too icy for the horses and there were no rain clouds in the sky. They'd ridden out before dawn had fully broken, determined to match their prey's pace, and at least she was well rested now, thanks to Erik.

The warmth of his back against hers had given her the comfort she needed to sleep deeply. It was an embarrassing realisation to need him in such a way, but he'd not spoken of it since and she was grateful to him for that. He'd been right, she needed to stay focused and strong for the gruelling journey ahead, so she would try her best to put the pain of Helga's loss to the back of her mind. It was difficult, but she knew how to do it. In battle she had to forget Helga and her friends back at camp. If you fought well and won, then you ensured their safety anyway. Fear killed more warriors than the blade.

Brynhild only hoped Njal was right and that the Lady Alswn and her lover were headed to the north-west and not the north-east as they'd originally said. Their next step depended upon it.

She glanced over at the silent and brooding Erik, his back straight in the saddle, his hips undulating with the ease of a confident rider. At her sister's wedding feast, Halfdan had proudly explained that Erik worked the Volga trade route. He'd ridden across a sea of sand on a strange animal called a 'camel', he'd fought against nomadic pirates and met with eastern Kings and traders. He'd experienced more wonders in the years since they'd first met than she could ever imagine.

There would be no such adventures in her future. She'd fought in Francia for many years. Helping to secure the kingdom of Northmannia for Rollo, and the spoils of war she'd built up over time had been combined with her mother's. Stupidly, because they'd lost it all when

Porunn's lover had stolen their silver and disappeared into the night.

She wondered if Erik thought her life dull in comparison, bound to her family as she was, and focused solely on possessing a small patch of dirt to build a life upon.

'What is it like…in the east?' she asked, unable to shake off her curiosity.

Surprised by her question after so long travelling in silence, he took a moment to ponder. *Odin's teeth!* He was still the most beautiful man she'd ever seen… *Curse him!* Sculpted brows and a square jaw, with long, dark, silky hair like a raven's wing that reached just past his shoulders. And his eyes! So rich and warm they made a woman yearn for the pleasures of the night.

'Hot, dry and dangerous,' he replied.

'Sounds fun.' She laughed and he shrugged, offering nothing more on the topic. Brynhild looked away before he noticed her staring.

Confidence and decent meals had made him even more handsome than he'd been in his youth, filling out the breadth of his shoulders and thickness of his thighs.

He'd been so thin before, his muscles barely strung to his frame like cords of rope wrapped around the branches of a sapling. His scars, a symbol of his strength and courage.

She'd thought him beautiful then, breathtakingly so, but he'd been so brittle and intense, like a bow pulled far too tight. She'd been worried he'd snap at her like a whip when she'd asked to see the kittens, or worse, mock her like the other boys did whenever they saw her.

He hadn't. He'd taken her to see them without a word.

Four delicate bundles of black and grey fur, nursing against their mother, who'd regarded her with suspicion until she'd crouched low and spoken gently to her. The cat hadn't been bothered by Erik's presence, had even dipped her head for a scratch behind the ears when he'd sunk down next to her.

'She keeps the mice away,' he'd said, as if explaining why he would happily share his barn with a cat, something Brynhild understood all too easily. You knew where you stood with animals.

Later she'd wondered if that's what he'd told Ulf, too, afraid that otherwise the cat might have been used against him. Affection was a weakness in Ulf's mind.

She'd thought him kind and gentle then, had

*trusted him, gone back daily to see the kittens
and, if she were honest, to see him as well.*

How wrong she'd been...

Brynhild sighed, focusing her attention back
on the curving path ahead. Erik had apologised
and she'd told him that she had forgiven him.
Wasn't it time she forgot the past and tried
harder to get along with him? If only he wasn't
always so *silent*!

As if to deliberately contradict her thoughts,
he declared loudly, 'Look!' He kicked his heels
and rode forward. There was a woman working with an ox to plough a very large field by
the side of them.

'*Heill!* Did you see two travellers pass by
here yesterday? A man and a woman, both dark
haired?' he called out.

The woman frowned at him and stopped
driving the ox to wipe at her brow. 'I did.'

'And which way were they going?'

'Err, the same way you are going...'

'Thank you!' he called back cheerfully and
the woman muttered something angrily under
her breath about pointless questions from for-
eign men, before going back to her work.

Erik grinned at Brynhild. His face was unbearably beautiful when he was happy, she noted. 'We are on the right path. Njal was right!'

She smiled. 'Thank Odin! We owe Njal a hogshead of ale!'

'As long as that is all you give him,' Erik said gruffly, his broad smile dropping into a scowl.

'Oh, do stop gnawing on the poor man's bones!' She sighed. What had started off as a way of teasing Erik had become tiresome and old very quickly. She couldn't understand why it bothered him so much.

'He doesn't deserve you.'

'Really?' she retorted. 'And who does? *You?*'

'Of course not!' His eyes remained firmly fixed on the road ahead and she was grateful because somehow his retort had hurt more than it should have.

What did she expect?

That he would become jealous of her flirtation with Njal and demand she accept him instead?

Ha!

No, what she got was a rather concerned Erik, trying to explain to her that she didn't have to 'sell herself so cheaply'. She could find herself another man… Not Erik—*of course not Erik!*

A man as handsome as him desiring her?

Madness! The first time they'd slept beside each other—also innocently, because she'd been tending his injured hand—he'd jumped away from her as soon as he'd woken, embarrassed they'd been discovered together by the settlement boys. So fast, in fact, that she'd almost caved in her face against the floor, when he'd rolled away from her.

At least she wasn't a maiden any more with foolish dreams. She knew her limitations and her strengths.

'Njal was pleasant enough, but I'll never marry, not if I can help it.'

'You might find someone you…like,' Erik replied softly.

'Nei!' she scoffed, shifting in the saddle to ease the soreness in her rump from the long hours of riding. 'Besides, I don't like sex enough to make it worthwhile.'

'What?'

Erik's horse skittered to the side at his gasp, as if he'd pulled the reins too tightly. Instinctively she reached over and patted his horse's neck. When she rose, she saw the horror in Erik's expression and shook her head with wry amusement.

She'd always been blunt and honest with her

words. Men didn't like it, but she found it far easier than pandering to them. 'You think me so *beastly* that I could never manage to tempt a man into my bed? I am a grown woman, Erik. I have fought in wars. Led men in battle. I am no *innocent*… I have had lovers.'

Erik remained silent, his dark eyes fixed on the road ahead.

Shaking her head, she carried on speaking, although why she felt the need to confess something so intimate to Erik, she had no idea. Maybe, because she wanted him to know that she *could be desired*, or maybe, because she'd always felt as though she could tell him anything and he would always calmly accept whatever she had to say—as he had all those years ago. Or, maybe…she was just bored and needed to talk to pass the time, anything to make this journey more bearable. 'Two, in fact…possibly three now I think about it.'

'Three?' he whispered in awe, which only fuelled her irritation.

'Yes, although maybe it doesn't count…'

He didn't reply, but neither did he tell her to stop talking so she carried on.

'I wanted to know what it would be like. And, you know me, if Valda's done something and I haven't… I get competitive. Although, I think Halfdan must be much better at it than most men, as Valda said it was *wonderful*…' Her eyes sparkled with amusement, but he must have known there was more to it, as he waited patiently for her to elaborate.

'When I tried it the first time, I found it dull and awkward. So, I decided to try it with another man, in case I had picked a bad one. It was…better, but not wonderful!' She laughed again, hoping Erik would laugh with her, but he didn't. His eyes flickered to hers for a moment before dropping to the road, again.

'And the third?' he asked, his voice even and without judgement.

'I don't think that one counts as it was just kissing. I thought that maybe I didn't like men… So, I tried it with a woman—she was nice. But that wasn't for me either. Honestly, I'd rather spend my days alone than have boring sex or awkward intimacy. At least then I can please myself without someone else getting in the way.'

Erik cleared his throat loudly as he shifted awkwardly in his saddle. For the first time she worried she'd been a little too honest with him. Did he think her…odd? He wouldn't be the first, but it still bruised her confidence.

'Sorry,' she mumbled. 'You probably didn't want to know any of that and I've made you uncomfortable.'

To her surprise, he smiled for the first time since she'd begun speaking. 'No, I like your honesty. I admire you, Brynhild. You are...fearless.' His eyes caught hers and held them for a moment, before she looked away, a hot flush creeping up her neck.

Chapter Nine

~~~~~~~~~~~~~~~~~~~~~

They rode on in silence after that, the lush sweeping hills growing large and rockier with each new horizon. Then they came to a thick forest, the river meandering slowly beside them as it weaved down from the hills.

As the sun hung low in the sky, they decided it was time to find somewhere to sleep. Not being familiar with the area, they decided to make camp near the river. The horses could drink and graze, while they prepared a makeshift shelter from the fallen branches and they would be safer hidden away from the main path.

As Brynhild saw to the horses, Erik went to see if he could catch some fish. She tried and failed to avert her gaze as he stripped down to his braies and walked into the freezing water, barely flinching despite the cold, a makeshift spear he'd made from a sharpened sapling held high above his head. He waited patiently, watching the water intently for any sign of movement.

Dark skin laced with scars covered his back and torso, tattoos of hardship and suffering, but also triumph. Erik was strong now; his old wounds had paled. No longer a thrall, he had succeeded where others would have crumbled.

She admired him too, she realised…a little too much.

'I will go and set some traps for the morning,' she called and he gave a small nod of approval, not breaking his concentration to look at her.

Walking a little further into the thick trees, she searched for a good place. Although she wasn't a keen hunter, she did prefer to keep her belly full and nothing filled a stew better than fresh meat.

After setting a couple of traps, she went foraging, looking for any herbs or vegetables she might be able to use to bulk up their stew. They had some supplies from Njal, but it was always wise to use whatever was available first and that way they could stretch them out for longer.

Then something caught her eye and she grinned at the sight in front of her.

* * *

By the time she'd made her way back to the river, Erik was pulling on a tunic, with a pair of river trout at his feet.

'Well done!' she said, impressed, and he shrugged, although there was a proud smile on his lips.

'I think you will be equally pleased with what I have found.'

'Oh, yes, how so?'

She beamed back at him, unable to help the smugness in her tone. 'We will have to move the horses, but I think I've found the place where our couple slept last night.'

He raised an eyebrow and tilted his head with a sly smile that matched her own. 'Lead the way.'

She showed him the campsite she'd found. Many saplings, and thick branches of evergreens had been cut down and laid to create a little triangular shelter. A small campfire edged with stones sat outside of it. The ashes were cold and damp, but undisturbed.

He walked around it and then peeked inside the little hut.

'They made a good job of it. It will suit us very well for tonight, do you not think?' asked

Brynhild with wry amusement—the little shelter had 'lovers' tryst' marked all over it.

Erik nodded, turning to give her a wicked smile that released butterflies in her stomach. 'It will indeed. It must have taken them a long time to build it… Maybe they left a little later this morning, after being so busy the night before?'

'Maybe… He obviously wanted to pamper his lady. Look at the little mattress of soft leaves he made for her,' Brynhild said with a smile. In Francia she'd slept many nights in mud and filth, with only her shield as a cover. This was pure luxury in comparison.

'For *them*,' Erik said, pointing out the two dips in the pile of fern leaves.

Brynhild leaned into the space to take another look. It was small, but definitely built for two, and threaded through the green branches of the walls were red and gold leaves, in a shape that seemed deliberate, as if someone had taken the time to make the small shelter look…pretty. 'Definitely lovers then,' she mused.

What would it be like to make love to Erik here?

The unwelcome thought slid into her mind and dampened her amusement.

She would never know.

For some reason, seeing this lovingly made nest made her depressed. She should be happy. They were getting closer to catching their runaway bride and they were definitely on the right trail.

Except, now she felt…bad for them, and if she were honest, a little sad, too…for *herself.* No one would pamper her like this, she was the one who took care of people, not the other way around. But sometimes…she wished someone would care for her needs first, just like this.

'If you build the fire, I'll bring the horses,' Erik said, turning away, and she got to work pushing aside her selfish thoughts.

A short time later they were sitting together on a fallen log beside the campfire. A happy silence settled around them like a warm blanket, as they ate their fish stew and looked up at the stars.

Then, after deciding between themselves that a lot of fresh bread today and tomorrow was better than small chunks of stale bread over many days, they ploughed through most of it. It went against Brynhild's earlier plan for frugal rationing, but she didn't care. It was good bread and she did love bread.

Erik didn't care and happily agreed to most of her suggestions. For once she didn't need to think of another's needs before her own. They were both strong and capable, it was a relief in a strange sort of way. She could almost allow herself to enjoy this break from her usual responsibilities, although even thinking that felt wrong.

Their prey was close, she reminded herself firmly. It *did* take some of the pressure off her, knowing that they would soon catch up with their quarry—there was no shame in her feelings. They had a month to complete their task and at this rate they would have the Lady Alswn back with her brother in half that time. Helga's freedom felt more inevitable with each passing day, especially now that she had pushed down her own fears and focused only on what she could change in the days ahead.

Sighing with pleasure, she put her bowl down in the empty cauldron at their feet.

Erik passed her the flagon of mead and she drank from it gladly, before passing it back.

'Should we have a plan? For when we catch them?' she asked.

He thought for a moment. 'Probably best to read the situation first before attacking… They might recognise me, but they wouldn't know you. We will have to see what happens.'

She nodded. 'I've been so focused on finding them. I didn't really think about what I was going to do when I did.'

'It's simple. We take her back to her brother. Whether she likes it or not.'

'Yes,' she agreed, but then added, 'Let's try not to kill her man, though…not if we can help it.'

'No, not if we can help it.' His voice had a tenderness to it, as if he were holding back a smile. Although she couldn't be sure, sat beside him as she was and with only the small flickering flames to see by.

'Her grief would make her difficult to deal with,' she explained.

'True.'

'Because they love each other…' Brynhild said, although she didn't know why she felt the need to say it.

'True.' His voice was husky and barely audible over the crackling fire.

'Have you ever loved anyone?' she asked quietly, half afraid of the answer.

After a pause, he said, 'Yes… Halfdan and my mother.'

She smiled at his obvious avoidance. 'Never anyone else?'

There was an even longer pause, but eventually he said. 'I have never been with a woman.'

'Oh!' The gasp left her throat before she had time to stop it.

Surely not... A man like Erik...a virgin? Of course not, the idea was ridiculous! A man as handsome and as good as him? But then, why would he lie? Unless he meant...

'Do you prefer—?'

'I like women,' he added quickly for clarity. Then he cleared his throat, his words stopping and starting like a jittery horse. 'But...on the island... I was an outcast, no one even spoke to me then, not if they could help it...and then after... I... It never felt right.'

'Oh...' she said, unsure of what else to say. After her initial shock, she realised how unusual his honesty was. In Norse society, men bragged about taking women to their bed from a young age. Strange considering they didn't like their brides to do the same. 'You must think me—'

'Brave,' he answered firmly, silencing her from saying anything else disparaging.

A warm glow of pride filled her body at his compliment. Praise from Erik held greater meaning to her somehow—maybe because of their conflicted past. 'That wasn't what I was going to say.'

'But it is true… I was always afraid.'

Again, his honesty shocked her. 'Why?'

'I cannot be like my father…' He sighed before speaking, prodding the fire with a twig absently. 'My mother was a thrall. Captured and forced to bear his child.'

'But you would never behave like that!'

'No, never,' he agreed.

'Then there is nothing to fear,' she reassured him, placing a hand on the sleeve of his tunic and feeling the warm strength beneath. Her body responded and she moved her hand away as if burned.

Thankfully, Erik didn't seem to notice. He sighed and snapped the small branch into pieces, before throwing them into the flames. 'When I went sailing with Halfdan and was no longer under my father's influence, I suppose I could have… But I could not bear the possibility of leaving a child behind. A child in a distant land who would have no way of finding me… No. I could never do such a thing.'

Choosing her words carefully she said with a frown, 'There are ways to…not have a babe from it… They don't always work, of course… Valda is proof of that—but usually they do. There are also ways to find pleasure without the full…*act*, or you can try to stop yourself from spilling your seed inside a woman.' She stopped speaking as the heat of embarrassment burned her face and neck.

Erik shook his head, a few long strands of hair falling forward across his face. 'I know, Halfdan has said much the same to me—I am not completely ignorant.' He laughed at the doubtful look on her face. 'But I didn't want to take the risk. Not with a woman I didn't care for… Better to wait, at least until my freedom was bought and paid. Now, as a freeman, I can finally marry and my children will never know the life of a thrall.'

Brynhild flinched. 'I'm sorry. When Valda returned with Halfdan she told us how you were Ulf's thrall back then. What a hateful thing to do to your own child… I never re-alised that part of it… If I'd known…' She frowned. 'No, that is a poor excuse. I *should* have known. We all saw the way he treated you. It wasn't normal…or right.'

He didn't say anything, and she felt the si-lence keenly, like a boulder pressing down on both of them, crushing the pleasant atmosphere they'd previously enjoyed.

'Your bride will be a very fortunate woman,' she said softly, trying to ease the years of hurt that she knew could never be healed.

'As fortunate as Njal's?' he asked and she burst out laughing, the heavy gloom cracking like an egg.

'Oh, I should think so!' She laughed. It felt good to laugh with Erik, she could forget—if only for a moment—the worries of the future. 'You are far more handsome for a start,' she teased.

'But… I don't have good grazing land and rich soil?' he replied innocently, his voice suspiciously high as if he were mocking her.

She swatted him with her arm. 'Hush! You have a fine face and a fine figure. The women will be fighting each other just to catch your eye! *And,* Valda says you and Halfdan have plenty of silver—even after paying Ulf. You could buy as much "good grazing land and rich soil" as you want. I'd wager your lady, when you find her, will be the happiest bride to walk Midgard.'

'But… I do not know how to *please* a woman…' he said, turning towards her more fully, his eyes pleading with her to listen. A shiver of longing rushed through her, like a waterfall of heat. She prayed he didn't want her to explain bed sport to him.

She tried to laugh, but it came out weak and dry. Coughing to clear her throat, she said, 'I am sure you could learn…with time.'

'With the right person?'

'Sure.' She nodded, looking into the fire and hating that nameless woman more than she could have ever thought possible.

'You?'

The air rushed in and out of her lungs as she tried not to choke on her shock. To have a man such as Erik eager to please her in bed was a tantalising thought. One she dared not think about for too long.

She laughed bitterly, certain this was yet more jesting on his part. 'I think it is quite clear— I am definitely not the right woman to teach you. I haven't… I don't…you know…*enjoy* it!' She found herself glancing around the clearing suspiciously, as if she were afraid Sune and his sniggering friends would leap from the bushes at any moment to point and jeer at her.

'But you know how to pleasure yourself?'

he asked huskily, his body leaning slightly towards hers.

She cleared her throat. 'Well, yes... But...'

How many times had she thought about him while touching herself?

The image of him rising from his bed of straw all those years ago. Bare-chested, his dark hair falling into his eyes as he'd stared at her, long and hard. The sight of him reaching up above her head, the musk of his scent filling her nose as his golden arm flexed above hers to take down his tunic from a peg. Such a fleeting moment in her past and yet she'd thought about it over and over for many years.

Imagining all kinds of possibilities.

What if he'd kissed her there and then? Cupped her face in his hands and kissed her deeply...laid her down among the straw, and *taken her...*

But, no! She'd asked to see his kittens instead—like an idiot! *Urgh!*

Could she have been any more childish and pathetic at that moment? Probably not. But it was still her most treasured memory of their time alone together.

To her horror, Erik appeared to be warming to the idea of having her as his guide in the art of lovemaking, as he deliberately placed his hand on her thigh, the searing heat of his light touch like a hot coal on her skin.

'And you are honest!' he insisted. 'The most honest woman I have ever met. You wouldn't lie to me if I was doing it wrong, you'd tell me, because you always speak the truth…always!' His eyes shone with fire in the flickering light and she felt a lightning bolt of satisfaction burn down her spine at his compliment. It wasn't entirely true, of course—she'd told him in Jorvik she'd never liked him, which was the boldest lie she'd ever uttered. But she supposed in all other matters she did speak her mind.

Now, she wondered if Erik had lost his…

She became lost in his eyes, searching for lies or mockery and finding none.

Surely the most beautiful man she'd ever met wasn't asking her to sleep with him? It was simply…ridiculous.

His hand lifted from her thigh and her relief was quickly replaced with shock as his fingers lifted to cup her jaw. She sank into the heat of his palm with a sigh of longing, her eyes closing as she savoured the touch.

It had been so long since someone had touched her like this.

The fact it was Erik made it impossible to pull away.

They were back in the barn in her mind. This time she would do what she'd only dreamed of doing back then.

Her own hand moved to rest against his thigh—for balance, she told herself. He sucked in a breath between his teeth as her fingers gripped solid muscle. Ripples of pleasure washed through her and she opened her eyes to stare into his, waiting with tense anticipation for whatever might happen next.

His lips crushed against hers. It wasn't a delicate kiss, it was bruising and clumsy, but it was also intoxicating because it was filled with passion and longing. Her hand lifted to his jaw, pushing him gently back with her fingers to steady his kiss. Instinctively, he reined back his pressure and she opened for him in acceptance. His inexperienced tongue slipped between her lips to taste her tentatively and she met him with a sensual stroke of her own. He groaned into her mouth and she gripped the silky hair she'd yearned to feel for years.

They explored each other's mouths for a long time, until the hot arousal between her legs made her squirm. She pressed a little closer towards him, impatient for more. Their tongues slid in and out of each other's mouths, mimicking the mating they were desperate to experience with each other.

Nothing had ever felt like this.

No kiss, no person, had ever made her this wet with need.

It couldn't be real.

She moaned against his lips, but pulled away, bracing her hands against his chest as if to hold him back.

Part of her still feared this was all a jest.

Was he going to turn into Sune? Laugh at her and make grunting noises to tease her for her own naivety?

No. She'd long ago moved past those fears.

She was a shieldmaiden. Powerful and in control.

She had a mission to complete. *A sister to save!*

'We *need* to concentrate on our task ahead.' She gasped, sucking in a deep breath. 'Helga...'

Why did it feel as though she was reminding herself of this, and not Erik?

'You're right,' he grunted, shifting away from her and running a hand through his mussed hair, in a way so heartbreakingly familiar to her. 'I am sorry. I should not have done that. You have bigger problems to consider.'

'No, no,' she reassured him, trying to avoid staring at the impressive bulge between his thighs. 'I… It was…good.' At the dismay on his face, she added with a breathless laugh, 'Very good. But… We have a long day tomorrow… a long month, really…' *Oh, why was she talking about long things?* 'I think we should go to bed…to sleep. I think that would be for the best, yes?'

He nodded, disappointment written across his face, but also acceptance. 'You are right.'

Why did his agreement dishearten her?

They put a couple of small logs on the fire. And went to bed, fully clothed, the bedding rolls unfurled and wrapped around them tightly, their backs lightly pressed against one another.

Chapter Ten

The next morning, Brynhild's traps had caught a rabbit in the early hours, and so they roasted it on a spit for *dagmal*. Erik watched her with hungry fascination as she eagerly ate her final chunk of bread. It was the reason why he'd readily agreed to eating all of the bread now rather than stretching it out, because he liked to see her happy. It was charming how something as simple as a good meal could please her.

What did it matter if they risked a lighter meal later on? They could both hunt and forage if they needed to. Most of his childhood had been spent scrounging for food like a dog. He was proud that he no longer feared the threat of hunger, but it was obviously still a concern for Brynhild by the way she had worried about their supplies at first.

Brynhild always seemed at war with herself, conflicted by what she wanted and her concern for prudence. He supposed she'd always put her own needs last because she was the main provider for her own family. But she didn't need to worry about that with him, he could take care of himself. If anything, he longed to care for her instead, to ease her worries and allow her the freedom to relax. It would be a pleasure for someone as assured as Brynhild to need him.

She gave a cheerful exhale of her satisfaction as she put aside her bowl and stretched her arms above her head and arched her spine.

Quickly he shifted his gaze to stare intently at the trees, his mind suddenly spinning with lustful thoughts that he tried hopelessly to calm. Last night's kiss had awakened in him feelings he'd repressed for so long. The need for touch, heat and intimacy. Now that he'd had a taste of those denied feelings, he found the need for them had become all consuming. He longed to brush his fingers across her cheek and kiss her again. He'd spent most of his sleepless night savouring the memory of her lips against his and wondering how good it would feel to wrap her in his arms and press his weight against hers.

The slap of Brynhild's hands brought him

out of his fantasy. 'Come on! We must not let the day escape us.' She gathered up half of the cooking equipment. 'I will wash these and have a quick dip in the river. Then you can do the rest while you take your turn to wash. Yes?'

Before he could nod his response, she was sauntering off towards the river.

It wasn't long before they were back on the well-worn path as it snaked north-west through hills and valleys. His eyes drank in the nature like a man starved. He'd seen many wonders and stunning landscapes on his travels, but there was something comforting about this country, with its dips and rises. The winters here were less harsh than Gotland, the summers warm, but not like the desert. Not acrid and unforgiving.

It was always fertile and lush...wholesome.

The dips became more prominent as they passed several large lakes, the water shining like pools of liquid silver, reflecting the landscape around them with a pure clarity that shocked the senses.

The hills and mountains were blanketed in swathes of green, brown and red heathers. Scattered with clusters of trees dipped in gold, the leaves fluttering across the landscape on the breath of the wind. A few evergreens defiantly hung on to their lush green branches, oblivious to the rest of the world changing around them, but otherwise the world was aflame with colour. The only sign of the mild threat of winter was in the dark clouds rolling across the sky, promising darker nights and heavier rain to come.

They rode in silence for many hours and Erik felt every breath of them, the landscape the only comfort to his nerves. Brynhild had occasionally commented on the possible change in weather, but he'd never responded in much depth, unsure of what else to say. With every passing moment he became more convinced that he'd made some terrible mistake by kissing her.

Brynhild hadn't spoken of it afterwards and had instead gone to sleep while he'd spent a long time trying helplessly to calm his lust. As with all things she'd met his passion with confidence, showing him gently how it was done. As first kisses went, it had been perfect, for him at least, and he would treasure it for the rest of his life.

But had he gone too far? Been too honest?

He'd felt vulnerable telling her about his previous decision never to lay with a woman. Any other warrior would have laughed at his fears and even questioned his manhood. But she'd reassured him with her usual kind and pragmatic manner. No judgement, only compassion and honesty. He would always be grateful to her for that.

And for their kiss...

So hot and wet, he'd ached with fierce longing when she'd rubbed her tongue against his so sensually. She had guided his kiss, softened it and encouraged it, and he'd heard her moan... which meant she must have liked it, at least partly? Which was incredible. He was desperate to try again, to see what other cries he could draw from her body.

Would it be like that, if he moved inside her? Hot, wet and exquisitely pleasurable? His cock stiffened at the thought.

He wanted Brynhild to be his first, if she allowed it, and he hoped he hadn't ruined things between them. If things had been different, he knew without a doubt he would have courted her when they'd first met. But as it was, he'd hurt her instead. It had been for her own good, of course—if Ulf had seen even a flicker of desire in Erik's eyes for Brynhild, he would have used her to torment him because that's what he liked to do.

And now she was even more intoxicating

than she'd been then. So confident and fearless. Experimenting with her sexuality, and deciding without hesitation, or regret, what suited her best. He admired her for that.

Although part of him wished to cut those men in two for disappointing her, another part of him was glad. *He* wanted to be the one to please her and he was determined that if she should ever grant him the opportunity to prove himself, he would refuse to take his own pleasure until he had at least given her hers—no matter how agonising the prospect.

He would be better than those two men. In fact, he would ensure he was *so good* that no one would ever compare to him in future and Brynhild would be spoiled for all others. It was a challenge he would relish fulfilling with great delight…except he didn't know how.

Half the night he'd spent wondering all the ways he could so easily have turned around and pulled her back into his arms, while his lack of knowledge and experience chained him from reaching out to her.

What if she didn't want him to touch her again?

She'd been right to admonish him. They had

to focus on her sister, his desires were inappropriate.

Erik shifted in his saddle awkwardly to ease the chafe of his erection. He had responsibilities. They had one sister to catch and another to save. He shouldn't be confusing their already tender renewal of friendship with demands of his own. Brynhild had enough to deal with as it was.

Besides, he would rather cut off his own hands than do anything without a woman's permission. If he were honest, his father's treatment of his mother had soured his view of the intimacy between a man and a woman. It had always struck him as an imbalance of power. A cruel way for one person to dominate another. He knew that was because of his own twisted father's behaviour. But he couldn't help but fear he might do the same, without realising it. Even if he chose a wife now, most women were smaller and more fragile than him. He was a warrior after all.

What if, in the heat of the moment, he accidently hurt his partner? The repulsive thought made his stomach lurch and his arousal die.

Trapped by his own doubts and worries, he couldn't even consider a woman without fearing the worst. At least with someone like

Brynhild, he could never hurt her, not even by
accident. She was powerful, strong and coura-
geous. He'd never met a warrior more honourable…or as sweet and divinely feminine, too.
He wasn't afraid of physically hurting her. She
could match him in battle and she spoke her
mind. She was his perfect match in all ways.

Glancing over at her, he indulged in watching
her a while. She rode with a strong roll of her
hips, her spine straight, her face tilted up to the
weak sunlight of the autumn day. She focused
on the winding path leading up the hillside with
calm determination.

She would not be considered beautiful, he
supposed. Not in the way most men liked. There
was no delicateness to her features, or pretty
curves to her lips and eyes, as he'd seen in his
own mother's beauty. But there was a sharp
strength in her even features, her skin as clear
and as pale as the colour of cream. Her long hair
was tied back, smooth as Byzantine silk and
the colour of dried wheat, the lightness starkly
contrasted with the powerful blue of her eyes
that shone with bright perceptive intelligence.

People stared at her when she entered a hall
and it wasn't just because she was tall and pow-

erful, but because she was unique, commanding the space around her with her mere presence.

He thought of the thousands of beautiful stars in the sky and how the moon shared the night with all of them. In contrast, the sun's light was shared with no one else, so dazzling and powerful, nothing could ever compete with it. No one would dare.

Brynhild was the sun.

She turned to look at him, her gaze unwavering. 'What?'

'Nothing.' Erik blinked and looked away, feeling as if he'd been blinded by staring at her for too long.

'I think we'll be coming to a settlement soon,' she said, nodding to the sheep and goats grazing on the hill.

He nodded, his mouth dry as if he were crossing the sandy dunes of the eastern desert and not fresh green fields.

Brynhild gave a heavy sigh of disdain. 'You speak very little, you know. You should be called Erik the Mute, not Erik the Black.'

He smiled. He had been distracted by his thoughts, unsure of what to say to her. This finally gave him the opportunity to really talk with her once more. 'I think I would prefer it.'

'Then call yourself it,' she said with a shrug, followed more gently by, 'You do not have to keep the name your father gave you when he freed you. You could choose something else… something to honour your mother perhaps?'

'Sons are not called after their mothers,' he reminded her.

She huffed indignantly. 'Pfft! They should be. Especially after pushing your big heads out!'

He couldn't help but laugh at her crudity.

'You know…' she added thoughtfully, 'Valda's old commander named himself after his mother. She was a shieldmaiden, named after one of the frost giant's daughters. So, he called himself Jötunnson. I thought it a clever way of honouring his mother.'

'My mother wasn't a giant. She was a slave,' he replied drily.

To his surprise she glared at him. '*She* was your *mother* and she deserves respect. Most of all from you.'

'I respect her,' he said, his voice suddenly hoarse as he realised how true her statement was.

'What was her name?'

'Anahita.'

'And did she have a family name?'

'Anahita bint al-Khusraw.'

'You could use that,' Brynhild said, although her wince at the long name was telling, and he laughed.

She blushed and laughed with him. 'Sorry.'

'Don't be,' he said, 'Although…you have made me think. Maybe I shall call myself Erik the Free?'

'It is a good name,' she agreed, then sat up in her saddle as they crested the hill. 'A large farm. Do you think our friends stopped here?'

'Let us see.'

Below in the valley was a homestead, surrounded by a few smaller buildings that looked like barns or stables. There were pens for livestock, as well as a couple of fields of grain.

They approached one of the workers feeding the pigs in one of the pens. The man came over to speak with them. Young and strong, with a ruddy face and sandy beard, he looked at the weapons they carried with wary eyes, then the man spoke in Cumbric, a Brythonic language.

Brynhild and Erik exchanged a look—they were now in Rheged, one of the old kingdoms of the north.

Erik spoke first. Haltingly, but in the man's tongue, followed by some Saxon.

The man nodded and then went into the hall, holding a hand up firmly, as if to ask them to stay where they were. They nodded with what they hoped were friendly smiles.

'You speak Cumbric?' Brynhild asked, obviously impressed.

Erik sighed. 'A few of my father's thralls were Britons. I learned a little, but I speak it badly. How is your Saxon?'

'Not much better than your Cumbric, I would guess. I lived most of my life in Francia. But I have improved it a little over the last year of living in Jorvik.'

An elderly couple came out from the farmhouse. He noticed the crosses at their necks and how they frowned at their weapons, as well as Brynhild's clothing, with distinct disapproval.

'Greetings,' he said, 'My name is Erik the Free and this is my wife, Brynhild. May we ask for your hospitality tonight?' If Brynhild was shocked by his lie, she didn't show it. Maybe her Saxon was as poor as she claimed.

'We can speak Norse, if that is your *mother's tongue*?' said the woman, her lips pinched, as she looked at him.

'My father's,' he replied in Norse and the woman's eyes flickered with disdain.

Brynhild cleared her throat and leaned forward in what could only be described as a mildly threatening manner and the woman paled.

She was mature in age, her red-gold hair streaked with white. The man next to her had a grey beard and balding head—they both looked unhappy to see them. 'You may stay one night, as hospitality dictates…in the barn. We will send some food to you.'

Yes, very unfriendly. They would have to tread carefully with these people.

'We are grateful for the shelter. We slept out in the open last night. But I suppose, being so close to the road, you get lots of travellers passing by.'

'Not really. You are the first in a long time,' snapped the lady, a little too quickly.

'Not in these autumn months, at least… What's your reason for passing through these lands?' said the man with a smile, although his jovial attitude appeared forced.

He glanced around at the farm and noticed the worker was watching them with keen interest. 'We are visiting my sister. She recently married and we have come to wish them well. Their marriage was not approved by my family, but

my wife insisted we let them know personally…
they will always have a friend in us.'

'What are their names? We might know of
them.'

Erik smiled slowly. 'I do not think so. They
live far north of here. We have a long road ahead
and our journey has only just begun.'

Erik made a big show of taking a silver dirham out of his bag and flipping it in the air before dropping down from his saddle to hand
it to the man. 'For your kindness,' he said and
the man took it, although the woman scowled
darkly at her husband for doing so.

Brynhild also dismounted from her horse and
they led both animals towards the barn.

'So, *Husband*—what do you think?' asked
Brynhild under her breath. There was a twinkle
in her eyes as she spoke, which eased his worry
about calling her his wife earlier.

'I think we are getting very close.'

'I think you might be right.'

In the barn they saw to their horses first before laying down their bedrolls in the hay loft.
The worker came in, carrying a bag of oats and
vegetable peelings which he poured out for the
hungry horses, who gobbled at them greedily.

'There is a well behind the Hall,' he said in

Cumbric, or at least that's what Erik thought he said, judging by the way the man pointed at the empty trough and buckets.

'Thank you,' Erik replied in what he hoped were the correct words. The man looked at the purse hanging from his belt with interest.

'Have you seen a couple come through here recently?' asked Erik and then repeated the question in both Saxon and Norse for good measure.

The man only grunted in response before leaving.

Brynhild looked as confused as he was. 'Was that a yes, or a no?'

'I think that was a "let me think about it".'

They filled the trough with the buckets from the well, then washed their hands and faces. By the time they were done, the lady and worker had come out with two wooden platters of food for them.

There was no brazier or torches and they ate with the door of the barn wide open as the sun sank beneath the horizon.

The worker came back just as the last burning light of dusk filled the sky. Dropping a sack of supplies at their feet, he said, 'For tomorrow.' Then he took their platters from them. It had been a decent meal of thick pottage, and bread. The man kicked at the straw around their feet.

'Silver?' he muttered quietly.

Erik nodded and took one dirham out of his bag and held it up.

Red and gold light shivered across its surface and reflected in the worker's eyes. The swirling script of the Abbasid caliphate's stamp proclaimed with enticing certainty its weight in value. High quality, undisputed silver that could be cut up and used to buy whatever a man wanted from the markets. With a click of Erik's fingers, the coin shifted, revealing a second coin beneath it. 'Where?'

The man's eyes brightened and after a quick glance to the closed doors of the farmhouse, he squatted to the ground and began shuffling with the straw at their feet. Brynhild came closer to watch. It appeared the man was drawing a crude map.

He twisted up a bunch of straw to make a rectangle and then circled his hand above his head. 'Farm,' he said, placing it on the ground. He began to draw lines in the dirt with his fingers. Creating two sweeping hills to indicate the valley between the two mountainous regions they now sat between. Then he used pieces of straw to show the curve of the land where it met the sea, even drawing a little boat to show the difference between them.

'Quite the craftsman,' said Brynhild with a dry smile.

'Dragon's sister,' the man said, stabbing at an area on the coast, adding with a sweep of his hand over the whole area, 'Friends to the Cymru.'

Erik nodded—that was the word the Welsh used to describe themselves. The man was warning them that the region would be more favourable to the couple than to any Norse strangers.

'Alauna.' He pointed at the map again, at a specific place on the coast by the little boat.

Erik stared at the map, committing it to memory. He had done this many times before on his travels, when only a few common words and hastily drawn pictures could show the way.

'How far?' Brynhild asked.

The man shrugged, before pointing at their horses. 'Two days?'

'I guess it depends on the horses,' said Erik. 'Ours have lasted well the last three days, but they will definitely need a rest after five.'

She nodded in agreement.

Erik handed the man the two coins. Capturing his gaze with a hard look, he placed a hand on his sword for emphasis. 'Truth?'

The man shrank back a little at the unspoken threat and nodded quickly. Then he dragged his foot across the dirt, sweeping away the map in one movement.

'Truth,' he snapped back, before biting each coin suspiciously and then leaving with them.

Erik was inclined to believe him.

Chapter Eleven

Brynhild lay in the darkness, her back pressed against Erik's as was their custom since leaving Jorvik, when she'd first admitted to missing Helga by her side. Tonight, however, she struggled to sleep.

So much was unsaid between them and not only to do with their kiss the previous night. Which, honestly, she couldn't believe had happened in the first place. They were barely friends—how had things escalated so quickly between them? How had she felt more in one kiss with Erik than with three previous lovers?

The questions rattled through her mind, along with the other more obvious worries she had regarding the future plaguing her rest and making her shift awkwardly in her bedding. It was no good—she would have to tackle it, or find no peace.

'Erik?' she whispered so lightly that, if he were asleep, she would not disturb him. To her surprise he answered clearly and without a drop of tiredness in his voice.

'Yes?'

As the couple had left them with no brazier or torch to see by, the barn was so dark she could barely see her hand in front of her face. She turned to him, propping herself up on her elbow and shuffling back a little so that she wasn't immediately in his face. Except, they were already very close and she only managed to move less than an arm's reach away, both their big bodies filling the space between them with the scent of warm hay.

'We could be with them in two days.'

'Yes,' he repeated, his voice calm—a refreshing balm on her prickly nerves.

'I was thinking… We should see where they are first and watch them. Rest the horses, see about a boat, then steal her away as soon as she's alone.'

'A good plan.'

She sank back in the hay with a sigh of relief, glad that he approved of her suggestion.

Not because she needed his approval, but because it would make the execution of her plan far easier if they were agreed upon it…and, yes, it did reassure her a little that he thought it a decent plan.

'So, we will need to find a place close by… A hiding place to keep watch on them from, until we have those things in place.'

'We'll see what the land is like when we get there,' he replied.

'Yes,' agreed Brynhild, 'it will depend on the terrain. But… If I was young and wanted to hide away from my family with a man, I would pick somewhere secluded. A small house in the woods, perhaps?' She thought of the little shelter they'd made along the way. A fragile home, just for two. 'Or a place by the sea or river, near to a settlement, but not within it.'

'They might be staying with friends or distant family,' suggested Erik.

'True…they would need help at first. But… I would wager they've decided to hide away from the world completely.'

A smile warmed the breath of Erik's words when he next spoke—she couldn't see it, of course, but she felt it in the tender way he said her name, like a stroke of silk against her skin. 'What makes you think that, *Brynhild*?'

She swallowed hard and stared up at the ceiling, trying to ignore the flutters of awareness in her belly. 'The little hut they made in the woods. The woman decorated the sides with autumn leaves…did you notice that?'

'Yes,' he murmured and she felt him shift beside her, as if he were sitting up on his elbow as she'd previously done. 'But why does that make you believe they will choose to live a secluded life?'

She tried to ignore his movement and instead pondered on the other questions that had been pestering her. 'She was a lady. The daughter of a powerful warlord. You would think she would miss the security and comforts of her home…'

'Possibly. Could that be why she added the leaves, for decoration, to make it feel more… luxurious?'

'Maybe, but… I do not think so. I think she loved being there with him and it was her way of expressing her happiness being away from everything and everyone. She wouldn't want to spoil it by living with others, especially ones she doesn't know well… She's madly in love and wants to forget her life before, or her obligations.' Brynhild paused—sometimes she felt sorry for them, she knew herself how heavy the pressure of duty could be. But she forced herself to remember Helga's face and the reason why she was hunting this couple in the first place. 'I will remind her of that *duty*.'

'As will I,' Erik replied firmly and she smiled at his show of support.

'Thank you, Erik.' She reached out and squeezed the arm he rested on, her hand lingering on his tunic sleeve for a moment longer than she'd intended, enjoying the breadth of his muscles beneath. He leaned towards her, his shadow falling over her, combined intoxicatingly with his rich, musky scent to overpower her senses.

Her heart began to beat faster as she waited breathlessly in the darkness, wondering what else he might do.

'I am sorry, too,' she blurted out, not realising until then how desperately she wanted to bury her own regrets from the past.

'For what?' Erik asked, his shadow rocking back a little with surprise.

She sucked in a deep breath. 'For hitting you… You were already wounded with your hand… And I hit you…*hard*. It wasn't right.'

A throaty laugh rippled overhead and she frowned.

'Don't pretend I didn't!' she cried, offended that he would find the idea amusing. She rose up on to both of her elbows in irritation, ready to argue the point. 'The day after Sune and those bleating sheep of his found us together in your barn. I knocked you senseless in front of them and…' guilt washed through her '…it was in front of your father.' Memories flooded back and shame threatened to suffocate her. Erik had apologised and now it was her turn to face her past mistakes. 'I shouldn't have done that and I'm sorry.'

'I goaded you,' he said quietly.

She winced at his honesty—he'd more than goaded her, he'd ripped out her heart in front of everyone present. 'That *still* doesn't make it right.'

'It does.' His breath was as gentle as a summer breeze against her face, and she realised how close they now were, their faces reaching to meet one another. 'After you left that morning, I told Sune that you only stayed with me to keep an eye on me after my *accident*. That you were just being kind. But…you know what he was like.'

'*Pathetic.*'

'Exactly, and I was afraid for you. If Ulf thought I'd formed an attachment...*slept* with you... I don't know what he would have done. He might not have cared, or he might have beaten me for daring to bed a free woman. Worst of all...he might have hurt *you*. I couldn't risk it. He hated anyone speaking with me normally and I didn't want to put you in any more danger after you'd helped me. So, I thought it best to stop any rumours from building. That's why I did...*it.*'

That single word *it* encompassed the very worst day of her life. Not the day Sune and his friends had laughed at her stumbling from Erik's barn, her face aflame. That had been nothing.

No, *it* was what had happened the following day.

When she'd been walking alone back from training with her mother and she'd had to walk past Sune with his friends. They had been standing by the pig pens. The same pens Erik had been mucking out while Ulf watched, his poor bandaged hand fumbling as he gripped the pitchfork. Trying his best to keep it clean among the filth. He must have been in so much pain, but he hadn't let it show, especially not in front of Ulf.

Sune had started it, grunting at her as she passed. She'd ignored him, thinking that would be the end of it. But then the group of boys had rushed her. She was sure their intention had been to throw her into the muck and laugh at her. But she was quick and strong, throwing two to the ground before the others even knew how to react. Sune had grabbed a spare pitchfork from the ground and smacked her belly with its handle. She'd stopped herself from falling by grabbing hold of Erik. He'd caught her, held her, and for a moment she'd felt so safe in his arms.

But then Sune had sneered, 'It is no wonder you want her, Erik! You enjoy sleeping with beasts!'

That was when Erik's grip had turned from comforting to cruel and he'd pushed her away in disgust. 'I don't want her! You are mad if you think any man could want her. Get away from me, you unnatural beast!'

She'd stared at him, confused and horrified. That's when he'd mimicked a snorting grunt at her and blind rage had filled her vision at his betrayal. She'd struck out before she'd even had time to think, punching him square in the nose, knocking him clear off his feet and into the muck.

She'd hit him hard and fast, pure emotion throwing the punch with a sickening crunch, and she knew she'd broken his nose. Marring the beautiful face she'd previously been infatuated with.

Then, with her back straight, she'd strode through the crowd of young men, the cowards moving warily out of her way as she passed. They had never bothered her again after that.

Then she'd heard Ulf's hateful laugh and her stomach had twisted with guilt. He was amused to see his son, humiliated and lying unconscious in the dirt, and she'd shivered at the sound.

She'd never felt so hurt, or so shameful in all of her life.

'I broke your nose…' she whispered, cupping his face and running a long finger down its crooked length. 'Did you hurt your head, too, when you landed?'

'I have a hard head.'

She smiled, 'So do I.'

His hand curved around her face in the darkness, stroking his thumb across her lips as if to check where they were, then he dipped his head and pressed his lips against hers. Almost melting against him, she was surprised when he moved slightly away, his breath still warm against her lips, as if in question.

'I didn't mean what I said back then,' he said finally.

'What part? *No man could want her!*' she mimicked in a deep voice. 'Or *oink-oink!*' She snorted loudly.

He brushed his lips once more against hers in a tender apology. 'All of it…and I *like* the sound of your grunts.'

She gasped in horror and then slapped his shoulder. 'Shut up! Besides, I never grunt any more… I trained hard on my breathing after that summer. I'm as silent as the moon now.'

'And as bright as the sun,' he said, stroking her cheek once again. 'But you shouldn't have changed your behaviour because of that. You are beautiful. You do not need to change for anyone, especially not for disgusting men like Sune. He couldn't beat you in a fair fight and he knew it. You are a goddess compared to him.'

She chuckled. 'Are you practising, Erik? Because there is no need to use pretty words on me. Especially when I know they're horse sh—'

He crushed his mouth against hers and, for a reason she couldn't quite understand, she opened for him with equally eager passion. As if they hadn't just been needling each other like old friends only moments before. As if every word, look and thought had been building up to this moment of rapture. Maybe it had.

Their laboured breaths mingled, becoming one. Hot and desperate tongues stroked against one another in sultry pleasure. It was clumsy and erratic, but also delightful in its intensity. Brynhild's head spun with the sudden change. How she had longed for him to kiss her like this all those years before. To fling her down in the straw and make love to her with urgent and all-consuming lust.

Was this a dream?

She pulled slightly away to drag some air into her tight lungs and tried her best to focus. An impossible task when his dark hair brushed against her jaw and he licked the pulse at her neck as if to soothe her racing heart.

'Show me how to please you,' he whispered against her neck, 'Teach me what you like... How you make yourself...*come*,' he gasped. 'I want to know. I *need* to know.'

Their bodies were so warm against the soft hay and the bedrolls beneath them, the thin blankets they'd laid over their bodies pushed aside and forgotten in the heat of the moment.

Brynhild was so hot and wet between her thighs. She'd never been like this before with any other man. With her own fingers and her own imagination, yes, but never with anyone else. To even get half this aroused would have taken a long time with a partner. But it was different with Erik, maybe because she knew he meant every word.

Her byrnie and belt were already off, as she didn't like to sleep with her weapons and purse attached, preferring to have them in easy reach by her side and not to be restricted by them if it wasn't necessary. So, it wasn't difficult to undo the ties around her waist. She took his hand in hers and brought it down beneath the fabric of her trousers and between her thighs.

A low groan ripped from his throat when he felt her wet heat and she gasped with pleasure as his big hand cupped her, instinctively massaging her mound. 'Here,' she whispered, laying a finger over one of his own to touch herself. 'I like to stroke, slowly at first and in tiny circles, like this…there…' The words died in her throat as he moved in the way she liked and suddenly she was panting against his mouth, as he rained kisses against her face and neck.

Her hips began to arch against his fingers.

'I have heard,' he said, his voice almost lazy as he stroked her, 'a woman is ready when she is hot and wet...'

'That is true,' she gasped and he groaned into her neck, the sound causing a thousand shivers across her skin.

'I have also heard...' he rasped between kisses, 'that you can kiss a woman between her legs to satisfy her... Do you want me to do that?'

She moaned. 'Let us just keep to one lesson at a time, yes?' she said, unsure if she could take any more as it was.

'I wish it wasn't so dark,' he whispered against her ear, as his fingers never deviated from the bud she'd shown him. He followed her instructions well, adding his own twist to her pleasure as he breathed sultry words into her ear. 'I love to hear you pant for me. I want to watch you climax. Should I get a torch?'

Her breathing became erratic, coming out in soft desperate gasps. She gripped his forearm tightly, afraid that he might move away from her. 'Don't stop!' she pleaded, and then, 'A little faster!'

No sooner had he changed his pace than her thighs were clenching, gripping his hand tightly, as waves of pleasure rushed through her. She cried out, her neck arching with her spine, delicious tension breaking into waves of pure ecstasy.

Afterwards she slumped into her bedding, spent, her body boneless and light, like warm honey cakes fresh from the oven. She sighed happily as he removed his hand.

'Was it good?' he asked, his voice rich and husky.

'Very, *very* good,' she mumbled, turning towards him in the darkness and pressing a light kiss against his lips. His arms wrapped around her and before she knew it, she'd fallen into blissful sleep, all previous tension and worry forgotten.

Chapter Twelve

Erik stared into the darkness, his body stiff and aching with need. But he didn't care about his mild physical frustration. He was too damn satisfied with himself!

Taking Brynhild to the heights of her pleasure with only his fingers and a few kisses had been a revelation. One he was unbearably smug about. If Brynhild could see the grin on his face right now, he was certain she would roll her eyes at his male pride. But he couldn't help it, he'd never been prouder of himself!

Although he couldn't be certain. He hoped he'd succeeded where her previous lovers had failed—but he refused to disturb her rest to find out.

As it was, she slept in his arms peacefully unaware of his arrogant and conceited thoughts.

It was enough that she had accepted him—he would not press for more.

No. It was more than acceptance, she had *welcomed* him. He'd never imagined such a perfect moment could even be possible between them.

Happiness was an unusual emotion for Erik and he savoured it like a cool drink in the desert. Even when he had paid for his freedom, it had tasted like a bittersweet victory, a goal that he never should have had to accomplish in the first place.

Not this, though.

This had been pure pleasure. The satisfying fulfilment of a long-held fantasy. One he would treasure for years to come.

After how he had treated her, he didn't deserve her acceptance. His arms tightened around her, as shame crawled over his skin, chilling him to the bone. Brynhild gave a soft sigh of contentment against the dip in his neck and he breathed her scent in deeply, seeking comfort in her closeness.

Hay and sunshine. That was what she smelled like. And *freedom.*

He remembered the first day they'd met. How she'd stood in the doorway of his barn and assessed him in the summer light. Strong and fearless, and so free… She'd embodied everything he'd ever wanted for himself and then she'd shyly asked to see some kittens. An intriguing contrast of sweetness and power.

All of Porunn's daughters had this strange, mirrored personality, but none so sharply as Brynhild. Even if he spent a thousand days with her, she would still surprise him and he liked that about her.

They'd talked over the kittens and he'd even indulged in petting them with her.

Normally he wouldn't have taken the risk. The settlement cats were his only companions, apart from Halfdan. They didn't care where he slept, or who his mother had been. They were a necessary part of island life, as they kept the pests under control. There was no risk of Ulf killing them out of spite. But he'd still kept his affection for them a closely guarded secret. Except when he was with Brynhild, because he'd somehow known she would not tell anyone about his weakness for them and she never had, even after she'd hit him.

The cats looked after themselves, stole scraps from the Jarl's table, and slept in the barn…

just like him. Sometimes he would hold and pet them at night, just to ease the loneliness in his heart and to feel the gentle touch of another living creature.

Brynhild had been delighted by them. Pressing their soft fur into her face and talking to them in a light and soothing tone the entire time, as if they could understand her, which sometimes he imagined they did. She'd not cared about his lowly status and had come back regularly to speak with him and see the kittens. Sometimes she would spend more time talking, and helping him with his chores, than she did petting the cats.

He'd warned her once. *'The others will shun you for talking to me.'*

But she'd shrugged away his concern, unbothered. *'Shame on them for treating you so poorly. I do not care for the company of mindless cowards anyway.'*

Then, after his punishment, she'd stayed with him, tended to his wounded hand and not told anyone about the horror he'd suffered. Even when Sune and his friends had found them together the next morning, she'd said nothing. Leaving silently with dignity and grace, she'd left it up to him whether to deny or confirm what had happened between them. He'd known he could say whatever he liked and she wouldn't have argued it. Accepting the jeers of puny braggarts without question—if it kept his own honour intact.

That's when he'd known how dangerously close he was to loving her.

His Valkyrie.

Even when the boys had pushed her into the pig pen, trying their best to intimidate her with their teasing harassment, she'd remained invincible. Refusing to fall at their feet, or shed a single tear of humiliation, and not even a flicker of fear entered her eyes. She'd turned on them with unshakeable courage. A goddess.

Throwing two into the very muck they'd tried to push her in. Sune had shown his own weakness by using the handle of a pitchfork against her. He must have realised she could have bested them all easily and sought to use a gutless advantage.

Even after being struck, she'd only staggered a few steps backwards. That's when she'd grabbed his tunic, reaching for him, her friend, to help steady her balance.

Rage and fury had flooded his veins at the

sight of her being attacked, but he was paralysed to help. As a thrall he could be executed for striking a freeman's son and Ulf stood watching only a few feet away. If he found out Erik cared for her...the consequences could be dire. Ulf had already threatened his brother regarding his relationship with Valda—he would show no such lenience with Erik.

Brynhild would have been dead before the end of the summer and for what?

She didn't *need* him. She didn't need anyone.

Was that why he'd said what he'd said?

Angry and bitter that she would never need him as much as he wanted her to? Or was it really to save her from Ulf's wrath?

Whatever his reasons, he'd never forgotten the look on her face when he'd pushed her away from him.

The shock and hurt, as he rejected her openly in front of the very people she'd protected him from. The betrayal.

And now she'd forgiven him, let him touch and pleasure her?

It was unbelievable and humbling. He clasped his iron arm ring in the darkness, the only gift he'd ever received from his father. It symbolised his newfound freedom and honour. Silently in the darkness he swore an oath on the cold metal.

Never again will I betray you, Brynhild. Never.

Chapter Thirteen

Brynhild woke him as she rose from his arms. Sleepily he watched as she donned her byrnie, weapons and purse in the fragile light of dawn. As he sat up on to his elbows, his hair fell forward, obscuring his eyes.

'You look more tumbled than I!' she said, as she tossed him his sheathed sword.

Catching it easily, he used the pommel to brush aside his hay-strewn hair to smile up at her. 'Maybe I am a little dazed…'

With a dismissive huff she tightened her belt and headed towards the ladder. 'Remember, it is probably wise for us not to linger here.'

Sighing, he put on his own weapons and rolled up their bedding, tossing them down to her as she waited below. Everything was so easy between them, as if they had been travelling together for years and not days. They used the wash bucket and saw to their needs at the farm's waste pit before packing up their belongings.

A simple *dagmal* of apples and bread with butter were the only offerings they received from their reluctant hosts. The bare minimum of hospitality expected by travellers and left out on the farmhouse's doorstep in a covered pot. Encouraging no further discussion and a clear hint for them to leave as soon as possible.

As they rode out of the sleepy farm the cockerel crowed. They didn't bother saying farewell.

A low mist on the horizon promised heavy rain to come. So, they wrapped their cloaks more tightly around themselves and pressed forward as much as they could.

They rode up and down countless rocky hills and heathered valleys, the horses' breath heavy with steam, so that they had to stop regularly to allow them time to rest.

Erik didn't mind the slow progress. It gave him more time with Brynhild and who could say how much longer they had together? Especially once Helga was freed. It was wrong to want more days and nights with Brynhild at her sister's expense, but he couldn't help it. Today especially had been pleasant, their conversations easy and open, despite the miserable weather.

'I never asked,' she said, as they waited beneath a coppice of trees during a particularly heavy bout of rainfall. The leaves were all turning from green to red, golds and browns and blanketed the ground beneath their feet. 'How will you get my mother her farm? I presumed you knew a jarl...one who might accept us without a marriage alliance?'

Speaking of the future deflated his cheerful mood a little—it was an unwelcome reminder that their time together was fleeting. They would not be riding across this green country for ever, and eventually they would have to part ways.

Pushing aside his own selfish feelings, he gave great thought to her question. 'There are a few options. Depending on what you would prefer. There is plenty of land in Iceland and Greenland. It is a long and treacherous journey to get there, but there are fewer rules about who can and cannot own land. There is also land in the east near Halfdan's settlement, but that would be more for grazing animals and is always under threat from passing nomads... I, personally, would not choose to farm there.'

'What sort of farm would you choose?' she asked curiously. Her eyes watched him closely, as the patter of rain fell lightly on the red leaves above her head. Some tendrils of her hair had escaped from her tie and they fluttered around her face like the branches of a willow. She brushed them away roughly, as if irritated by them, and he felt their loss keenly, deep in the pit of his stomach. He would love to see her hair loose.

What would she have done if he'd brushed them away and kissed her?

'Maybe I will run Halfdan's trading post— that's what he wants me to do, it's a prosperous settlement with a large fort. A great prospect for any man...' He paused, with a frown, as always unconvinced about taking on such a responsibility despite its obvious benefits.

'But it's not yours. It's Halfdan's...and you don't want that,' she answered perceptively.

'Yes...' he said, shocked that she would see into his heart when he hadn't understood his own doubts until now. 'How did you know?'

'I would not want to live in Valda's shadow either. No matter how great a prospect it would be for me.'

Erik smiled. 'Exactly... I have some silver.

It's not much. My father took most of our silver in payment for my freedom. But Halfdan always put aside half of his profits for me, even though, officially, I could not earn silver as my father's thrall. Halfdan still considered us equal partners and now that I am free, I have decided I wish to try farming. I plan on buying land with my half of our remaining silver, eventually. I thought somewhere near Jorvik, but...'

Brynhild nodded, closing the cloak around her a little tighter. 'There is too much discontent between the Jarls and the Saxons. I suspect there will be more battles ahead.'

'Not good for anyone wishing to secure a home for the future.'

'No,' she agreed with a sigh.

After a moment of companionable silence, she brightened. 'You should buy land close to the land we settle on! That way we can support each other.' Triumphantly she repeated the old Norse saying, 'One's back is bare without a brother.'

He smiled weakly in response. He didn't want to be thought of as a *brother*, but he appreciated the sentiment. 'Perhaps.'

At first the idea was appealing. To have Brynhild so close? But then another sudden and uneasy thought soured the suggestion completely in his mind. 'Why do you think you'll never marry, Brynhild? You could have land easily if you did so.'

She laughed. A deep throaty sound that warmed his heart, until her words hit him like a hammer in the chest. 'Do you not remember the man I told you about? The one Ivar offered us and who ran from me in fear? I am not a tempting prospect for most men.'

'Most men are stupid and weak.' Erik growled and then he looked at her shrewdly. 'What if a man asked you to marry him? One you liked...'

She stared at him, all amusement gone, the pulled-back blonde hair appearing dark from the rain, her eyes sharp and cool, like the blade of a sword. 'I would say no.' Then she looked away from him, out at the drizzle dropping from the sparse red-gold leaves above their heads, and said firmly, 'As I've said, I will never marry.'

'Never?' All his pride and hope died within his chest.

She smiled wryly at his horrified exclamation. 'Is that so outrageous, Erik? Honestly, I have never *wanted* to marry! A woman is owned by her husband... I would not wish to be owned.' She tilted her head thoughtfully. 'No. Marriage is definitely not for me and I could never leave my mother. She relies on me... She'd never admit it, but her old wounds plague her and she needs a more peaceful and settled life for her old age.

'You know...when we were children, my sister Helga once cast runes—to see who our future husbands would be. It was part of her dream—the one with the dragon. She was convinced that one day we would all be married with flowers in our hair.' Her lips twisted into a sneer. '*Flowers!* Can you imagine anything more ridiculous? It would be more likely for me to turn into a bear and dance than I would ever willingly marry with flowers in my hair!'

He laughed at the disgust on her face. At Valda's wedding she'd worn a ringlet of ivy at her sister's insistence and she'd tossed that aside as soon as the ceremony was complete. Curiosity got the better of him, and he asked, 'What did *your* rune say?'

'Never mind,' she said, lightly shrugging off the question, 'I know what it meant. It meant I shall never marry and I am glad of it. It is not the life that I would want for me.'

He nodded, although he hated that he understood her reasoning. He'd been in half a mind to ask her to marry him. But it was marriage itself that she could not accept and not the man, so he had no chance in offering for her. He could understand it. Freedom was everything and no one fully understood that unless they themselves had had their independence threatened or taken.

But… Could he settle near her and be content with that? Find a wife, build his family, complete his own goals, when the woman he really wanted was his neighbour? It would not be fair on anyone, especially his new wife.

Living close by to Brynhild and her family was impossible. He would be caught in a spider's web of the past, unable to move forward, when the woman he wanted was so close and yet still so far out of reach.

Just as Brynhild knew she would never marry, *he knew that he would.*

A wife would give him the family life he craved. The dream he'd promised himself, for many years, and in many cold and empty beds.

I will be free and my children will be free.

But was that truly freedom? If he were forced to walk away from someone he cared for? Someone who made him…happy?

Brynhild paused thoughtfully, oblivious to

his conflicted thoughts. 'Helga might marry one day. She's pretty and sweet... A little strange, some might say, what with her runes, herbs and spells. But there is a well of kindness within her that will never empty. Someone is bound to sweep her away eventually, with some romantic nonsense, I suspect. I only hope she doesn't go too far from us... Now that Valda is away travelling with Halfdan, I would hate to lose Helga, too.'

She sighed miserably. 'I should make more of an effort to spend time with her—before she marries. I can't believe I've only just realised it! She'll leave us, too, eventually... After all, she is the only one of us with an acknowledged father and so will have a good bride price and fine prospects...although that might change...'

Brynhild suddenly looked very ill, as if she were about to be sick. She must have realised the possibility that her sister could be suffering terrible abuse at this very moment and that such mistreatment would affect her bridal worth later on. It was a horrible truth, but he hoped it would not come to that.

Taking her hand in his, he squeezed it gently. 'It would go against all codes of decency to hurt a female hostage,' he said firmly, although he knew that the cruelty of men could very easily forget the codes of honour.

Brynhild nodded with a pained expression. 'True, and as the Lord is relying on us capturing his sister...he would not risk his own sister's safety by hurting mine...would he?' She looked down at the scars on his hand and he realised he'd reached for her without thought for which hand would hold hers. 'They've healed well. Is there any loss of feeling?'

He shook his head, dizzy from the sudden change in conversation. 'The skin is dry and itchy sometimes. But otherwise, it is no different from my other... Your balm helped save it.'

'Why did he do it?'

Erik blinked, realising that he'd never once explained to her *why* it had happened. Only that Ulf had been responsible. His heart ached as he realised how good she'd been to him, to help him regardless of knowing if he deserved it or not.

'To punish me. Although he called it a trial by ordeal.'

She shook her head, a flash of vengeance in her eyes. 'What could you have *possibly* done to warrant that kind of punishment?'

'Halfdan saved the blacksmith's family from

starving. We were forbidden to help them in any way, but Halfdan could not bear it. So, he secretly gave them grain. Ulf suspected what he'd done and he used me as a tool to try to force the truth from him.'

Brynhild gritted her teeth with barely contained rage, 'And Halfdan allowed—'

'No,' Erik replied firmly. 'I was the first to deny Halfdan had anything to do with it. I knew that even if we did tell the truth, the family would be punished for accepting our help. It was worth it, taking the punishment. I have never regretted it.'

'You sacrificed your hand to save them?' she said softly, as understanding dawned across her face.

'They had three children,' Erik said simply. 'Wouldn't you do the same?'

'One day,' she vowed through gritted teeth, 'Ulf will pay for this. Odin will have seen his crimes and will surely rain vengeance upon him.' She straightened her spine. 'He *has* to... When I think of all the harm he has caused...'

Erik smiled gently and raised her hand to his lips, kissing each of her fingers in turn. 'I used to dream of killing him,' he said quietly, a little shocked that he would openly admit to such a terrible thing. Another woman might have been horrified, but Brynhild understood, she looked at him without judgement or reproach.

'That's understandable after what he has done to you.'

'Oh, I hate him for that…it's true. But the reason I wanted to kill him was for my mother.'

She waited, allowing him to tell it in his own words.

'He brought my mother back from raiding in the east. My mother once told me that she was a nobleman's daughter, a man of power. A Persian connected with the Abbasid Caliphate who'd met with him for trade negotiations on the Volga route. But he'd laughed at some mistake my father had made when they first met. In revenge, Ulf attacked their camp and murdered everyone within, taking his daughter as his only prisoner. She was only a child herself when she fell pregnant with me… Helga reminds me a little of her…she was also wise beyond her years and kind, with a skill for the healing arts.

'Sigrid, Halfdan's mother, was horrified when Ulf returned with her. Tostig is her cousin and he once said that her love for Ulf died when she realised what horrors he was truly capable of. I think that's why Ulf hated my mother so much, because his wife stopped loving him the day he brought my mother home. Then when Sigrid became friends with Anahita, he couldn't stand it, despising and punishing my mother at every opportunity. I'd thought it awful then, but now I realise Sigrid tempered him and could at least reason with his moods.

'When I had seen eight winters, and Halfdan six, Sigrid fell ill during her second pregnancy. My mother fought so hard to save both her and the child. But there was nothing she could do and the baby girl died. Sigrid appeared to recover for a little while afterwards, but then died of a sudden fever herself. I will never forget my mother's cry when she found her dead. She howled like a wounded animal and then Ulf came and things got so much worse.

'They were both stricken by grief from Sigrid's loss, but Ulf raged at my mother as if she were to blame. He said she had struck her down out of spite with her magic. And that she would soon curse Halfdan, too—all so that I could inherit instead of his legitimate son. She denied it, but he murdered her anyway and called me outcast and slave from that day forward. That's when I started to really hate him. I thought about killing him daily—until Tostig spoke with me and said that my mother would have thought it a terrible crime. Knowing her, even for the short time that I did... I knew he spoke the truth.'

Throughout his speech he'd not dared to look at Brynhild. But when his eyes met hers, he was shocked to see tears running down her cheeks. Reaching forward, he touched one of the drops of water, hoping to brush both it and her sadness away with one stroke.

Stumbling through her words, she asked, 'You talk as if you saw it happen. Were you there?'

'I was,' he said, quietly.

Brynhild jumped forward, wrapping her arms around him so tightly his ribs hurt. She held him close and the rain continued to drip around them, the trees weeping with Brynhild while he stood motionless in her arms.

'It was a long time ago,' he said, soothingly as he rubbed at her back. But for some reason his words only made her squeeze him tighter.

'Would you mind if I killed Ulf one day?' she mumbled into his neck and he sighed.

'Maybe the Welsh Lord will do it for us and save us the bother?'

She moved a little, holding his biceps tight and facing him, their misty breath mingling together. Reaching up with one hand, she plucked a blood-red leaf from his hair. She rubbed the stem lightly and the leaf danced in the air. A flame of nature, a fleeting splash of colour in a darkening world. It reminded him that their time together would also pass.

She let it go and it was snatched up by the wind. Lifted up in the air for a moment before fluttering to the ground.

He wanted to enjoy every moment of this flickering time together. Snaking his arms around her waist, he pulled her close once more. Her eyes moved from the crimson ground to his face, and a flush of colour rose up her cheekbones.

Leaning forward, he brushed his lips against hers. It was enough to fire the blood in his veins and had him aching for more. Was it strange that they'd just been discussing the death of his father and now he wanted to lay her down and make love to her?

Brynhild must have thought so, because she stepped out of his embrace. 'Well, the rain is easing,' she said, looking up at the grey sky and ignoring his gaze. 'We should carry on, don't you think?'

'Of course,' he replied, guilt twisting his stomach in knots. They had a duty to her sister. It wasn't right of him to push her for more. What had happened the night before was a brief and exquisite moment. A lesson that she'd enjoyed teaching him, but there was nothing more to it than friendship. He shouldn't expect anything more from her.

'Thank you, for listening and…for everything,' he said, unwilling to end it without at least showing his gratitude for the kindness she'd shown him both past and present.

Later, when they approached a farmstead at twilight they decided to appear as unassuming as possible and definitely not to ask about a young couple fleeing Jorvik.

'We'll tell them we're just travellers heading north-east, a brother and sister visiting relatives,' Brynhild said as they approached the main hall. Two little boys were feeding hens in a pen and stared at them with wide eyes as they passed by.

A man and woman, about the same age as them, walked out of the hall.

The woman had a plump soft figure, with ruddy cheeks and light brown hair pulled under a cap, while the man had a barrel chest and short sturdy legs, his dark blond hair in a short crop with a clean-shaven face.

'Heill!' Brynhild called, and the couple greeted them back in Saxon. This land was obviously a mixture of all kinds of people. Brynhild smiled warmly at them as she responded in surprisingly good Saxon, considering her earlier claim to be poor in the language. 'May we beg your hospitality tonight? We are travelling north-east beyond the wall and have a long journey ahead.'

Erik added quickly when he saw the suspicion in their eyes, 'We are heading north-east, my wife and I are visiting her newly wedded sister. We can pay you.' The couple relaxed a little then and they felt welcome enough to drop down from their horses.

'You may rest your horses in our stable. I am Eadburg and this is Godwin, my husband. Please come and join us after your horses are settled, our evening meal is almost ready,' said the woman and the husband gave a pleasant nod, but nothing more—he seemed a naturally quiet type.

As they led their horses into the stable, Brynhild whispered, 'Would it not be better to say we are brother and sister?'

'We look nothing alike.'

'Neither do you and Halfdan,' she pointed out with a raised brow.

'True...' He paused, unsure whether to admit the truth, then decided that there was no shame in it. He would not pretend what happened the other night was a mistake, nor would he ask her for more, but he could not hide his feelings. 'I do not look at Halfdan the same way I look at you.'

She blinked at that. 'And how do you look at me?' she asked quietly.

'Like I want you.'

She cleared her throat awkwardly and he smiled at the blush on her cheeks. It wasn't often that she looked like that, sweetly uncertain.

'I see...'

'Better not to draw attention to ourselves by behaving out of character. Do you not think? As I cannot look at you as a brother should and I have no hope in pretending otherwise, then I will say that I am your husband, although I do not expect anything in return. Except to admire you, as I always have.'

Brynhild's blush deepened to a bright crimson as she stared at the barn ahead of them. 'I think last night addled your brain.'

He laughed, and their eyes met. 'Perhaps it did.'

Brynhild shook her head with an indulgent smile before leading her horse into an empty stall. 'Be careful, Erik. You do not want to make the mistake of falling in love with me. You would ruin yourself for all other women.'

She had tossed away the comment in jest, immediately busying herself with preparing her horse for its well-deserved night of rest and no longer paying him any attention. But his stomach clenched, as if bracing against an invisible punch.

Was it already too late?

Removing his saddle, he rubbed his horse down thoroughly to remove the sweat and dirt. Deciding to take his own advice, he would focus on one step at a time and worry about the future later.

Once they had both ensured their animals had plenty of food and water, they carried their packs into the large farmstead.

Chapter Fourteen

Brynhild admired the farmstead as they approached it. It was a comfortable and beautiful home that anyone, including herself, would be proud to own.

Rectangular, with a thatched roof, it was reasonably large and looked as if it had been built many years ago. An ancestral home that had probably been owned by this farmer's family for several generations. Lovingly expanded, repaired and improved by each new pair of hands. It would last this generation and probably several more into the future.

The walls were made from solid planks, the wooden floor scattered with fresh rushes mixed with dried heather, giving it a pleasant smell. Tools, barrels and clay pots lined the entrance to the house. One wall had a large tapestry on it and there were piles of fleeces up on a large platform above, which had a ladder for access. Dried heathers and herbs hung from the beams throughout, always a good sign of an exceptional cook or healer.

The fire was in the centre of the room and raised up on a platform, with a large cauldron suspended over it. The hole in the ceiling above was just large enough to let out a small tendril of smoke. The south-facing window was open and let in the last fading light of the day. There were benches and chests against one wall, while a loom and a small table for food preparation lined the other.

Any spare room was filled up by the plentiful baskets of autumn fruit and vegetables from the recent harvest. At the very back of the house were two large bed boxes, sectioned off with hazel screens and covered in blankets and warm fleeces. Presumably one for the adults and one for the children.

'You can sleep either on the benches by the fire, or up with the fleeces,' said Eadburg with more confidence now than before. Maybe the promise of silver had warmed them to her?

Erik answered the lady with a respectful bow, 'The fleece loft will suit us fine, thank you.'

Eadburg nodded and went back to preparing the meal, placing several bread cakes to cook on the cauldron's lid. Erik took Brynhild's pack from her and climbed the ladder to deposit their things.

She saw the couple's children peeking through the open window at her and so she smiled at them. Immediately the two faces ducked down, their furious whispers like a swarm of bees.

'You'd best come in, boys, it's almost ready,' called Eadburg sternly, without even looking up from her task.

There was more shuffling and muttering from the boys outside the window and their mother tutted with impatience. They'd passed Godwin in one of the nearby pens still working, so Eadburg was alone with her chores.

'Can I help?' asked Brynhild, before hastily adding, 'Shall I move the benches nearer the fire?' Child herding wasn't a skill she was familiar with and she wasn't much of a cook at the best of times. She feared she would only get in this woman's way if she helped with either of those tasks, but she still wanted to help.

At her nod, Brynhild began to move the benches closer. When Erik was back down from the loft he helped her, giving her a warm smile as he did so. Brynhild felt her chest squeeze as if someone had stood on it.

Erik's behaviour was beginning to worry her. She hoped she would not hurt his feelings later. He'd suffered enough in the past and she did not wish to be the first woman to break his heart. She'd been clear, hadn't she? Marriage was not something she wished for…a relationship was not something she wanted either. She had to concentrate on her sister's freedom and not her own desires.

It was true that the pressure to find the couple had been significantly eased, now that they knew where they were headed. But she had to remember what was important to her and that had always been her family. They came first, even before her own needs.

No matter how pleasurable her time with Erik had been, and it had been *very* pleasurable, she had to remember her priorities. She was also afraid that, if she encouraged his attention, their friendship would be broken somehow and that felt too awful a prospect for her to risk.

Then again, maybe she was worrying for no reason?

Men seemed able to walk away from relationships far easier than women. Hadn't all of her mother's love affairs taught her that?

She took a seat at one of the benches and Erik joined her, the wood beneath them creaking a little at their combined weight. She almost laughed at the conceit of her earlier thoughts... As if she could hurt Erik—she was hardly a seductive beauty to blind men with lust!

Scampering in like excited puppies, the two boys ran in and sat on the bench opposite them, staring at them both with open curiosity, especially Brynhild. She stared back and finally one of the boys had the courage to ask, 'Why are you dressed like a man?'

'Eadric!' gasped his mother, horrified.

Brynhild chuckled and his mother relaxed a little. 'I am a shieldmaiden.'

'But girls cannot fight,' said Eadric, more with confusion than malice.

'Brynhild can,' Eric said firmly and then, with a loud whisper, as if she couldn't possibly hear him, 'She is a great warrior, who has earned her place in the shield wall... Do not tell her this, but I would be afraid to meet her in battle.'

Brynhild peered at the little boys through the flames and the younger swallowed nervously.

'Women are all fierce and strong—whether they wield an axe or not.' She glanced at Eadburg and the woman gave her an amused smile of agreement.

Godwin came in from outside then, shutting the door after him and stamping the mud from his boots repeatedly before entering the main living area.

'Father says Mother will skin him like a rabbit if he ever brings muck in from the pens—she's fierce,' said Eadric.

His younger brother nodded enthusiastically in agreement. 'He's afraid of her, too.'

Godwin laughed and ruffled the boys' hair as he passed, before heading to his wife to peck her cheek.

'Thank you for sharing your meal with us,' said Erik.

Eadburg shrugged and piled the cooked bread on to a platter. 'I always make too much,' she said, ladling the stew into wooden bowls.

As she handed them out, she tucked a bread cake into each one. The fragrant steam from her stew made Brynhild's mouth water. Thick with chunks of salty bacon, creamy vegetables, grains and fresh herbs, it was as delicious to taste as it was to smell.

Brynhild sighed with pleasure after her first bite of dunked bread. 'We are fortunate to stop at your home. Your stew is the best I have ever eaten.' Usually this would have been a necessary compliment for their show of hospitality, but Brynhild meant every word and hoped her admiration showed.

Godwin spoke in heavily accented Saxon as if it weren't his first language, 'Eadburg is the best cook in all of Rheged.'

Eadburg blushed, but didn't argue. Instead, she asked Brynhild curiously, 'Your sister is newly married?'

'Yes, to a sheep farmer north-east of the wall. Erik and I were hoping to see her before her baby comes in the spring.' She had been pondering what to tell the couple and felt that the closer she remained to her own life the easier the lie would be to tell.

'And…you wish to help with the baby?' the woman said with a frown, as if she didn't quite believe her capable of such a thing. Granted, she was a heavily armed shieldmaiden and had the body of a person more than capable of wielding them, but Brynhild stiffened at the assumption she couldn't possibly help in such matters.

'I've helped deliver many,' answered Brynhild and bristled a little more at the woman's disbelieving face. She *had* helped deliver babies in the past! It was a fact of life in a travelling army, filled with families and settlers.

Still, why couldn't a shieldmaiden help a new mother?

She'd helped Porunn often enough with Helga as a babe. There were seven winters between them and she'd been left with both Valda and Helga in the camp when her mother had had to leave them to fight. But this woman was not to know that and had probably never met a shieldmaiden before, so Brynhild tempered her response. 'Most of the time a mother just needs an extra pair of hands.'

Eadburg laughed. 'That is certainly true!' She touched her stomach and then looked adoringly at her two sons. The boys seemed to be inhaling the food with incredible speed and Brynhild suspected there would be another mouth to feed in the near future. At least the family seemed well prepared.

'Have you been married long?' Eadburg asked, as she took her seat and began to eat. 'Godwin and I have seen six winters together.'

Erik answered, 'Only since this summer.'

'Ahh, then it will not be long until you have children of your own.' She smiled.

'If we want them,' Brynhild said sharply, unable to help herself. For some reason this pretence had riled her temper. It reminded her of the odd jealousy she'd felt at Valda's wedding. The sense that she was missing out on something, a life she'd thought she'd never wanted in the first place.

Maybe because these people had the married life she knew she would never have... And it also felt wrong to pretend she and Erik were married, too, deceitful even. As if the lie were a cruel way of mocking her, like Sune might have done.

'Oh!' Eadburg gasped and she looked at her husband, who shrugged.

Erik cleared his throat and took Brynhild's hand in his. 'Brynhild has been a shieldmaiden many years. It may take her a little time to accept the life of a wife. We hope to settle near her sister.'

Eadburg raised an eyebrow. 'I can imagine.'

Brynhild hated Erik's words, of course, none of this was real, but did he really think a woman like her would only need a *little time* to accept such a life? When she'd been her own master for years?

'And was your sister...like you?' asked Eadburg.

'Yes,' she replied tartly and the woman smiled weakly back, a flush of embarrassment on her cheeks.

Brynhild realised then that she was not only being rude, but unkind to the woman who'd accepted them into her home, and so she added more gently, 'Her husband accepts her for who she is and loves her in spite of it.'

'*Because* of it,' Erik corrected her firmly, his eyes flickering with the light of the fire. 'He loves her *because* of it. A person cannot help who they love and if they want to honour them, *truly* honour them, they will accept them as they are and be grateful to have them in their lives.'

Brynhild felt suddenly hot and light-headed as she stared into Erik's eyes. She could almost believe he was saying it about her. *But...no...he wants a wife,* she reminded herself. After all, that's why he wanted her to teach him how to please a woman. So that he could one day please his wife! At least...that's what he'd said.

Eadburg sighed happily, 'How lovely. Close

the window, Godwin. The weather has definitely turned, has it not?'

Brynhild looked reluctantly away from Erik. 'Indeed, it has.'

Godwin closed the window shutter with a bang, bolting it closed. The shadows around them lengthened and Eadburg tidied up their empty bowls, presenting them with bone cups of mead and honeyed oat cakes for dessert.

Brynhild was about to eat them with relish as she loved the taste of anything made with honey. But then the cakes reminded her of Helga's abduction and her stomach churned. She offered hers to the boys and they took them happily, gobbling their share in the blink of an eye.

Maybe she should do the same? Enjoy whatever pleasures came her way, and not think too heavily about them...like Erik.

Erik began telling the family about his travels in the east after they'd asked about his ancestors—at least these people did so with more politeness than the last. He wasn't much of a storyteller—unlike his charming brother, Halfdan. But the family were still fascinated by his tales and asked many questions. Eventually the children began to slump on the bench and the couple picked up a boy each and went to bed.

Brynhild and Erik made their way to the loft, rearranging the fleeces to form a nest for their bedrolls. As it was warm in the fleece loft, they stripped off their outer clothing, so they could sleep comfortably in only their undertunics and braies. There wasn't much room, but there was enough space to lie comfortably side by side.

They lay facing each other at first, both not ready yet to sleep. 'You didn't enjoy the life of a merchant at all, did you?' she asked quietly. He'd said that he'd wanted to try the life of farmer, but she suspected there was more to it than curiosity. He'd spoken of his wondrous travels as if they were a hardship rather than a joy. The fire had died to glowing embers that didn't quite reach the darkness of the loft, so she couldn't see his expression clearly when he answered.

'No.' He sighed.

'It sounds exciting.'

'In some ways it is… But travel can also be dull, with lots of waiting.'

'Was there nothing you enjoyed about it?'

He sighed again. 'Not really. I do not have an adventurous heart like Halfdan. Besides, I always knew that nearly everything I earned would one day be handed over to my father in payment for my freedom. That took away some of the pleasure for me.'

'That's understandable. But...you wouldn't consider going back to it, though? You could buy your own ship, begin again? This time you would be earning silver for yourself.'

'True. But I would still always be travelling and I find that tiresome... I want a place where I can belong...' He paused and the weight of it caused her heart to lurch painfully. 'I never felt comfortable over there. People treated me differently. Here I am an oddity, but now that I have my arm ring I am mostly accepted regardless of my ancestry.

'But in the east, nothing I do will ever change me in their eyes. I am the son of a barbarian, ungodly and a shame on my mother's name. They saw me as even less than a thrall and only traded with me because I could speak my mother's tongue... I did not belong there...'

She reached for his hand and clasped it in the darkness, hearing the pain in his voice and wishing she could slay all of his enemies with a single swing of her axe.

'They did not deserve you.'

He squeezed her hand in response, his voice rough with emotion. 'I am sick of being alone. I want a family. I have to marry... I *need* to.'

The pain slipped like a knife between her ribs, smoothly piercing her heart in the darkness and robbing her of breath. It shouldn't hurt, but it did. Now she understood why this farm had put her on edge.

It represented the life Erik wanted. A wife and children. Brynhild wasn't a home-maker. She couldn't make Erik delicious stews, or complain about the state of his muddy boots. She wasn't even sure if she wanted children, or would even know how to mother them if she did. Not like Eadburg, for example.

When she had her mother's farm, she'd always known she would be the one taking on the role of the man in the family. She would be the one mucking out pens and labouring in the field, defending their land if needed with axe and shield.

'I understand,' said Brynhild softly. 'It is important to be happy in yourself... I could never be a wife...' She let her words sit between them for a moment. 'It is hard to be different... But, if you are true to your heart, you can never fail.' Then she nestled closer, deciding that now things were clear between them she would savour what little time they had left. Slowly easing one leg over his, she whispered, 'Erik…even though our time together will be short. I will never regret it.' She held her breath, wondering what he would make of her invitation, now that she'd been clear about their future.

'Nor I,' he replied huskily and, without hesitation, he gripped her leg to keep it in place as he rocked his hips against the apex of her legs.

She gasped, already feeling the stiffening of him against her, and her body responded with equal intensity. Her nipples tightened beneath the strips of linen, and she ached to tear them from her body. Unfortunately, she couldn't do that easily in such a tight space. They could barely even sit up, so close to the roof as they were.

But at least she could give him some pleasure to remember her by.

She tugged at the ties on his waist and his hand closed over hers. 'No,' he whispered, 'I want to see you when we do that.'

She kissed him until they were both breathless. Then she whispered, 'Stay silent, you don't want to wake them.' She shuffled down the bed-roll, and heard his breath catch in his throat when she stroked the front of his braies posses-sively with her palm.

Tugging at the ties at his waist, she was able to loosen his clothing enough to release him.

'Brynhild!' he cried in warning, trying to raise himself up on to his elbows, and she pat-ted his strong stomach reassuringly.

'Shh, Eric. You deserve this,' she whispered, 'Now, be silent.'

She took his member in her hand and stroked the silk of his skin tenderly, learning the mea-sure of him despite the darkness. Erik fell on to his back with a muffled sigh of pleasure and she grinned, more pleased with her plan with every passing moment.

He was big and nicely shaped and she took great delight in stroking him. His hips bucked repeatedly against her hand and his cries of ec-stasy were muffled by the hem of his tunic that he'd dragged up to stuff into his mouth.

Brynhild loved the power she held over him, as well as the delight in returning the favour he'd given her the previous night. She pressed light kisses on his stomach, his muscles tense and straining as she worked him with her hand.

Then she began to lick a leisurely path down his stomach and his hips stilled, and she could hear his laboured breath even with the cloth stuffed in his mouth.

She raised herself up a little, gripped him tightly in her fist, and then lowered down to close her lips around the head of his erection. It was too much for him and with a muffled curse he climaxed.

After discreetly cleaning up with a nearby cloth, she laid down beside him with a sigh of satisfaction. Erik was struggling to regain his breath, then turned to kiss her face and neck with reverent thanks.

'That was…' he whispered.

'I know,' she replied, unable to hide the smug pride in her voice.

'Let me please you now.' He began to tug at the ties of her braies.

'There's no need,' she whispered, although her blood was already pumping with excitement at the possibility of him touching her like he'd done the previous night.

'I need to!' he demanded and she sighed happily.

'If you insist…' She helped him with the ties and then gasped as he pushed his hand down into her braies, his fingers quickly finding the wet and eager heat of her arousal.

Erik wasn't the only one who had to stuff the hem of their tunic into their mouths that night.

Chapter Fifteen

When Brynhild and Erik left in the morning, Godwin and Eadburg were far more generous than the last home they'd stayed at, offering them two large sacks of supplies. Brynhild gave them an extra dirham for their kindness.

By noon they had crested a large hill and saw the sea stretching out in the distance, the arc of a harbour and a large settlement clearly visible from their vantage point. A shepherd they'd met on the road earlier had confirmed they were on the right path for Alauna.

'So, where are they, do you think? Shall we make a wager?' asked Erik, thoughtfully, as they scanned the vista before them. The land was reasonably flat, the harbour curving in around itself as if pulling the sea inwards.

Wooden jetties lined with boats stretched out into the water, muddy sand banks rippling towards the small fort, homes and workshops. The buildings were a mix of stone and timber, some rectangular like Norse longhouses, while many others were round or oval in the Saxon way.

A strange mix of a place, but everything in the north had been an odd blend of cultures, languages and beauty. Brittle people, suspicious of outsiders and yet happy to help a young couple running from their fate. Beautiful sweeping landscapes that became awe-inspiring or miserable depending on the weather.

Most of the land was used for pasture, the houses scattering further apart as they moved away from the sea. At the other side of the harbour, and covering the entirety of the opposite hillside, was a large woodland that dipped down to a thin shingle beach. 'There,' Brynhild said confidently, pointing at the trees. 'If we ride through the settlement, news will spread quickly of our arrival.'

'True.'

'Let's swing around it,' she said, indicating the fields and meadows behind. 'Get to the woodland that way. It would be best not to give them any warning of our presence, if we can.'

With a nod and a click of his tongue, Erik urged his horse back down the hill, Brynhild following closely behind. They circled around the settlement, deliberately choosing the lower fields and meadows to cross without being seen.

As they entered the wood, they were rewarded by the sight of an old timber building, possibly used by the woodcutters during the summer months. It was small and empty, suggesting it hadn't been used for some time.

Brynhild and Erik tied their horses outside it and each of them scouted the area around the building, coming back to meet by their horses once again.

'It's not been disturbed in some time,' said Erik.

'I thought the same, no paths or worn walkways. There's a stream not far away. It will do us well for a night or two.'

'As they have seen me before, I will stay here. Look after the horses and prepare the camp. You go, see if your gut was right.' And then, as if thinking better of it, he added firmly, 'But do not grab her without me.'

Brynhild raised an eyebrow at his command—Erik rarely made any demands of her.

'And there I was, thinking you would never doubt my skills or common sense.'

'I would never doubt your abilities... I just don't want to miss out on the fun.' He shrugged, but there was a twinkle in his eyes and then he smiled mischievously, the effect devastatingly attractive, and she laughed, feeling a little flustered.

Despite the urgency and importance of their need to capture Lady Alswn, she couldn't help but admit it. She *was* having fun with Erik.

She sobered a little at the thought and walked out into the woods with a renewed determination. Shouldn't she be thinking of poor Helga? Kept captive by this woman's brother. Only Odin with his far-reaching sight knew how well she fared. What if he had hurt her, kept her in a cage, or mistreated her? She shook her head as if to try to clear the images from her mind, but it didn't work. Then she thought of her mother and her words of wisdom.

They were shieldmaidens; they would accept whatever destiny the Norns of fate weaved for them. If that meant suffering, then they would take it with pride and honour, knowing they would be rewarded for their courage in the next life. Helga might be more vulnerable than Brynhild, but their mother was right, she did not lack courage.

She had seen Helga tame hawks and falcons. Feed wolves from her bare hands and heal the sick with herbs. She would not crumble in the hands of an enemy. She would thrive.

As she walked through the trees, Brynhild touched the bark of the trunks gently in greeting as she passed them. It was not something she did often, but here in the woods she felt closest to her sister. Helga was always happiest in nature. When she touched the moss of a particularly old oak she smiled, pressing her hands firmly against the soft dampness of it, and then watching as it sprang back, unbothered by her roughness. Moss was flexible, useful and resilient. It wasn't strong, but it could embed itself in the mightiest of oaks and flourish, *like Helga*.

'I will come for you soon, dear sister,' she whispered, patting the moss, and for some reason she felt better.

She moved slowly through the dense growth, occasionally using her axe or her seax to cut through the thicket. She didn't mind the labour, it only reassured her that their place at the edge of the woods was secluded from the rest of the settlement and rarely used.

After a while she came along a thin, well-worn path that led up from the harbour to the top of the woodland. She followed it down to a fork in the path. One side led to a shingle beach, the other to the harbour settlement. She retraced her steps back up to the woodland, more confident about where the path might eventually lead, and taking care to walk in the deepest part of the thicket.

She was glad she had, when she heard someone approaching up from the path with heavy feet. Crouching low, she waited. A dark-haired man, matching Erik's description of the Lady's guard, came walking up the path, a rabbit at his belt and a sack slung over his shoulder. His cap was low, but he was whistling through his teeth in a carefree manner. No weapons at his side, save a long dagger.

Brynhild waited for him to pass her a good distance, before she followed him slowly up the trail, being sure to stay low as he led her unwittingly to his new home at the top of the path.

A reasonably large and round homestead sat on a flat part of the hill. Made from the timber of the woods with a thatched roof, it was surrounded by an untidy vegetable garden that looked as if it had grown wild from lack of care.

The soft sound of rushing water not too far away indicated a waterfall nearby.

A perfect plot, for a family, thought Brynhild drily, not sure why it made her feel sad to see it.

'Alswn!' called the man cheerfully as he arrived outside the homestead.

'Hywel!' came a girlish cry and Lady Alswn sprinted towards him, from the direction of the running water. She wore a simple woollen dress in a reddish brown, her hair damp from bathing. Hywel laughed as he saw her, sweeping her up into his embrace. Kissing her deeply with a hungry passion.

They spoke in the Welsh tongue, their words a happy melody as they hugged and kissed. Alswn exclaimed over the rabbit as if he'd brought her a chest filled with silver and, in turn, he looked admiringly at the wild mess of the vegetable plot—Brynhild supposed Alswn must have pulled up a few of the weeds in his absence. There was a handful of upturned plants in a bucket nearby that the girl had pointed out to him.

Looking at the garden, Brynhild couldn't help but compare it to Helga's plot back in Jorvik. Helga would have had this cleared and sown ready for spring in a single day.

Bile twisted in her stomach as she watched the exchange—not because of the sickly sweetness of their young love. Usually, she would have laughed at such ridiculousness, but because, for once, it made her long for something she could never have.

I do not want this! she reminded herself firmly.

The pleasure she'd had with Erik was fleeting. A training exercise to help him win a maiden later on, not that he needed help, and she felt a little guilty about that. Erik obviously didn't realise how fine a man he was to a woman's eye. How handsome, strong and honourable others would see him.

But how could he? He'd been treated no better than a dog most of his life. Her heart ached as she realised that he'd never felt his father's love or pride, and although she'd been disappointed by the stream of fathers Porunn had plagued their childhoods with, at least Brynhild's mother had remained a constant and devoted parent.

In contrast Erik's father was the cruellest of beasts and his mother had died painfully young. However, she must have forged his heart well, because despite their lack of years together, he

had grown into a man both noble and coura-
geous to the very marrow of his bones.

Shaking off thoughts of Erik, she concen-
trated on observing the lovers. They kissed and
embraced as if they'd been parted for weeks.
But by the little he carried, she doubted he'd
been gone more than a day. They must have had
help from friends or family down at the settlement—there was no way these two fools could
have managed otherwise.

Brynhild couldn't understand a word they
said to each other, as they spoke the language
of the Welsh, and so, for her own amusement,
she found herself translating their conversation
in her head.

*'Look, my sweetling, I have been the best of
men and returned with one skinny rabbit and
a bag of grain that will last us barely a day!'*

*'Oh, Hywel! How impressive! All I need to
do now is learn how to mill it without creating
bread so full of stone that it breaks our teeth!
Now, look at what I have done today, my love!
I have pulled out a few weeds and washed my
beautiful raven hair!'*

*'Ah, your hair is very pretty! What a won-
derful use of your time! We will definitely not*

starve this winter. What with my excellent hunting skills and your hard work in this garden!'

The couple embraced tightly, their kisses quickly turning from loving affection to burning lust, and Brynhild looked away. Her mocking observations lost all humour now that she could see their obvious depth of feeling for one another.

Hywel wasn't a big man, Brynhild had noticed, short and slim, but still young and strong, with wiry muscle. Even so, she was certain she could overpower him if she needed to.

Only…she wasn't sure if she wanted to. He seemed to genuinely love his lady and she felt a twist of pity for them as they stumbled into their home, tearing off each other's clothes.

Once she was sure they were settled inside, she made her way slowly and quietly away from the hut, walking around it in a large arc. She wanted to see all that was nearby—better to know too much than not enough. Behind the roundhouse and down a steep hill, another woodland path led down to the secluded beach. Pulled up on the shingle was a small fishing boat, laid upside down.

Brynhild made her way over to it to get a better look at it. It was old, but appeared watertight and sturdy, with a pair of strong oars inside, a tattered sail and room for at least three people.

She walked to the base of the woodland and crossed the path back into the trees, heading directly back to Erik and their camp, noting as she walked the base of the hill, that the path Hywel had come from did lead towards the harbour settlement below. That must be where he went during the day. Probably to work for the people who had helped them with the empty house and the grain. An escape by sea would be the best route for her, Erik and Alswn, otherwise they risked a whole settlement chasing after them.

When she made it back to camp, Erik was sat a little outside of the shelter, a small fire burning with their little cauldron above it. The horses were merrily grazing beneath a hazel, foraging for nuts. A large wooden trough beside them was filled with water and scattered on the ground were a pile of half-eaten oats.

'Find them?' he asked quietly and she nodded.

'They matched your description and he called her by name.' She sat on a log beside him in the doorway with a heavy sigh that had nothing to do with the long walk she'd just done. 'It should be easy enough. I suspect he goes out daily to work in the settlement. We can take her then.'

Erik frowned at the resignation in Brynhild's voice. He wondered if something had happened to depress her spirits, but if that were the case, she would have told him…wouldn't she?

'Are you well?'

She smiled weakly. 'They are very happy together. It is…disgusting.'

He laughed at her words, but could sense the deeper sadness beneath them.

It went against her sense of honour to steal a woman away from her home and happiness. Even if it was for Helga, it must hurt Brynhild to go against her beliefs like this. To take the freedom of one innocent in exchange for her sister's. He felt the same, but what else could they do?

The small flames of their fire licked at the cauldron, slowly cooking their evening meal. He'd only built a little one deliberately, not wanting to draw attention to their presence with too much smoke. If they gave away their location it could lead to bloodshed…not theirs, of course, but still…

A sudden chilly unease rippled down his spine.

It was clear Brynhild didn't want to hurt these strangers, but she would do what she must, to ensure her sister's safety.

However, that didn't mean she had to like it. He wished he could console her in some way. But there was nothing he could do to comfort her.

Unless…a lustful thought entered his head and he immediately cast it from his mind.

He was mad! Thinking of his own pleasure, rather than her needs?

He checked on the stew, feeling utterly ashamed of himself. At least it was finally ready to serve. No meat, because he'd spent his time preparing the shelter for a decent night's sleep and looking after the horses. But the stew consisted of the autumn vegetables the young farmers had given them, as well as a handful of grain to help thicken it into a more satisfying meal. He stirred it thoughtfully, as Brynhild drank from the bucket of water he'd brought back from the nearby stream.

When she was done drinking, he handed her a bowl of stew. With a distracted 'thank you' she took it and began to eat. He did the same.

'They have a fishing boat and the winds are blowing in the right direction for the moment.

It is small and old. It may only get us halfway down the coast. But it's a quick escape that will leave no trail… I suspect he's only gone during the day, so it would be best to move quickly.'

'So, we take her at first light?'

Brynhild nodded.

'We'll have to release the horses.'

Brynhild looked sadly over at them. 'Shame. But we'll point them in the direction of the settlement. Someone will have use of them… they're good horses.'

He nodded, sensing the idea upset her far more than she liked to admit.

When they'd finished their meal, they took the cauldron off the fire and put the dirty dishes inside, sealing it with the lid for the night. They would eat the remainder for *dagmal* the next day.

Frowning at the fading light, she said, 'I think I will go wash in the stream before we sleep.' She wrinkled her nose as she plucked at her tunic. 'It is past time that I washed this.'

He nodded. 'I will need to do the same. I think my smell will alert the Lady to my presence long before I get within a foot of her. Would you like some soap?' He began to rummage in his saddlebag, but stilled when her next words finally filtered through.

'Come with me.'

The air froze in his lungs and he looked up at her, startled. Then he glanced at the fire, uncertain. Brynhild kicked some dirt on the flames to dampen them.

'It will keep. I would rather bathe and enjoy our last night alone together. Wouldn't you?' she asked quietly and the simple question suddenly felt heavy with meaning.

He nodded and stumbled to his feet, checking the rocks around the glowing embers with his boot to reassure himself that the fire wouldn't get out of control.

Brynhild picked up one of her blankets, slung it over her shoulder and sauntered in the direction of the stream.

'Don't take too long, *sweetling.*'

He blinked at the unusual term of endearment, but then grinned and leapt to his feet to follow her.

Chapter Sixteen

∂∞∂

The stream that rushed down the hillside collected at a small deep pool before pouring onwards to the settlement below. The banks were rocky and covered in lush moss and delicate white lichen. The colours so vibrant and deep that, combined with the gentle melody of the running water, it immediately soothed the soul. In summer it would have been a delightful spot for long leisurely baths. In autumn, with the trees shimmering gold, red and brown, it was stunning, but cold.

Brynhild laid her blanket on a flat grassy area and then glanced over her shoulder, as if to check Erik had followed her. When she saw him, she turned away and began to strip off her clothes.

Erik's step faltered and he stood paralysed.

She took off her boots and leg wraps, then undid her belt and dropped her trousers. Finally, she pulled off her byrnie, long tunic and undertunic.

Her arms were sculpted with muscle, her shoulders broad. Taking off her tunic had revealed the dramatic curves of her waist and hips—usually they were lost beneath her thick clothing. Something he'd only felt in the dark and his imagination had not done her beauty justice.

For all Brynhild's powerful build and size, she was incredibly feminine. Strength and sweetness combined so beautifully, like her personality, she took his breath away. She was naked now, except for her breasts that were restrained by strips of linen—for practical reasons, he presumed. 'Do all women wear those?' he asked.

She glanced over her shoulder, a light smile on her lips. 'Not many—it is a shieldmaiden's secret, keeps them secure and out of the way.' A look of uncertainty crossed her face. 'If you don't want to…'

'I do,' he replied firmly.

'Can you help unwrap them?' she asked with a shy smile, as she turned fully to face him.

He cleared his suddenly dry throat and joined her. 'Yes.'

She untied the knot just below the swell of her breasts and handed him one end of the linen. 'Hold this and I'll do the rest.'

As she turned, the linen began to peel off her skin. As if she were an apple being turned on the blade of a knife, her pale flesh revealed itself to his hungry eyes.

There were marks on her skin from the cloth, pink impressions of the fabric on her skin. As he dropped the linen on to the blanket, she rubbed at them with a blissful sigh of relief, closing her eyes with pleasure. 'I'd almost forgotten how good it is to take the bindings off.'

He stepped forward, stroking his thumb across one of the pink blemishes, wanting to soothe her ache and satisfy the one that now surged in his groin.

Bending his head, he kissed the tender flesh and she let out a low moan of pleasure. His hands dropped to measure her waist, his fingers callused and dark against the creamy skin. An outcast like himself had no right to touch such beauty...

'Kiss me,' she murmured, draping her arms around his neck, and his uncertainty eased.

They stood eye to eye, equals and opposites at the same time. But she looked vulnerable standing there naked and he felt compelled to restore the balance between them.

He quickly untied his belt and dropped it next to hers, then pulled off his tunic and undertunic in one fluid motion, eagerly casting them aside. His back and front were scarred from his father's many punishments and he waited, breathless, to see if she would flinch at the sight of him. She hadn't before, but many years had passed since she'd last seen him.

To his relief she didn't flinch. 'You are more beautiful than I remember,' she said, her eyes brightening with desire, and she wrapped her arms around his neck once more. Her long pale lashes fluttered closed as she pressed her lips against his.

Their mouths danced against each other, firing the blood in both their veins. He could have happily drowned in her kisses.

But after a while had passed, she pulled away with a breathless chuckle. 'I have to wash first. I feel too disgusting to go any further with you like this!'

He groaned as she moved away. 'I don't care about that.'

She grinned at his tortured expression. 'I do!'

Walking to the pool, her hips swaying delightfully as she did so, she spoke over her shoulder at him. 'I am a little bigger than most women.' Her voice was confident as she spoke, as if daring him to question it. He found himself staring at her lower body as she walked to the pool. Strong thighs, muscled calves and a rounded bottom with full hips. Enthralled, he tried his best to focus on her words. Sadly, he failed, but she didn't seem to mind. In fact, when she turned back to see his clear admiration of her, it only seemed to ignite her own passion.

The words were stuck in his throat and he sounded hoarse. 'You are strong and powerful, Brynhild. What man wouldn't want a woman who was his equal?'

'Quite a few,' she said drily.

He strode to meet her, taking her face in his hands. 'Then they are not confident in their own abilities. I think you are...perfect.'

She beamed at him, her eyes brighter than any sea he'd ever crossed. 'I'm glad you like me as I am. I...' she stroked her long fingers up his body, her nails scratching into the hair on his chest '… I like you, too… I always have… *very much so.*'

'You do not care that I was once a thrall and an outcast?' he asked softly. For some reason he needed to hear her say it, before they took the next step together.

Her fingers cupped his face, her thumb stroking against his roughened jaw. 'I care…because you should never have been treated like that. It wasn't right, and I think Ulf should be punished for it. But…do I care about the status he unjustly forced upon you? No. I admire you, Erik. I would be honoured to lay with you. Although…*after* I have bathed…' She kissed his nose playfully and jumped down into the pool, gasping at the ice-cold water and laughing with girlish delight.

'Quick, grab our clothes so we can wash them!' she said. 'I don't know how long I can stand the cold.'

Smiling, he went back to their belongings, stripped off his remaining clothes, and tossed their clothing where Brynhild leapt into the air to catch them. He took two small bars wrapped in linen from his bag before following her into the water.

'Argh!' he gasped, sucking the air between

his teeth as the bitter cold shocked his skin with a thousand goose pimples.

She took the soap from his hand and furiously washed her clothes. It was coarse soap made from animal fat and ash, but together they made quick work of cleaning their clothes. Rinsing and wringing them out before throwing them over a nearby rock took very little time. Later, they would put them out on sticks in front of the fire to dry.

Now their clothes were scrubbed, Brynhild untied her hair and shook it out around her with a toss of her head. He didn't have long to admire the sight of it however. So as not to lose the tie she strapped it around her wrist, then submerged herself in the deepest part of the pool.

Erik reached for the other bar of soap he'd brought with him to the pool. When she broke the surface gasping, he held out the linen parcel to her. 'It's perfumed. I bought it on the Volga route. It is from Asia, I believe, although I am not certain…'

He held it up for her to smell and she breathed it in, holding the scent in her nose for a long moment before releasing it with a happy sigh. 'Oh, that is beautiful! It smells like warm earth and spiced flowers. I've never smelt anything like it before. Thank you, Erik.'

He lathered it in his hands and then smoothed it through her hair, then over her skin, cleaning the grime away from their last few days of gruelling travel. Savouring the touch far more than he probably should.

She dipped beneath the water, rinsing away the residue, and stood to face him as she smoothed the water from her hair. He handed her the soap and she used it on him, their bodies and height so similar that it felt as if they were one person, so close and easy were their movements.

No awkwardness, only quiet, exploring tenderness.

It was almost too much for him. He wanted to feel her whimpers of pleasure against his. Indulge himself in touching and kissing every part of her.

How many times had he imagined her legs wrapped tightly around his waist? Gods!

It was too much and not enough all at once, overwhelming his senses with aching need. He *needed* to feel her hips beneath the press of his fingertips, her chest pressed hotly against his, as they struggled for breath.

Unable to take any more of her slow tempting caresses, he pulled her to him, so that she could feel the press of his desire against her. Even the cold water around his thighs no longer bothered him. Feverish with passion, he kissed her hard, his breath catching in his throat when she pulled away to look into his eyes.

'There is no rush,' she said gently. Her palm was against his heart. It felt as if it belonged there, like a hand in a glove. Warmer, and safer in her possession. 'I know how men are about such things—but you shouldn't feel that you *have* to be experienced with a woman. In truth, it makes very little difference. I have already had more pleasure with you than anyone else I have been with. You are a natural.'

Heat bloomed across his cheeks and he silently preened under her praise. 'I want to please you. But it is more likely that I will be the one rushing our time together, not you. I fear I will come undone at the smallest touch.'

She laughed. 'Then you should rinse yourself in the cold water to cool your lust and then come join me...' She moved her hand slowly down his chest, tickling over the hair around his nipple, before sliding over the scarred flesh of his ribs and down past his stomach. He closed his eyes, unable to bear it, her hand moments away from his hardness, from gripping him, as she'd done once before. *Would she...?*

When he could no longer breathe or think, her fingers fluttered away. 'But... Don't make me wait too long,' she teased. He groaned at the loss of her touch, opening his eyes to see her walk away and out of the water, her bottom swaying delightfully. 'Come quickly,' she said.

'That is what I am afraid of...' he muttered and heard her light laughter as he dunked himself in the water.

When he resurfaced, she had put on her boots and wrapped her cloak around her, her lips trembling from the cold as she gathered up their clothes in the blanket.

'I will bring those,' he said, pulling himself up among the rocks to the bank.

She shrugged and hurried away, calling behind her as she did so, 'Good. I will rebuild the fire. We will need warming up after that freezing water.'

Somehow Erik wasn't so sure. His blood was pumping hotly through his veins and all he could think about was having Brynhild beneath him.

Back at camp, Brynhild had reignited the fire

and it burned merrily. She'd poked sticks in the ground nearby for their clothes. Erik dropped the bundle of their clothing and they made short work of putting their clothes out to dry.

Afterwards Brynhild crawled into the shelter through the small triangular doorway. There was only enough room for their bedrolls and it reminded him a little of the romantic shelter in the woods that the man Hywel had made. Except this one was sturdier and made with timber instead of branches.

The twilight was succumbing to the approaching night and soon it would be dark except for their small campfire. Erik busily moved around their camp, breaking up some timber and gathering up a large pile of logs in his arms. At least now people would be in their homes for the night, so their smoke would not be seen.

He piled up the wood in his arms and then went for more.

'What are you doing?' asked Brynhild and he realised she sounded a little disgruntled, her cloak wrapped tightly around her as she peered at him through the entrance with a frown.

'I wanted to make sure there was plenty of firewood.'

'I'm sure we'll be warm enough tonight, Erik,' she said. 'I'm not a lady you have to pander to.'

'Oh, I know. But… I couldn't see you very well before. I want to be able to see you. Especially, this time…' His words trailed off, and her eyes softened.

'Then see me…' she said and unwrapped her cloak boldly and lay down, revealing her long and beautiful body to the flickering gold light.

The lump in his throat suddenly felt as if it had doubled in size and he nodded, dropping the log he was holding absently into the flames and causing sparks to dance up in the air.

'My beautiful Valkyrie,' he whispered. Then tossing aside his cloak, he jumped naked through the flames. 'See how I walk through fire for you?'

She giggled. 'A mighty inferno indeed!'

He ducked into the shelter, placed his arms behind her back and pulled her up to meet his kiss. Her hands smoothed up his chest and around his neck as she arched her spine to press against him, just as he'd imagined she would.

Everything had been building up to this moment and it felt perfect. Brynhild was in his arms and to his surprise he didn't feel nervous about what was to come. He only hoped he could pleasure her first like he had before.

His breathing was already ragged as their mouths joined and he felt her soft curves press against his hardness. He moved to nip and suck the sides of her neck and she sighed blissfully, pulling him down so that she could feel his weight on top of her.

Their sighs of pleasure filled the quiet clearing as they explored each other's bodies with hands and mouths. When her hand gripped his length, he growled against her collarbone in warning, 'I will not last if you continue to touch me like that.'

'Autumn nights are long and dark. We have plenty of time,' she teased, squeezing him gently.

He took her hand and moved it up and over her head, kissing her disappointment away tenderly as an apology. 'Not yet, I want to know what it's like to be inside you first.'

She moaned and wriggled beneath him. 'For a man who said it would be quick, you are frustratingly restrained.'

He smiled at that, moving to lie beside her. Parting her thighs with the gentlest push of his hand, he began to move in the circular motion that she liked and she began to squirm against him. Her wet heat slid against his fingers in a rhythm that called to him, rocking his own hips against her side to feel the delicious friction against his own body.

Her hand reached up to cup the back of his neck as he kissed her shoulder and, with a needy moan, she whispered, 'I'm ready!' She gripped his face tightly as she kissed him thoroughly, moving her body against his and turning so that she could drape her leg over his hips in blatant invitation. 'Please, don't make me wait.'

Rolling her on to her back, he still held her leg in the palm of his hand—because, *Odin's teeth, he loved her thighs!* He thought about telling her, but she was arching her spine in such an alluring way that he couldn't think straight. Soon, he would finally sink into her body and finally know what it was like to have her in the most intimate of ways. The anticipation was almost too much and he had to take deep steadying breaths to stop himself from spilling his seed before he'd even started.

'Don't move!' he ordered in a deep and husky voice that he barely recognised.

She closed her eyes and groaned at his command, but she did as he asked and stayed still, her spine still slightly curved, her breasts swollen and flushed with tightly budded nipples. He took one in his mouth and lightly sucked. She whimpered, but remained motionless. Realising that she took pleasure in his control, he slowly stroked a palm down her chest and stomach, in the same way she had done to him in the pool. Her moan was enough encouragement on its own, but when his thumb brushed over her soaking wet entrance, she clenched her teeth as if holding herself back from the precipice of her climax.

Taking her hips in his hands, he raised himself up and over her. Positioning himself at her entrance, he paused. 'Not yet, beautiful,' he whispered, as her body arched like a supple bow in his hands, ready and begging for him to release her from his grip.

He rubbed his thumb over the bud she'd shown him and she jerked a little in response, but otherwise didn't move. Instead, she stared at him, her blue eyes bright in the darkness, capturing him in her gaze.

'Yes, that's good, *sweetling*,' he groaned and smiled at the way her hands fisted into the blanket beneath her.

He was so tempted to taste her, to let her ride

his mouth, but he wasn't sure if that's what she wanted. 'Would you like my tongue or—'

'You… Inside me… Now!' she gasped.

He couldn't take it any more. Thrusting his hips forward, he plunged inside her. She cried out in ecstasy and he withdrew a little, before plunging once more inside her glorious heat. It was the sweetest of pleasures and he began to thrust in earnest, unable to hold back a moment longer. Moving his body over and over against hers, taking all that she had to give.

Her body shuddered with her climax and he watched in wonder as raw ecstasy washed over her face in the firelight.

But then her legs wrapped around his waist and when she gripped him tightly, he lost his mind, having to wrench away from her body quickly before he accidentally came inside of her.

His hot breath misted the air, as his own climax swept through him like a wild horse, pummelling his strength beneath its hooves. He collapsed on his back, beside Brynhild's trembling body, and sighed with the smug satisfaction of a proud lover.

Chapter Seventeen

The next day they were waiting just after dawn in the trees and undergrowth surrounding Lady Alswn and Hywel's house. The horses had been released down the path towards the settlement on their way here. It would have been better to release them at night, but Brynhild hadn't wanted the horses to trip or fall in the dark. A horse could break its leg in thick woodland like this. She would not wish such a pitiful death on anyone, especially not a blameless animal, who had worked so hard for them.

She only hoped the horses would make some good progress down the path, otherwise Hywel might see them and think to turn back. Still, it was a risk she was willing to take and at least stealing their runaway bride would be quick and easy. Erik had already checked the boat was seaworthy and they'd filled it with their remaining supplies. All that was left to do was to grab the lady and sail away.

They watched silently in the undergrowth as Hywel and Alswn emerged from their home. After a loving kiss goodbye, Hywel left to stride jauntily down the path leading to the settlement, oblivious to what was about to happen to his lady, or that this morning would be the last time he kissed her goodbye.

Brynhild tried not to pity him. At least this way they wouldn't have to kill him. She had already decided not to tell the dragon lord where they had found them, fearing he might retaliate one day. She would give some vague explanation of finding them on the Northern Road. If he wanted revenge, he would have to go and get it himself. Brynhild was done doing that man's bidding after today.

They waited a moment longer until they were convinced Hywel would be far enough down the path to not be within hearing distance of any scuffle. They planned to creep up on the Lady, and prevent her from even screaming, but it was always wise not to tempt failure.

Alswn began to bring outside tools for the garden, cheerfully humming a little tune as she did so. The next time she went inside would be their chance to snatch her. With a nod, Brynhild and Erik rushed out of their hiding place and into the garden, each taking a different direction, so that when they reached the house, they stood either side of the doorway.

When Alswn stepped out of her house for the final time, Erik grabbed her, wrapping one arm around her body, while he covered her mouth with his other hand.

Brynhild stepped out from the side to face her. The lady struggled against his hold, but Erik was far stronger and she could barely move within his grip.

'Lady Alswn, we do not *want* to harm you,' Brynhild said firmly. 'Or Hywel...'

The Lady paused in her squirming.

Brynhild spoke in Norse, noting that the woman seemed to understand her. Well, the lady was meant to have married a Norse man, so she supposed the girl had learned their language for that reason.

'But...' Brynhild took a step towards her with a strip of linen in her hands. 'I will do whatever I have to, to ensure my sister's release from your brother. Is that understood?'

Alswn's green eyes flashed with shock and

horrified understanding. She managed a quick nod, before tears began to fall freely down her cheeks.

Brynhild ignored them. *How many tears had Helga shed in the last few days?* 'I will gag you if you scream for him. Will you scream?'

Alswn shook her head and Erik dropped his hand from the lady's mouth. She sobbed, but thankfully did not cry out.

'Good girl,' Brynhild said, trying to sound kind, 'See, no one has to die.'

She sobbed a little louder at that and Brynhild rolled her eyes. With a steely hold on the lady's arm, Erik led her towards the back path, the one that led down to the cove and their boat below.

'I cannot go back there,' whimpered Alswn as they walked. 'I will die!'

Erik gave Brynhild a concerned look over her head, but the girl's words reminded Brynhild of how she had been as an earnest young woman. Alswn didn't look as if she'd seen more than nineteen winters and she had the dramatic countenance of a woman who'd never seen true hardship.

'Your brother will kill you?' Brynhild asked mildly. 'That seems a wasted effort—to force me to drag you back to him, only for him to murder you. If he'd wanted you dead, he could have just told me.'

The woman glared at her, no doubt sensing Brynhild's dry amusement was at her own expense. 'He will break my spirit!'

'Your spirit?' Brynhild flinched a little at that. 'Does he beat you?'

'No,' Alswn said with a bad-tempered huff. 'But he does not care for me. He was happy to give me away to a barbarian, a heathen, a—' She stopped speaking, realising her mistake too late, and Brynhild laughed.

'Be careful, my Lady, the man who holds you is Halfdan's brother.'

Alswn glanced up at Erik and paled. Shrinking considerably in his grip, she stumbled over a rock in the path and with a grunt Erik steadied her before dragging her forward again. Brynhild felt a little guilty at that, not for Alswn, but for making Erik uncomfortable.

'What your brother does to your *spirit* is not my concern. I care only for the release of my sister. If Hywel loves you, he will petition your brother for your release.'

'Rhys will kill Hywel on sight for betraying him!'

Brynhild couldn't blame Lord Rhys for being

angry at Hywel. The man had stolen his sister—the woman he was meant to be protecting, and not only that, he'd slept with her. Still…maybe things could still be put right between them. 'Are you wed?' asked Brynhild.

'We will be.'

'Hmmm,' replied Brynhild.

'We *will* be!' Alswn snapped, finally showing a little courage. 'We have to wait for the return of a priest, that is all.'

'I'm sure,' Brynhild said drily, not really caring any more, her eyes flitting back and forth from the path ahead and behind them for Hywel.

'I don't even understand why he wants me back!' snapped Alswn. 'He never liked me anyway. My brother always considered me to be a burden. One he needed to marry off as soon as possible.'

'I am sure he was worried about you. When you disappeared, he wouldn't have known if Ulf told the truth. If you had left with Hywel, or if Ulf had murdered or stolen you for himself, after all, it was Halfdan who broke the treaty.'

Alswn stumbled again, this time on some twigs across the path as they walked down into the cove. She had paled considerably, and looked even younger, in the bright morning light. 'Halfdan broke the treaty? I thought my brother had.'

'No, it was my brother,' said Erik, 'Why does that matter?'

'My aunt…' she whispered, and then with more force, 'What of the captives? Ulf held some of our people hostage at his fort. Did Rhys get them out? That was the plan, and if he got them out, he would break the treaty and come for me. But…if Halfdan broke the treaty first…'

'I do not know about any captives,' said Erik. 'I only know your brother couldn't spare men to search for you because he had his own troubles back in the west… I presume that might have something to do with it.'

Alswn frowned, her face pale and sickly. 'His army is too stretched across the Kingdom to attack Ulf's fort directly. Our marriage was meant to be a last resort—if he couldn't free them himself, then the alliance would ensure their release.'

'Hywel didn't tell you? That it was Halfdan who broke the treaty?' asked Brynhild and the girl shook her head. Then her eyes widened at something behind them and instinctively Brynhild turned.

Hywel was running down the path, sword

and shield in hand. Brynhild unsheathed her axe and turned to face him as he came charging out of the woods.

'I'll handle this, get her in the water,' Brynhild ordered, and Erik nodded. Picking up the Lady as if she were a bag of feathers, he ran with her towards the little boat. For some reason that simple acceptance of her command filled her with pride and affection.

Erik was a powerful warrior in his own right, but he did not doubt her.

She focused on the man screaming a battle cry as he ran across the shingle towards her. She'd already judged his speed, strength and level of skill before he was even within arm's reach of her. The way he held his sword and shield, how he ran, and leapt over obstacles. He was impressive.

But she was Brynhild the Hammer and she showed the reason for her nickname as she met him head on. Angling her shield, she deflected the force of his blade easily, then hooked the handle of his sword with her axe and twisted it downwards, punching the metal boss of her shield into his face to unsteady him. To his credit he didn't drop his weapon, but it forced his body downwards.

She swung her axe hard and the wood of his shield shuddered against the blow as he raised it high to protect his head. She jabbed him with her shield once more, this time with the edge and against his exposed stomach. He crumpled, losing grip of his shield, and she took the advantage and swept his feet from underneath him with a deliberate kick, so that he sprawled flat on his back.

Desperately he raised his sword, but with another twisted hook of her axe she threw it several feet away. There was a moment where she could have carved his head in two and ended it there. But instead she tossed the axe in the air and grabbed it so that she now held it just below the razor-sharp head of the blade. With a mighty swing, she smacked him hard across the head with the blunt wooden handle and the man fell limp.

There was a scream from behind and she saw Erik struggling to keep hold of the distraught girl as he tried to bundle her into the boat.

'Do not fret. He is still *alive*,' she shouted back in irritation and the girl sagged with relief against Erik's strong arms. Brynhild glanced at the man at her feet. 'At least I think he is…' she murmured to herself, kicking him with her foot. Hywel groaned. 'Yes, definitely alive,' she called back, this time with a bit more cheer.

Then she ran across the shingle to join them at the little boat.

'Stay in!' she ordered Alswn and the girl sank down upon the deck, tears running down her cheeks.

'Raise the sail!' Erik said. 'I'll push us out.'

She didn't question him, as he had not questioned her. Jumping into the boat, she began to rig the sail. Her hands worked quickly as Erik grunted and strained to haul the boat into the sea. The tide was in, so at least he didn't have to drag them far. Even so, Brynhild was shocked at the sheer strength and speed with which he dragged them out into the waves.

Picking up an oar, she began to strike out into the surf, pushing them off the rocky bed to be buoyant in the water. Once the boat had lifted, Erik pulled himself up into the boat with a loud grunt of relief.

'Damn that stupid fool!' growled Brynhild as her eyes caught something on the beach behind them.

Alswn began to weep even louder and Erik sighed.

'What is *wrong* with him?' cried Brynhild

to no one in particular, as she watched Hywel stumble into the surf, his sword held limply in his hand, and his body weaving from side to side, as if he were confused.

'He is in love,' Erik said grimly. Falling back against the side of the boat, he stared at Brynhild silently and a weighted look of understanding passed between them.

They knew Hywel was going to drown if he didn't turn back.

The wind caught the sail and the cloth swelled with air. Hywel continued to struggle through the waves. His sword was gone now, taken by the relentless sea, his arms flailing as he tried to swim, as well as shake off the knock Brynhild had given to his head.

'Please,' begged Alswn, 'please, don't let him die. I beg you!'

Brynhild watched as the man struggled to keep his head above water and then one of the breaker waves hit him, and he disappeared beneath the surface. Erik knew by the grim look on her face what had happened and he grabbed Alswn before she tried to leap from the boat.

Holding her tight, he looked at Brynhild from above her wailing head. His expression calm as he waited on her order.

Brynhild glared at the spot where Hywel had submerged. His head broke the surface and he managed to gasp a breath or two to regain his last remaining strength. But instead of heading to the shore, he carried on trying to swim towards them, even though it was hopeless.

She hesitated and Erik held Alswn firmly to his chest, as the young woman began to plead for her lover's life.

'Damn him!' shouted Brynhild and she swung the boat with an angry pull of the steering oar. Jabbing a finger at Alswn, she said, 'Take one step off this boat and I will gut you like a fish!'

'I will do whatever you say, but please help him!' she cried, her voice hoarse with tears.

With more curses, Brynhild and Erik used both wind and oar to make it to the spot where Hywel fought not to drown. The man was losing the battle to stay afloat, let alone swim, the large welt above his eye swollen and bleeding into the salty water.

Erik gripped him by the shoulders of his tunic and hauled him aboard in one smooth motion. He flopped on the deck half-dead, barely able to gasp for breath, or keep his eyes open.

'Alswn...' he moaned.

'Idiot!' Brynhild said, followed by a flood of

foul curses that would have made even a sea-
soned raider wince. She thumped the side of
the boat with her fist, as Erik allowed Alswn
to comfort her lover.

Erik hated to see Brynhild battling with her
conscience like this. Struggling to do what was
right, when it might condemn her sister.

Erik had waited for her decision, willing to
follow her regardless of her choice. He would
do anything for her. He was bound to her in a
way that even his father could never have managed, because it was a willing surrender, an
eternal loyalty.

She owned his heart.

Whatever she decided he would accept, although he was secretly glad she'd chosen to save
Hywel. Not because he thought much of the
man, but because he knew how Brynhild would
struggle to live with herself if she had let him
die. She was incapable of murdering a man who
was only trying to protect his partner, just as she
had taken a risk by releasing the horses in the
morning, fearing they might break a leg in the
dark. A risk he suspected had ruined their plans
and brought Hywel back to find Alswn gone.

'You *will* help me save my sister!' Brynhild

glared at Alswn, as she rained kisses against Hywel's face and tried to revive the now unconscious man.

Her wide green eyes were overflowing with tears, this time with gratitude rather than pain. 'Thank you!'

Erik couldn't help but smile at the confusion running across Brynhild's face. It was the same emotion he'd felt many times growing up with Halfdan. When he'd taken yet another punishment or allowed his little brother to win a contest at his own expense, each time he'd wondered why he'd done it. Why he hadn't let his brother fail in their father's eyes. It had made no sense at the time, but now it did, when he saw Brynhild facing a similar dilemma.

Because it was the right thing to do.

He and Brynhild were built the same. Hard outer shells and soft hearts. She'd saved a man who had been an obstacle, and a threat, because ultimately she couldn't live with herself if she didn't.

Compassion. It was a curse he knew all too well—at least he wasn't alone suffering with it.

They made their way back to the shore, the hull scraping against the shingle as they landed. Hywel—the madman that he was—tried to fight them when he awoke, his bare feet scrabbling against the deck as he tried to raise himself to his feet. He threw a weak punch, which Erik easily dodged considering the man's poor condition. Not surprising considering the crack Brynhild had given his head.

'Control your dog, woman!' snarled Brynhild and after a few soothing words from Alswn, Hywel collapsed back on the deck, sinking into Alswn's arms with a groan.

Once they were back on dry land. Erik carried Hywel back up to their roundhouse, his lover worrying over him the entire walk. Alswn fluttered around Hywel like a butterfly, lighting the fire and soothing his head with cool linen cloths as he lay on the pallet in the corner of the small room.

'My family will come looking for me,' he croaked in Norse. 'When I do not arrive today...'

Brynhild took an angry stride forward and hissed in his face, 'Then maybe I should kill you and then *finally* we can be on our way!' It was all bluster, of course, but Hywel wasn't to know that.

Alswn raised her hand, as if such a weak gesture could stop a powerful woman like Brynhild. 'Please, I swear I will help you with your sister.' She tugged at a gold chain around her neck and pulled from her dress a gold ring. It was covered in beautiful engravings and knot work. 'Take this…and I… I will also write a letter to my brother.'

'A letter? What good will that do me? He wants *you* back, not parchment!'

The girl sighed. 'I cannot go back. I am carrying Hywel's child.'

Brynhild laughed. 'You have been with him less than a week! You cannot know you are already carrying his child!'

'I have been *with him* longer than a week,' whispered Alswn, her green eyes shining without regret in the dim light.

Brynhild gave a long-suffering sigh. 'I see. But that does not change anything, he will not believe you are safe until he sees you with his own eyes. That was the deal.'

Alswn held her gaze. 'He will believe you. I swear it. When he sees this and my letter.'

Hywel spoke up. 'I saw your horses. It will not be long until the settlement realises you are here and then my family will come—'

'And what will they do?' barked Brynhild, exasperated with the young man. 'Will they force me to save them from drowning, too? Carry me up a hill and put me to bed?'

Hywel sighed and took a ring off his own hand. 'Give this to Lord Rhys. He will realise the significance. Tell him *I wasn't strong enough.*'

Brynhild threw up her hands. 'Finally! Something we can all agree with!'

Erik failed to cover his stifled laugh at Brynhild's sour tone. When she glared at him in warning, he couldn't help himself and his rich laugh echoed around the room.

Alswn dropped to her knees. 'I swear by the holy mother, and by the life of my unborn child, Rhys will understand when you give him our rings and letter. He will realise I am no longer of use to him. He will no longer care or want me back. He cares only for his Kingdom—even family must come second to the honour of our house.'

'Then why don't you come with us? Tell him yourself,' asked Erik quietly, all humour gone.

There were more fresh heart-breaking sobs. 'I cannot face him! He will kill Hywel for bedding me. He will see it as the ultimate betrayal… from both of us!'

'And I will not let her face him alone!' Hywel growled from the pallet.

'Mighty words from a man flat on his back,' said Brynhild in disgust. As if to prove her point he rose up on his elbows and promptly collapsed back on the bed with another groan.

Grimly Brynhild folded her arms across her chest and said, 'Give it to me then! This apparent missive that will free us all of each other's company.'

Alswn hurried to a small chest in the corner and took out a scroll. She then grabbed some charcoal from the edge of the fire that had yet to catch. 'This was the treaty,' she said, holding and unfurling the scroll up to the light, before placing it on a table in the centre of the room and flipping it over to write on the only blank side. 'I kept it, intending to write an apology to my brother, to try to explain what we have done and why.'

'Indeed,' said Erik drily. 'You could have sent it *before* you ran for the hills…saved Brynhild's sister from being kidnapped.'

'I am truly sorry that your sister has been taken. But I assure you, for all my brother's faults, he would not harm a woman.' She paused, looking uncertainly at the big body of Brynhild.

'My sister is nothing like me…she is…*delicate*.'

Erik saw the twist of pain in Brynhild's eyes and he felt a sudden rush of anger towards the couple.

Alswn nodded enthusiastically. 'Then he would definitely not harm her.'

'How *comforting*!' Erik said. Why would her body make any difference? Helga had nothing to do with this, yet she was the one being punished instead of these fools? It wasn't fair.

Brynhild shrugged coldly. 'Write your note, then… But if you lie and my sister *is* harmed, I will return with my mother and sister—they are not *delicate*. And we will kill your man and anyone else who stands with you. Understood?'

Erik added his own show of support. 'My brother and I will join with Brynhild and her family. We have longships. Even if you run, we will raid this place and leave nothing but smoke and ruin. Then, we will hunt you down…and seek our *full revenge*.'

The couple looked at Brynhild and Erik with wide terrified eyes, and the note was written quickly. Again, Alswn reassured them it explained everything, but as it was written in Welsh, they couldn't be sure. They had to trust the couple's fear of them was enough to keep them honest.

Alone they walked down to the beach and Brynhild asked Erik quietly, 'Have I made a terrible mistake?'

Erik shook his head. 'No.'

'I will never forgive myself...if this doesn't work.'

Erik wrapped an arm around her shoulders, pulling her to his side. 'You would never have forgiven yourself if you had let him die.'

She sighed and leaned into his solid warmth, allowing her anger and frustration to be released in one long breath. 'True.'

Chapter Eighteen

They sailed their little boat out of the cove and on to the sea. The waves were choppy and the wind brisk, biting at their clothes and faces. They huddled together for warmth, glad the wind was blowing south and filling the sail.

They kept close to the coastline as they travelled. When the sun began to dip, they reefed the sail and rowed towards land, pulling up their little boat on the muddy sand of a small inlet. Once they had dragged their boat out of the tidal reach, they created a shelter among the rolling dunes, soaring black cliffs behind them. They had plenty of fresh water in their supplies and some fish they'd caught in an old net they'd found among the boat's belongings. Using some flotsam, they pitched up a makeshift tent, using the hull of the boat and the sail to create a shelter from the wind.

'At least it's not raining,' Brynhild said through chattering teeth as she dropped an armful of wood and some sticks beside Erik. He'd gutted the fish and had them cooking in the pot with some sea water.

After lighting a fire, Brynhild took out the parchment and rings. 'Can you read it?' she asked hopefully, already knowing the answer, but staring at the strange text as if she might somehow learn its meaning anyway.

Erik glanced at it and shook his head. 'No, but I do not think they are stupid enough to betray us. I am sure her message explains to her brother why she left and he will have to release Helga when he reads it. And there is always your silver to offer, or Helga's father may bring assistance… Do you think he will help us?'

Brynhild rather enjoyed the way he said 'us', as if they were now a partnership. But would this end once Helga was free? A little voice whispered in her ear that it would. There was nothing to keep Erik with her once he'd served his duty.

Strange that he should ask about Sihtric—it was a timely reminder that men were as seasonal as the tides, flowing in and out of your life. 'Jarl Sihtric did love my mother in the past and he is a man of his word. He swore to offer his aid if Helga ever needed him.'

'Was he with your mother long?'

'Three winters. The longest Porunn has ever been with a man.'

'Why did they separate?'

Brynhild sighed. 'My mother grew restless. She wanted her own path, her own glory, and he could never offer her that. He was a good man, kind to all of us… Valda found it especially hard when he left. She had always longed for a proper father, even if he couldn't be hers by blood.'

'And you?'

Brynhild smiled. 'I was older and more used to my mother's ways.' An image of Sihtric waving goodbye from his ship suddenly came into her mind. Followed by another of Valda weeping in her bed each night, and Brynhild trying to comfort her even though her own heart was breaking. Her smiled dropped.

'But I know our mother did the right thing. She couldn't have stayed with him and it was best Helga grew up not knowing her father well, especially as he had already sworn to marry another woman. His legitimate children would always have come first, which would have been hard on Helga. Porunn knew that it was better to keep our family together and separate from him. Just the four of us.'

'Did you know your own father?'

'No. Although he must have been a big troll by the size of me!' Brynhild chuckled, but Erik didn't laugh at her jest. It soured her mood and she kicked at the sand beneath her boot absently.

'You are perfect as you are,' he said.

'Thank you,' she replied softly, feeling more awkward and vulnerable than if he'd just laughed at her as she'd intended. It made her feel weak and she hated it. Easier to keep herself safe behind a wall of indifferent humour, than to admit this man made her feel…fragile.

After clearing her throat, she tried her best to sound indifferent and purposeful. 'Your task is almost complete and soon you will be free to begin your new life.' At his frown she added, 'You have helped me find Lady Alswn… It is not your fault I decided against bringing her back with me.'

'I will see it through to the end,' he said, his eyes as black as an endless night.

She stiffened, although she tried not to show

it. He had just confirmed their relationship would end. It was what they'd agreed, but it still hurt to have it confirmed. 'And I suppose you will need to meet up with Tostig first, though?'

'Yes.' He smiled as if his mood were brightened by the prospect. 'And I did promise your mother a farm.'

'Yes.' Brynhild smiled, too, if shakily, before wagging her finger at him. 'I still demand that from you, my mother's *damn* farm.'

'You will have it.'

If only their time together were as endless.

'And will you join us…near our farm? I meant what I said before…' She prodded the fire with a stick to avoid his gaze. 'You would be welcome to settle near us, if you wished…' It was a secret hope of hers that he would say yes. That he would always remain close by and be her friend. The idea gave her comfort in an otherwise grey and dull future.

Erik was silent for a long time and she felt as if the flames burned at her face and throat as she waited for his response.

'No,' he said gently, 'I will find another place. I want to have a family of my own.'

Of course! Why would she imagine it to be any different? He didn't want her! He wanted a sweet bride. One he would know how to please...because of Brynhild.

It hurt. But she refused to be his victim. She stamped down her disappointment and summoned every piece of her shattered pride into a shield.

It wasn't as if she wanted to be his bride! That wasn't the life she wanted... Was it?

At least they still had some time left together and Brynhild would enjoy what little pleasures she had while they lasted.

Moving closer, she took his face in her hands and pressed a tentative kiss against his lips. 'Will you keep me warm tonight?'

His black pupils flared with lust. 'As long as you want me, I am yours,' he promised.

Sweeping her leg over him, she sat upon his lap, straddling his thighs. His long legs stretched out in front of him, a little to the side of the fire. She undid his belt and gripped the bottom of his tunic, but when she tried to tug it off, she realised he was sat on the hem. She sighed forlornly, about to get off his lap so he could undress.

But he gripped her bottom firmly with one hand, while pushing up with the other. Their hips pressed against each other as he raised himself up off the ground so that she could drag up his tunic from beneath him. When he sat back down, she had his top gripped firmly in her hands and she pulled it up and over his head, his display of strength firing the lust in her veins that was only intensified by his bare chest beneath her fingers.

Acres of golden muscle, dark wiry hair and fine scars were laid out for her indulgence. She loved it all, the power and the vulnerability. He had survived so much and she thought him the best of men because of it.

'At least…until we have my mother's farm?' she teased, a little breathless, as his fingers untied her belt and dropped it to the side.

'Your mother's *damn* farm,' he corrected.

Unable to help herself, she lurched forward, clasping his neck and pulling his face towards her for a greedy kiss. His arms wrapped around her in a tight embrace as he opened his mouth for her, stroking his tongue against hers with low groans that reverberated through to the depths of her soul.

His nimble fingers worked at the linen strips beneath her tunic, but she found the layers of fabric between them frustrating and she pulled away to help him remove them until only their trousers and braies remained between them.

Again, she fell into his kiss, this time with his hands around her neck pulling her gently closer. The sail hung over their shelter shivered with wind, but she didn't feel it, her body too enflamed with desire.

Erik's dark head dropped to her breast, his long hair sliding tantalisingly over her skin. He licked and caressed her nipple, drawing it into his mouth with teasing flicks of his tongue, while she arched and moaned beneath his touch.

Running her hands through his hair, she pulled him up to her lips, unable to take his teasing a moment longer.

They tasted and explored each other's mouths, relishing the freedom and intimacy they shared— no matter how fleeting it was.

When she could no longer take the press of him without wanting more, she moved to the side, and on to a nearby bedroll. Feverishly she began to remove the clothing below her waist, tugging off her boots, leg wraps, trousers and finally her braies.

Erik did the same and, breathless, she straddled him once more, their hands and lips reaching for one another eagerly. One of his arms wrapped around her hips, even as his other slipped between their bodies to stroke her.

She moaned, rocking against him with happy sighs of pleasure. Reaching around her waist, she took his scarred hand from where it was on her hips and pressed it to her lips, stroking the rough flesh with a loving caress of her fingers. Then she stroked her hand up his arm to the mark of a blade against his shoulder. Leaning forward, she pressed a kiss there, before touching and tasting the scars against his chest. She wanted to replace the pain of each spot with a tender memory of her.

'I need you inside me,' she breathed, reaching down between them to wrap her fingers around his length.

'You are not ready yet,' he said huskily, as he pushed one finger inside her.

She moaned as his finger slipped out and circled her clitoris. He cupped the back of her head and pulled her down for another deep and passionate kiss, as if she were precious to him and he needed her more than food or air. She would never get enough of him, she realised— there would be no one after him. No one saw her like he did.

He stroked her until she was rocking, hot and wet against his hand.

'I am ready,' she whimpered, reaching between them to slide her hand down his hardness.

'Are you sure?' he whispered against her ear and she moaned as he pushed first one and then two fingers inside her.

'Yes,' she gasped. Then, as she rose up on to her knees, he released her and it was her turn to drive him mad with lust.

She positioned him at her entrance and then pushed down on his manhood, her body slowly taking in his impressive size with an achingly glorious rush of heat. Using his shoulders for leverage, she began to slide up and down against him, welcoming the feel of him stretching and filling her. He didn't move, allowed her to use him in whatever way she wished.

'Just tell me,' she panted, 'when you are... about to...'

He shook his head, his teeth clenched, his head thrown back, neck straining, and his eyes fixed on the sail cloth above their heads. She smiled and stilled her hips, stroking a palm tenderly down his face to draw his eyes back to hers. As if she were soothing a wild stallion, she said gently, 'Let me please you, Erik. As you have pleased me. Don't you like to watch me ride you?'

He sucked in a sharp breath, as if she'd punched him in the gut. *'Odin's teeth!* You are killing me, woman! Ride me as long as you like, sweetling. But please do not ask me to watch. I will be done far too soon if I do.'

She smiled, a delighted spark in her blue eyes. 'I want you to watch me.'

He groaned, but followed her command, and she began to move.

'No one else sees me like you do,' she confessed, leaning down to kiss him softly.

He gripped her hips, unable to stop himself from touching her. He jerked against her body, pounding his pelvis up against hers with an increasingly erratic pace. The sheer display of his passion was enough to bring her to a soaring climax and she cried out his name to the night.

Cradling her trembling body in his arms, he rolled her on to her back. He thrust once, twice, and then with a curse, pushed away from her to spend his seed against her thigh.

Later, after they'd cleaned themselves up, the wind had died down a little and they ate their stew outside the shelter, wrapped in a blanket and each other's arms beneath the stars.

Brynhild was certain that she would treasure the memory of this night for the rest of her life.

Chapter Nineteen

They set sail early the next day, flowing with a swift wind down the coast. When the land began to jut out to the west with the shadow of mountains in the distance, they knew they'd reached the land of the Welsh. Soon they would walk into the black dragon lord's lair and hopefully free Helga.

When they saw a large settlement on the coast, they rowed towards it and into the harbour to find their bearings, the sea as blue and as sparkling as Brynhild's eyes. Erik wasn't sure if he would survive the gut-wrenching parting from her. He tried not to dwell on it—no good ever came from fearing the future. He would take each day at a time, as he'd always done.

They'd agreed they would stay together until he had found her mother a farm. There she would live with her mother and sister, enjoying a life free from men.

He wished things were different, that he could take her as his bride. But then she wouldn't be Brynhild, the fierce shieldmaiden who valued her independence above all things.

She'd asked him to join with them. But not as part of her family, more that he would live 'close by'. He didn't want that, to live once more as an outsider, he needed a place where he belonged. A wife and children, but Brynhild didn't want any of that...

He understood her need for freedom. Hadn't he dreamed of the same thing for years? He didn't want to *own* her—even the idea of it made bile churn in his stomach. He would never demand obedience as if she were a dog. In his mind she would always be his equal...better even, and with him she could do whatever she wished whether it be farming or battle. But... his heart ached when he thought of a life without children.

The need to have his own family was a clawing hunger that he could never ignore.

An ache he could easily satisfy if he chose... someone else.

Anyone except Brynhild.

It was what most women wanted—wasn't it?

To have a husband, a good provider, a man who would cherish and care for them. Erik knew without a doubt that he would be loyal and devoted to any woman who accepted him.

When he pictured a woman lying beside him in a bed made with his own hands he could only see Brynhild's face and body. The one woman who would never accept him as her husband.

Brynhild didn't need anyone. It was why he thought her so special and breathtakingly beautiful. Unlike him, who feared loneliness, she embraced it, finding glory in the freedom it gave her.

Even now she had set to work, gathering up their few possessions and preparing to step off their little boat without a backward glance. It could sink down to the seabed and she would not miss it. Would she feel the same about him when they parted?

He hoped not. He wanted to be branded on to her memory as clearly as she was burned into his. To never forget him, long for him even.

Maybe he didn't really want a wife and children after all? Maybe he just wanted someone to *love* him, unconditionally.

They knocked against the jetty with a light

tap, their boat looking like a pitiful bucket among the larger ships. The men on the harbour looked at them curiously as they stepped from their humble vessel with their sacks of supplies tossed over their shoulders.

'Where are we?' asked Erik in Saxon to a nearby man. The man glared at him and then walked on.

'Gwynedd,' said a man not that far away from them. He was mending a net with a young lad beside him, 'Are you Norse?' he asked in the Norse tongue. He was a thickset man, with curly dark hair, and a swarthy complexion.

'Yes,' replied Brynhild.

'Then you would do better to speak that. We hate your people, too, but not as much as the Saxons,' the man replied mildly, barely looking up from his task of rethreading the rope on his net. He nodded at their boat. 'If you want that *ship* to still be here when you get back, I can keep an eye on it for you...for a price.'

Brynhild smiled. 'We don't mind if it's not. Although if you can point us in the direction of where we could buy some horses, there'd be some silver in it for you.'

The man put down his net and looked at them shrewdly. 'Plan on travelling far, then? Did you come from your brethren in Ireland? Be warned, there have been attacks on our shores before from your kind and we have already beaten you back once... However, if you wish to trade...'

'We have an important message to deliver to Lord Rhys Draig ddu Gwynedd regarding his sister.'

The man's eyes widened and he jumped to his feet, casting aside his net. After speaking to the lad in Welsh, the boy leapt to his feet and began to tie their boat more securely to the jetty.

He turned to Brynhild and Erik. 'Come, I will see you settled with supplies and horses. It is getting too late for travel. Better we give you a hot meal and a bed for the night. It is not safe to travel up the mountains in the dark. Especially at this time of year.'

They hurried after the suddenly energetic man as he weaved through the muddy paths of the settlement. The whole time he spoke to them over his shoulder, with the same brash manner as his walk. 'It is fortunate you ran into me and not someone loyal to Seisyllwg, or one of the other kingdoms. Most in these parts owe fealty to Lord Rhys, but not all.'

'Lord Rhys is at war with a neighbouring Kingdom?'

The man glanced at them and laughed. 'The kingdoms are always feuding. But Lord Rhys has more sense than to let their quarrels get out of hand. He crushes any dissent quickly enough.'

Erik noticed Brynhild stiffen at that. Lord Rhys did not sound flexible, or given easily to forgiveness—which did not bode well for them. He tried to soothe her with a light touch of his knuckles against the back of her hand. No one watching would have noticed its significance, but Brynhild did, as there was a slight drop in the stiffness of her shoulders after his caress.

'My name is Dafydd. Our chieftain is away at the moment. There is trouble in the eastern borders. Maybe something to do with your message?' He stopped momentarily to raise a brow at them in question.

'Possibly,' answered Erik with a shrug that offered no more information. If there was trouble in the east, it was probably because of Ulf.

Were they already out of time? 'Has there been news of bloodshed?'

Dafydd frowned. 'Not yet, although there is talk of a Norse army approaching. Are you something to do with that?'

Erik and Brynhild exchanged a look, then he answered, 'Indirectly...'

At Dafydd's scowl Brynhild added, 'We do not wish to fight against Lord Rhys... Which is why we must deliver our message *soon*. We will need the swiftest horses you can find.'

Dafydd nodded glumly. 'Swift *mountain* horses. I can see you right in that regard. But there truly is no point in you travelling at night, it is too treacherous, and will only lead to injury or worse.'

They came to a large stone building with a thatched roof. No cheery smoke or light came from its darkened centre.

'Stay here for the night, the chieftain will not mind—as you are on a mission for Lord Rhys,' said Dafydd, opening the door and ushering them in. 'I will go and see about your supplies for the journey tomorrow.'

Exhausted from sailing out on open water and in bitter winds, they made their way straight to the empty firepit. Brynhild lit the kindling, while Erik raided the larder for food. Before he'd left, Dafydd had said they could use whatever they liked, as important messengers for Lord Rhys were welcome in the Chieftain's home.

So, they searched together to find what they

needed for the night. If Dafydd had known the real reason for their presence, he might not have been so accommodating. Erik searched and gathered supplies from the storage chests along the walls, then made his way back to Brynhild.

Her teeth had begun to chatter, so she pulled her cloak tighter to ward off the chill and prodded the flames with an iron poker. Erik brought over a bucket of water and poured some in the cauldron above the flames. Next, he brought over two boards—on each of them were a handful of vegetables. He handed one board to Brynhild and they sat on the bench side by side, dropping in the roots as they chopped them up with their daggers.

They worked in companiable silence. She loved how easily they worked together on chores. He never expected her to do all the cooking and cleaning. Which was rare—even as a shieldmaiden some of her fellow warriors had expected her to do such things, solely because she was a woman. She'd always deliberately disappointed them, but with Erik it wasn't even an issue, he never expected such things from her.

Usually, he was the one who cooked and she

suspected it was because he enjoyed the chore. Even now he offered her a spoon to taste the broth and she nodded enthusiastically when he suggested adding a few herbs. In fact, he'd probably only shared this task with her because they were both ravenously hungry and the quicker they filled the pot the sooner they would eat.

'There's some dried bacon and grains over there that we can add, too,' he said. 'I will find us something to drink.'

She headed towards where he'd pointed and Erik went to look at the barrels by the door. Searching around in the pots and sacks, she managed to find what she was looking for. A sack of barley and the salted bacon, which was covered in linen and kept cool in a clay pot. She cut a good chunk off and diced it, then poured the pieces as well as a large handful of grains into the cauldron.

The stew bubbled and she gave it a stir with a sigh of relief. She couldn't wait to eat something hot and filling. She still felt as if she were bobbing on the waves and her stomach ached with hunger. Their little boat had felt like a leaf, floating helplessly on the whims of the sea. They'd had to work hard to keep it afloat, bailing out water regularly and rowing when they strayed too far from the coast.

Erik came over from the barrels by the door, a triumphant look on his face, his arms full of produce. 'Cheese, milk and ale!'

'Great! We can have porridge in the morning. I found some oats and dried fruit in one of the sacks.'

Erik walked over and she took the parcel of cheese from him so that he could sit. After pouring her a cup of ale, he then poured one for himself, and made a show of knocking it against hers in a toast. *'Skol!'*

'Skol!' she replied before taking a sip. They wrapped themselves in their cloaks and blankets and nibbled on the cheese while they waited for the stew to cook.

'What do you think this chieftain is like?' Brynhild asked as she curiously looked around her at the man's home.

'He's well stocked with good ale at least,' Erik said, looking thoughtfully around at the sparse furnishings.

'No family at home with him,' Brynhild pointed out, as any wife and children would have still remained even in his absence.

'No.' Erik nodded, then gestured around him.

'I would wager he's never been married. He lives like a man who has a simple life.'

'Young or old?' she asked curiously.

'Definitely old.'

'What makes you say that?'

'Look how old his furniture is. I swear this bench has been repaired a hundred times.' Erik bounced in his seat to prove his point and it creaked loudly.

She stilled him with a firm grip of his arm. 'Stop that! How does that make him old? He could have inherited it.'

Erik shook his head with a smile. 'Possibly, but a young man wouldn't keep such an orderly home. Our chieftain has lived alone for many years, I think.'

Looking around her at the humble home, it struck Brynhild as a rather lonely existence.

Would her life be like this, eventually?

If her sister married and when her mother eventually passed? Who could tell? No one knew their fate but the Norns who wove them.

Unaware of her melancholy, Erik added cheerfully, 'He's not a big man either. Look at his bed.'

Pushing aside her gloomy thoughts, Brynhild looked over at the short pallet pressed against the wall and forced a chuckle. 'I think we will break that if we both try to sleep on it!'

Erik nodded. 'I will sleep on the floor, then. You should have the bed.'

Brynhild stared at him thoughtfully. 'I would rather sleep by your side.'

Their eyes met and he smiled warmly. 'As would I by yours.'

Chapter Twenty

The next day they rode out on two ponies. Sturdy animals covered in a thick wiry coat, more suited to the chill of the mountains than normal horses, and surprisingly strong despite their size.

Dafydd gave them clear directions about how to reach Lord Rhys's fortress up on one of the larger mountains, explaining that it would take them at least a day's ride to reach it and that at the base of the mountain was a lake, with an old fishing hut that they could use to rest in before they made the climb up to the fort the following day.

Brynhild was tempted to ride through the night up the mountain if needs be, but already she could see how dangerous that might be.

The terrain was rocky, the path littered with

boulders and shingle. The ponies plodded forward at a slow and steady pace. They moved away from the coast and into the forests, diligently following the path Dafydd had said led to the mountain.

The huge giants of rock loomed over them black and cold. She could almost imagine fiery dragons curled up within their stone hearts. A rumble of thunder filled the slate sky and she shivered.

Was Thor beating his hammer, or had the dragons awoken?

Dismissing her fanciful thoughts, she urged her pony forward. Light rain began to splatter against her hands and she tugged on her woollen mittens, determined to keep riding for as long as possible.

The weather turned for the worse, but they rode on, not pausing to rest or eat. The rain seemed to fall sideways, so that no matter how heavily they wrapped themselves in their cloaks it still managed to soak them to the bone. Hammering down hard on their bodies, like a bucket of nails poured down from the sky. She could barely see the path ahead, so dark were the clouds smothering the noon sun.

They passed the lake, but Brynhild refused to

stop at the shelter. She urged her mount on and upwards, and Erik silently followed her lead. Brynhild was grateful for his support. Now that they were so close to her sister, she couldn't wait to end this nightmare—no matter how gruelling the final test.

'I hate this place!' spat Brynhild, after they'd cantered up a particularly hard bit of terrain, where the pebbles and earth had shifted dangerously beneath their mounts' hooves. They paused to let the ponies catch their breath and squinted up at their destination through the sleet. It felt as if the black rock had grown in size since the last time she'd looked and she had to glance behind to reassure herself how far they'd climbed.

'What?' shouted Erik, obviously not hearing her through the wind despite only being a few feet away.

'I *hate* this place!' she shouted again, spluttering against the icy rain that filled her mouth as soon as she raised her head.

Erik nodded, before shouting back, 'It makes me long for the desert!'

She nodded towards a nearby ash tree and they walked their animals over to it, glad to be out of the worst of the weather, if only for a moment.

'Does it,' she asked, 'make you long for the desert?' She wondered if there was any part of his mother's land which he might have visited on his travels that he missed. It seemed so exotic and exciting in comparison.

He paused, as if contemplating his surroundings. The freezing cold, the rain, the unforgiving terrain. Then his dark eyes fixed on her face and he smiled, the white of his teeth flashing in a flicker of distant lightning. 'No. Why would I want sunshine, when I could have this?'

She laughed—it sounded rusty in her throat and she realised how much she relied on him to lighten her mood. Erik had brought the sun to her and she felt warmer already for it. She clicked her tongue and urged her pony forward, tackling the mountain ahead with renewed vigour.

The afternoon passed painfully slowly, as the ponies climbed up the mountain with heads bowed low against the freezing wind, their breath misting up with each laboured snort, and yet they were dependable animals and Brynhild was grateful for them.

The day, which hadn't been particularly bright as it was, quickly faded into darkness. Brynhild's misery was complete. They would have to find a tree or cave to shelter in soon, or risk laming the ponies.

But then Erik stood up in his saddle and pointed into the distance. 'I think that's the fortress up ahead!'

She squinted through the rain and saw several tiny lights up ahead, like the flickering of beacons, or torches. Faint but clearly there.

Kicking her heels lightly, she urged her animal forward into a trot.

'Odin,' she whispered into the night sky, *'I beg you, bring my sister back to us.'*

The fort was substantial, ringed by built-up earth, and a wooden wall so high she could only just make out the torches in the guard towers above, let alone see whatever was beyond it. However, it must have been a large settlement. Smoke billowed up from behind the walls and she realised why they might call him the dragon Lord. His lair was high up in the mountains, heavily defended and billowing with smoke.

They made their way to the gate. The huge doors were closed against them, but as they approached a small shutter opened in one of the gates and they saw a flickering light. Brynhild hopped off her pony and went towards it.

An old woman stood glaring at them through the small iron grate.

'Heill,' Brynhild called, having to shout to be heard over the howling wind.

There was some bad-tempered grumbling from behind the woman and then the wooden shutter snapped shut. Brynhild stepped closer, wondering if they were ordering the gate to be opened, or more likely, they'd been denied entry. As she couldn't hear any ropes pulling, or levers being cranked, she presumed the latter.

She banged on the shutter with her fist. *'Heill!* We have a message for your master. A message from his sister Lady Alswn!'

Nothing happened and she slammed her fist even harder against the wood, causing the shutter to rattle, depressingly not by much. Erik came to stand at her side, both the ponies' reins in his hands. 'What is happening?'

'I'll be damned if I know,' she exclaimed with frustration, before hammering her fist against the door once more. 'Open up! We have a message for your master!'

The shutter snapped open again and this time

the torch flashed across a wizened man's face. He didn't look happy to see them either.

'Who are you?' he snapped, showing a couple of missing teeth and a barrel full of attitude, his Norse heavily accented with the disgust of having to use it.

'We have a message for Lord Rhys from his sister Lady Alswn.'

The man appeared unimpressed. 'That's not what I asked. I asked, *who are you?*'

If her sister's life wasn't at stake, she might have tried punching through the iron grate to throttle the man.

'Brynhild Porunndóttir and Erik the Black,' she shouted, although this time out of anger rather than to be heard above the wind. 'We have a message for your master.'

'What message?' croaked the voice.

Brynhild sucked in a deep breath of outrage. 'From his sister the Lady Alswn. We must speak with him.'

'Where is the Lady Alswn?' hissed the voice and then they heard an old woman's voice—presumably the hag who had originally opened the shutter—grumbling to him in the Welsh language.

Brynhild glared at the old man with bloodthirsty eyes. She had reached the end of her patience with both of them. 'Let us in, or you will never know!'

The shutter snapped closed again and Brynhild thumped the gate with all her might. 'Damn you! Let us in, we must speak with your master!'

'Come on, then!' croaked a voice to the side and Brynhild jumped as she saw a narrow doorway open up in the wall beside them. 'Or do you wish to spend all night in the rain?' It was the old man, wrapped heavily in cloaks, and he had the audacity to be tapping his boot impatiently.

'What about the ponies?' Brynhild asked, walking across to tower over the little old man, who stared up at her without an ounce of sense or fear.

'Well, you are a big one, aren't you? Wouldn't have imagined someone like you to be *her* sister,' he said, seemingly unaware of the rudeness of his comment.

At the mention of Helga, she breathed in a sigh of relief. *Did this mean she was alive?*

Brynhild only hoped she was also unharmed. She'd have asked, but the man didn't appear the helpful type. He nodded at the ponies. 'Bring them, they'll squeeze through… You two might struggle, though,' he said with a snide chuckle.

Brynhild gritted her teeth, took hold of her pony's reins from Erik and followed the old man through the doorway. Immediately her ears began to sting, as they came out of the elements and into a reasonably sheltered area.

After passing through the wooden door, they arrived at a narrow strip of land, followed by another wall, built up with earth and wood. She had never seen anywhere so heavily defended, and Ulf thought to take this? Men walked the palisade, although admittedly not as many as she would have expected. But maybe the weather kept them inside? It seemed unlikely, but these were strange people.

She supposed with enough men anywhere could be defeated. Still, she hoped Ulf died trying. She had never loathed anyone quite as much as Erik's father and would gladly have met him in battle.

They reached a long guard house with a stable attached. A fire was burning in a brazier just inside the stable, illuminating the fresh hay and troughs within. She could have sworn her pony picked up its pace as soon as it saw it.

'Remove your weapons. They and your ponies can stay here.' The old man fixed them with a stern look that defied his hunched and withered frame. 'Otherwise, you will go no further this night. Understood?'

Reluctantly, Brynhild and Erik stripped off their weapons and left their ponies to be attended to by a couple of youths who looked as if they'd been dragged from their beds only moments before.

They were taken through yet another small gate into a large central area. It didn't look much smaller than Jorvik if Brynhild were honest. This was the home of a king surely, not a lord? There were several halls, workshops and stables, all within the defences. She could see now that the fortress was built on a reasonably flat step of land, the steep cliffs of the mountain behind. She could even see a waterfall running down from the wall of rock in the distance, so the fort had both fresh water and natural defences on one side.

In the centre of the fortress was a very large stone building, with many smaller buildings surrounding it. They were led towards it. The roof was timber and had several smoke holes. A striking hall that even the gods would find impressive.

As they entered, the heat and light of the room hit her senses hard. The aches of their many days of travelling began to pull at her bones in the same way that the keel of a ship creaks and moans during a storm. She dragged back her cloak from around her head and a drop of rain dripped from her nose on to the clean floor. She glanced at Erik and he was stamping his feet and clapping his hands as if to beat the blood back into his veins. He looked pale and tired, but he gave her a supportive smile as he moved to stand by her side.

The hall was separated into different sections by large wooden dividers, though each section was bigger than some of the homes they'd stayed in recently. More like a palace than a lord's hall. The Saxons liked to think themselves superior to the Britons—the people who had settled on the land long before them. But if this grand hall was anything to go by, they were mistaken to do so. A gold and silver Christian crucifix decorated in the Celtic style was hung above the entrance. It wasn't the only symbol of wealth and expertise.

Beautifully carved benches and long elaborate feasting tables filled the immediate entrance, with large kitchen areas and pantries to the sides of the hall, including a clay oven. The tapestries were huge and some were even decorated with Byzantian silk, depicting their people's legends and tales, as well as stories from their holy book. Braziers and torches, as well as a central fire, illuminated the carvings on the timbers, some of which were even painted in reds, whites, greens and golds.

They were led to the far end of the hall, where there was a raised dais and a throne-like chair, intricately carved with dragons. The beasts' mouths were open and breathing fire as they coiled around the chair. In the flickering light of the oil lamps, they appeared to be moving. It was stunning and intimidating in equal measure.

However, nothing compared to the Lord who sat upon its throne. Long legs clad in rich leather boots. Dark woollen hose, a gold-buckled belt, a long deep blue tunic edged with gold embroidery in the Celtic style. His wrists draped over the arms of his chair, a gold ring shining from his hand in the firelight.

A warrior prince, for he couldn't be much older than Brynhild and yet he looked older. Slim of build, but still powerful by the breadth of his shoulders. He had the fine-boned frame of an elvish king. A crown of black loose curls fell to his shoulders, but unlike Erik with his golden colouring and earthy eyes, this man was pale, his skin almost luminescent, his bone structure masculine, but fine, as if cut from marble. Gem-like blue eyes, deeply set, shadowed and as piercing as a blade, stared back at her. He was breathtakingly beautiful, but also deeply unsettling.

Brynhild shivered to think of her sweet sister in this predator's company for any length of time.

The man leaned forward as if to see her better and she felt as if someone had placed a bejewelled hand around her neck. She shivered, wanting desperately to reach for Erik and the warmth of his embrace.

Then she felt him, Erik's shoulder brushing against hers, subtly letting her know he was still by her side. Her hand flexed and she felt his scarred knuckles slide against hers. Immediately she felt stronger.

'*You* are her sister?' asked Rhys, for that was who he had to be.

Brynhild raised her chin. It wasn't the first time someone had questioned their bloodline. 'Yes, I am. My name is Brynhild.'

'You do not look anything like her,' he accused, as if beauty was something she'd simply failed to acquire.

'You do not look old enough to be a lord,' she answered drily, 'and yet life is full of surprises.'

Rhys raised a jet brow at her tone. 'You certainly sound like her.'

Her chest tightened and her stomach lurched—she should take care. After all, this man held her sister hostage. 'May I see her?'

'Where is my sister?' he hissed, his eyes flashing like a serpent before it strikes.

Erik spoke, stepping forward as if to somehow shield her from his words. 'We found her. But she did not wish to return to you.'

'Lies!' he snarled, his fingers curling into the wood of his armrest like claws. 'What of Hywel? Is he dead?'

'Alive and well. He was the one who took your sister north.'

'Now I know you are lying. Hywel would never betray me.'

Brynhild took the bag from her belt and held it up in her fist. 'Here is your proof, words written by your sister in her own hand. She was not taken, she ran away. I say again, Hywel is the man who has her now, but as you will soon learn, he had her long before.' Anger pushed her forward despite the murderous look in his eyes. 'My sister has nothing to do with your petty grievances with Ulf! You behave as if we owe you something when we do not! You stole a young girl from her family! You are the monster here, not us. Why should we have brought another frightened girl to you for punishment?'

'Frightened? Give me that!' he snapped, lurching from his seat, and stalking towards her, his long legs eating up the ground between them in only a few strides.

Erik moved a step forward, but she stopped him with a touch to his arm. She shoved the bag outwards to Rhys, who took it with a snap of his wrist and then turned away to look at the contents: the two rings and the parchment.

Her breath caught in her throat and she found herself grasping for anything that might save her sister. 'Hywel said he was sorry, that he wasn't strong enough...that you would understand.'

There was only silence in response. His shoulders tensed and she saw the guards around the walls exchange worried glances among themselves, their hands moving to rest on the pommels of their swords.

Brynhild took another step forward, hoping to ease her earlier words with some form of comfort. 'She seems happy...your sister. They're expecting a babe together.'

Rhys's hand fisted, crumpling the parchment into a ball, which he threw into one of the nearby braziers that lined the path to his throne. 'Hywel is wrong. I do not understand.' He stalked back towards his chair, sweeping his cloak to the side as he returned to his seat, his eyes cold and unfeeling as he stared down at her from the dais. 'Helga will be staying.'

Brynhild's throat tightened painfully. Her worst fears were coming true and she was helpless to stop them.

Erik's voice boomed through the hall. 'Your sister was taken by your own man! You have no right to hold Helga hostage.'

Rhys's eyes flashed upwards at Erik. 'Helga is no longer my prisoner. She stays with me willingly. She says I am her *fate*.'

A cold shiver ran down Brynhild's spine. *Fate*. The runes they'd cast as children flashed before her eyes and she felt sick.

'Let me see her,' she gasped, her voice hoarse.

Rhys raised his chin and stared down at her with defiance. 'No.' A bronze medallion on his chest caught the light, to show a dragon with its wings unfurled.

'Why not?' barked Erik, striding forward. A guard stepped forward from the shadows to halt him and Erik threw him to the ground with a curse. More men melted from the walls, but Rhys held up one of his jewelled fingers and they stood still, hands lightly resting on the hilts of their swords.

Brynhild's strength was shaken. 'Please,' she begged, 'let me see her, I need to know that she is safe.'

Rhys leaned forward, his expression unmoved. 'You will have to trust me when I say that she is well. As I will have to trust *you* regarding the welfare of Lady Alswn.'

'How much?' shouted Erik. 'You honourless wretch! How much silver for her return?'

Rhys snarled at Erik with cold fury, 'You cannot buy me with gold or silver, Ulfsson! It is time your people learned that a man's soul cannot be bought like cattle! We were here long before the Saxons came to our shores and we will remain long after you have crawled back to your pits. Remind your father of that before he thinks to attack my lands!'

Erik glared at him. 'Ulf is not my father.

He disowned me long before he disowned my brother. We are nothing to him.'

'And yet *here* you are!' snarled Rhys, his hands gripping the arms of his throne tightly. 'In *my* lands, demanding I do *your* bidding! I know Ulf means to attack us again. I will defeat him and burn away your people's plague from Gwynedd.'

Brynhild placed a calming hand on Erik's shoulder, before turning once more to Lord Rhys. '*Please.* Helga would not want us to worry about her. Let us speak with her, if only to reassure us that she stays so willingly.'

'No.'

Frustration and fear caused her voice to rise. 'Please, I beg you—I cannot understand why you will not let us speak with her! We are her family.'

A flicker of pity flashed in Rhys' eyes for a moment and Brynhild held her breath, only for her hope to be shattered by his next words. 'You may stay within the first wall tonight. But I expect you gone at first light.'

'I will not leave without seeing my sister!' Her shout rang out across the golden Hall like a battle cry.

'One night. Now leave me!' Rhys said firmly,

then, with a dismissive click of his fingers, the guards from the walls rushed towards them.

Erik charged forward to meet them, flattening two men with brutal punches before they'd even unsheathed their swords. He snatched both their weapons as they fell and met the remaining three with a growl of fury. Retreating only to cover Brynhild's back, he twisted both swords in his hands to demonstrate his skill and made the guards think twice before taking another step. Uncertain of what to do, the men pulled back and looked anxiously up at their leader, who had risen from his chair.

Brynhild glared at Lord Rhys and then, hoping that wherever Helga was she would hear her sister and know that they would never give up on her, she shouted with a voice she'd used countless times to command, or intimidate men in battle. 'Helga is an honoured and beloved sister! You cannot treat her as a spoil of war—she is worth far more than you could ever imagine. You may throw us out tonight, but soon *all* of her kin will come for her. You will see, Lord Rhys! We shieldmaidens will save our sister or die trying!'

The room began to fill with more armed warriors, some with arrows already notched and aimed at Erik. Without removing her gaze from Rhys, she placed a hand on Erik's shoulder and gently squeezed.

Erik dropped his swords and the men rushed towards them. Erik snarled and lashed out at the men who grabbed him roughly by the arms. They punched him in the gut and head to try to subdue him, but it was like hitting stone and he barely flinched, striking back until they managed to wrestle his arms to his back.

In contrast, Brynhild didn't fight them as they pulled her arms behind her back. Never once did she take her eyes off her sister's captor. 'You have made an enemy of us, *Lord Rhys*. You have made a *terrible* enemy...'

Then something entirely unexpected happened.

Helga walked into the room from an antechamber behind the throne. She wore a gown of matching blue to the tunic Rhys wore and she moved to stand beside her captor, placing her small hand on his shoulder.

Lord Rhys smiled coldly at Brynhild and reached up to cover her hand with his own. Brynhild stared in horror at her sister's easy acceptance of her captivity.

'I am happy here. Please, do not fight,' Helga

said gently, then she turned to Rhys. 'May I speak with her?'

'No.'

Then, with a dismissive wave of his hand, Brynhild was dragged from the hall. She shouted Helga's name, but could see nothing through the armed men as they forced her out of the room.

Chapter Twenty-One

Back at the guard house and stable behind the first wall, they were shoved into the building by a guard with a bloody nose and no patience.

'We will come for you at dawn. Don't even think about causing any more trouble, or I will burn this place down with you in it!' snapped the guard, as he bolted the door. By the sounds of the men huffing, and the scraping of furniture outside, Brynhild imagined they were barricading the entrance, not wishing to take any more chances with their unruly guests.

'Our weapons are gone,' Erik noticed as he looked around at their surroundings.

Brynhild nodded numbly, staring at the contents of the room as if she were in a dream. It was as if the rage and grief from moments before had burned away all of her other emotions, leaving her cold and hollow inside.

There was a comfortable pallet on a raised platform in the corner, covered in blankets and soft furs. The firebox in the centre of the room had a small fire burning, with plenty of logs in the store beneath. An array of pickled fish and dried meats were placed on a table at the side of the room, with bowls of apples and plums, as well as platters of bread and cheese, beside them.

But Brynhild's mouth felt as dry as ash. For the first time in her life the sight of such a plentiful meal did nothing to please her. She crossed her arms, hugging herself tightly, as the misery of her failure threatened to crush her.

Erik took hold of her arms gently, turning her to face him. 'We *will* get her back.'

'How?' she whispered, her voice cracking beneath the strain. 'And what if Ulf attacks here in full force? There will be no way to protect her.' Brynhild sucked in a shaky breath. 'She is not like us, Erik. She is not a warrior, just a girl who picks flowers, and believes in myths and magic.' She gave a rusty bitter laugh. 'She probably thinks this is her *destiny*. That he is the one she was meant to marry from her prophecy.

She doesn't even realise how he is *using* her. I am not sure what will be worse. Trying to force her away from him, or how she will feel when she discovers the truth. Either way, she will be broken by it.'

Erik frowned. 'No rune could have foretold this.'

Brynhild sighed. 'It wasn't even a rune! That is what makes this so ridiculous! Her dream was of a dragon, remember? A black dragon with blue eyes. So, she drew it on one of the bones and, of course, she picked it. She is risking her life with this man! All because of some silly game we played as children! I never should have let her believe in such nonsense.'

Erik wrapped his arms around her tightly. 'We will find a way.' He wiped the tears on her cheeks and she realised for the first time that she'd been crying.

How long had she been crying? Since the hall—in front of that monster?

A wave of revulsion washed over her. She hoped not.

All the certainties in her life suddenly felt fragile and meaningless. She had always thought of her family as the one constant. But even that was no longer true.

Erik undid the cloak at her neck and laid it on a stool. Then he worked on her clothes, gently removing them piece by piece, as she stood numbly in front of the fire. There was no lust in his gaze, only concern for her welfare.

When she was naked, he wrapped her in blankets and settled her among the furs on the pallet. Then he took a trencher and filled it with a little bit of every food available, before handing it to her. 'Eat, you will need your strength.'

Never had she felt this helpless before. It shook her to her core and made her question everything, including her own courage.

How many more times would her family be shattered by their own mistakes?

Their mother had lost them their status and wealth in Francia by falling in love with the wrong man. She had lost Valda to marriage and a merchant's life.

Was Helga lost, too?

'Do you think she will ever come back to us?' The possibility pierced her heart like a thorn.

'He must have lied to her. Why else would she stay with him?'

Brynhild nodded. 'She takes everyone at their word.' Sucking in a deep breath, she tried to steady herself, to focus on what needed to be done rather than the mistakes of the past.

Erik's voice was soothing as he said thoughtfully, 'Helga is clever. She will learn the truth eventually...maybe she already has...and was lying for his benefit? And he wouldn't let you speak any longer with her—there must be a reason for that.'

She looked at Erik and felt a pang of guilt at his concerned expression. He had fought by her side, had vowed to help in any way that he could. But things were going badly for her family and she could not imagine how this mess would ever be resolved.

She should cut this bond between them and quickly, before it hurt either of them any more than it had to. She had no right to delay him from beginning his own life, or to weigh him down with her own problems.

She had to set him free.

Erik couldn't think when she looked at him like that, as if she were begging for him to do something. To somehow make everything better.

But what could he do? He was a nobody and

his connection to Ulf had only made matters worse. He had to offer her something.

'We should make camp down at the base of the mountain tomorrow. In the fishing hut by the lake. Your mother and Tostig are sure to come past there and they may have help from Helga's father. If not, at least we will show Lord Rhys that we will not leave until he allows you to speak with her properly... Please eat.'

Brynhild looked away from him, staring at the wall as if it might offer her some better guidance.

'I mean it, Brynhild. Eat. This may be our last good meal in a long time and we will need our strength.'

His worry eased when she began to eat, shovelling the food down absently as if she were loading logs on to a pyre.

Reassured that she was at least taking care of herself, Erik stripped off his wet clothes and went to sit on the bed with her, dragging a blanket around his own shoulders as he settled down with his own meal.

'You should leave. Once Porunn and Tostig arrive, you can go with him. Begin your new life,' Brynhild said quietly, her eyes meeting his with a pained look.

He stopped chewing and forced himself to swallow the mouthful of bread and cheese so that he could answer her. 'You want me to leave?'

Her gaze returned to the wall, deliberately avoiding his. 'You have completed your task. You were meant to help me find Lady Alswn and bring her back to her brother. I was the one who decided against doing that and that made him angry. He might have let me at least speak with her if we'd done as he asked. It is my fault Helga is not free.'

He shook his head. 'That is not true. I agreed with your decision. You are not solely to blame. Besides, I do not think Lord Rhys has any intention of giving up Helga easily.'

Brynhild shrugged. 'Maybe, but if we had brought his sister here, he couldn't have refused us then.'

'I'm not so sure. He seems a hard man. I am not certain he would have forgiven them for their betrayal. We might have saved their lives by not bringing them here.'

'But you don't *know* that, do you?' she said angrily, finally looking at him with raw pain in her eyes.

'No. I don't,' he admitted grimly.

powerful house. I believe he hoped to wed his sister to the ruler of Seisyllwg…'

'He wanted his sister back, just so that he could marry her off to another?' Brynhild asked, shocked.

Sihtric nodded. 'I suspect he will now have to offer himself to the King's daughter.'

His reluctance in allowing them to speak with Helga made more sense to Brynhild. 'So, he has not been honest with Helga…'

Sihtric sighed. 'Probably not. Maybe I can offer an alliance with him?'

Porunn shook her head. 'No, Helga must be freed. This man is not worthy of her. He is without honour and she deserves better than that.'

Tostig took a deep breath and looked to Erik. 'Then you must make a deal with Ulf. The southern Lords refuse to deal with the Norse… But Ulf will—especially for more warriors to storm the fortress with. It may be the only way of ensuring Helga's safe return.'

'Nothing is guaranteed with Ulf!' Erik said.

Brynhild nodded. 'I agree.' She looked to her mother. 'But what choice do we have?'

Sihtric nodded, and turned to one of his men. 'Send a messenger to Jarl Ulf. Let him know we wish to discuss an alliance.'

'My Lord, you may wish to delay that order,' said a red-haired warrior who was striding towards them. 'Jarl Ulf's army has marched to the base of the mountain. He has heard of your arrival, and has come to discuss combining our forces.'

As they stood and walked away from the shelter, they saw Ulf flanked by thirty warriors—all of them on horseback—waiting patiently at the edge of the forest.

'Tell them they may approach,' said Sihtric. 'Let us hear what he has to say.'

The red-haired warrior ran back with his message and soon Ulf was riding into camp, an arrogant look in his eyes as he counted their numbers.

His numbers must have swelled considerably to be unbothered by their presence.

It was a disturbing thought.

When he saw Erik, a cruel smile curved slowly on his lips, before he looked away, waiting patiently for Sihtric to move forward to meet him, one Jarl to another.

Sihtric turned and spoke quietly to Porunn and Tostig. 'I will do what I must to secure Helga's release.'

Tostig sighed. 'He cannot be trusted. You may as well make an alliance with a serpent.'

'Please, do what you can, but Tostig is right… be cautious,' added Porunn.

Her face was impassive, almost blank, but Brynhild knew it was the mask her mother often wore before battle. Once she had told Brynhild, *'Give your enemy no blade to cut you with.'* Brynhild tried to do the same, refusing to look at Erik, in case it revealed her true heart.

'Heill, Jarl Ulf!' Sihtric said, stepping forward in acknowledgement.

Ulf slid down from his horse and walked forward to meet him halfway. 'Jarl Sihtric, I am surprised you came all this way for a bastard— and a girl at that! Are you becoming sentimental in your old age?'

To Sihtric's credit, he didn't even flinch. 'I am surprised you are here at all, Jarl Ulf. I thought your lands were south of Jorvik?' It was a light barb aimed at Ulf's loss of land to the Saxons.

'I have new prospects.'

'Indeed, I heard you had bought yourself an army?'

'A thousand men,' Ulf boasted.

'Still… I hear the Lord's fortress is impressive. I would rather negotiate with him for my daughter's release, than fight... He might be willing to concede more land. If that is what you want?'

'No,' snapped Ulf. 'Even if he agrees, he will only try to regain it later—as he did with my first settlement. It is only ash and ruin now.'

Interesting... He has no defensive base. Which is why he must attack with full force.

Sihtric nodded, but frowned up at the grey mist that ringed the mountain despite the full noon sun. 'So you mean to attack soon. It is not the best time of year—'

Ulf lifted his hand to interrupt him. 'It matters not. I will have everything from him or die in battle against him. All or nothing. No concessions, no negotiations.' Ulf's fist closed tightly. 'I *will* crush him.' His eyes were like chips of ice as he shifted to look at Erik. 'I am done making deals with lesser men.'

Sihtric cleared his throat, drawing Ulf's attention once more. He stared Ulf down, his voice as hard as stone, proving his worth as a war leader. 'What of my daughter?'

Ulf shrugged. 'Out of *respect* I offer you the opportunity to join with me in the attack. When we breach the second wall, you may send your warriors out to search for her. If Lord Rhys hasn't killed her, and she is still alive, none of my warriors will harm her...not if you fight with us.'

The last was said as a clear threat—it seemed that no care would be taken in ensuring Helga's safety unless they fought with him.

Sihtric appeared thoughtful, but said nothing. Brynhild imagined he had not considered an immediate battle, otherwise he might have brought more men. His three hundred warriors had been a display of strength to ensure quick negotiations. Waging war against a Welsh prince had not been his original plan.

Ulf gave an oily smile. 'I will compensate you for the men you bring to battle. Afterwards, we can share the spoils of victory. You may even build on my old settlement if you wish. It would be advantageous for you to have land across the sea, would it not? You could develop a direct trade route between your land in Ireland and Jorvik.'

Sihtric inclined his pale head. 'That would be advantageous for me. However, I would struggle to maintain a second settlement with such a great distance between them.'

Erik spoke up, ignoring the disgust on Ulf's face when he did so. 'Other Jarls have made similar mistakes in the past, Sihtric, stretching themselves too thinly. In the end they have lost more than they gained. Are you sure this is wise, Ulf?'

It was a deliberate reminder of Ulf's past failings and he bristled with indignation. 'What do you know of my business, *runt*? You should never have been born and even now you *still* follow me like a curse!' His voice rose with anger. 'Be careful on the battlefield, Erik. I may forget the blood that binds us.'

Erik stared him down. 'Nothing binds us.'

That caused Ulf to pause and he turned to Sihtric. 'I will have the sworn loyalty of every man who fights under your banner.'

'My men are bound to me and me alone,' Sihtric replied sternly. 'But none will go against you in battle, or I will cut them down myself.' Sihtric fixed Erik with a hard look and he shrugged in what might be considered acceptance, although Brynhild suspected it only meant he would not deliberately seek to kill him.

Regardless, it appeased Ulf. 'Then we have a deal?'

Sihtric's head tilted, as if he were listening to the counsel of the wind.

Brynhild remembered a saying he used to

favour, *'No one is a total fool if he knows when to hold his tongue.'* Sihtric had succeeded as a jarl because of his intelligence. He was a decent fighter and an expert with a bow. But his true strength lay in his intelligence and his eerie ability to know his enemies better than they knew themselves.

Tostig moved to his side and spoke quietly, so quietly, in fact, Brynhild had no idea what he had said.

Neither did Ulf by the flash of irritation that raced across his features. His horse pranced at the tight grip he held on its reins and he jerked them viciously to control it. 'Well?' he barked.

Sihtric nodded at Tostig and patted his shoulder. Finally, he looked to Ulf and spoke with a calm and reasonable tone. 'I have already sent a request for my daughter's immediate return. If the messenger fails to come back with instructions regarding her release, than we will join your camp by dawn tomorrow.'

'Mark my words, your messenger will not return,' snapped Ulf. 'The man murders all offers of diplomacy.'

Sihtric nodded. 'Then you will not have long to wait, Jarl Ulf. I have my own troubles back home—if I can avoid war, I will. It makes far more sense than throwing my men to the wolves without a firm guarantee of my daughter's safe return.'

'Until tomorrow then,' said Ulf with a nod while getting back on his horse. Then he and his men rode away. Sihtric called for one of his men.

'Deliver this message to Lord Rhys.' Sihtric looked coolly up at the mountain as he spoke, an unflinching determination in his tone. 'The time for negotiation is over. He must release my daughter before sunrise, or I will join with Ulf and kill everyone inside his walls. If Ulf should fail to breach his walls, or Helga is killed, I will return with twice this number and burn his fortress to the ground. His people will be enslaved and all value stripped from them. All memory of his name and kin will be forgotten. This is his last warning.'

The messenger sprang on to a nearby horse and galloped up the mountain path.

Porunn reached for Sihtric and gripped his forearm. 'Thank you, Sihtric.'

He squeezed her arm and smiled gently, the savagery of his earlier words forgotten in the blink of an eye. 'You do not have to thank me. Helga will always have my protection.'

He looked towards Brynhild. 'As will all your daughters. They have a special place in my heart.'

Sudden and unexpected tears choked Brynhild's throat and she inclined her head with a respectful nod before looking away, unable to hold his gaze for long, as raw emotion threatened to overwhelm her. Thankfully, Sihtric and Porunn walked a little way from her then and she was given a chance to catch her breath.

Sihtric was the only real father she had ever known and, even though they had never been tied by blood, she had still found his parting from them hard—although she would never admit it. She had told Erik that Valda was the one who had found it difficult—and she had, she'd wept and asked for him every day for months, too young to understand why he couldn't stay—and so she'd had to push down her own grief for her sister's sake.

Erik's hand slipped into hers. He understood her, deep down to the very marrow of her bones. He knew how Sihtric's words would shatter her, even though she'd never confessed—even to herself—how hard she had found his departure.

Erik just knew.

As she knew how hard seeing Ulf would have

been for him. How impossible the idea of ever fighting or swearing an oath under Ulf's banner would be for him. There was no way that Erik could ever form an alliance with his father. To do so would be an insult to his hard-won freedom.

It was time to say goodbye.

She turned to him and Erik's eyes locked with hers.

'Erik, thank you…for everything you have done… But I…'

Sihtric began ordering men loudly, and Brynhild glanced at him, distracted. When she looked back Erik was walking towards their ponies' shelter.

He was leaving.

It was understandable, but she couldn't bear for him to go without first letting him know how grateful she was to him… Not just for helping with finding Lady Alswn, but for…everything. For showing her kindness, pleasure and… love. She only wished things could have been different between them.

If only *she* could have been different.

Chapter Twenty-Three

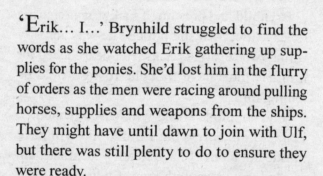

'Erik... I...' Brynhild struggled to find the words as she watched Erik gathering up supplies for the ponies. She'd lost him in the flurry of orders as the men were racing around pulling horses, supplies and weapons from the ships. They might have until dawn to join with Ulf, but there was still plenty to do to ensure they were ready.

Maybe it was seeing Sihtric again, but suddenly she felt as helpless as a child, with events and actions unravelling around her, while she could only stand and watch.

Sihtric had a sizeable force, otherwise Ulf would not have bothered inviting him to form an alliance. Still, it made her uneasy—would they really be able to guarantee Helga's safety if they attacked with Ulf? He was a cruel tyrant, a snake who couldn't be trusted. Did they really want to make him even more powerful?

But what choice did they have? Sihtric's force would not be enough to storm the fortress alone. If the messenger came back empty handed, then war was inevitable. Something about Lord Rhys's stubbornness made her question whether he would ever have the sense to release Helga, even if it were in his best interests.

Brynhild had presumed Erik was preparing to leave, but then she noticed he was actually filling two separate packs. Her heart ached for him. He must have thought Tostig would be joining him.

'I do not think Tostig will leave my mother, Erik… I am sorry, but I think you will have to ride out alone. I have to tell you…that I am so glad you were with me—finding the Lady Alswn, as well as the meeting with Lord Rhys. I couldn't have done any of this without you…' He didn't pause in his packing as she spoke and, frustrated by his lack of concern, she said sharply, 'What are you doing? I told you, Tostig—'

'I am coming with you.' His words were firm and pragmatic, as if he were volunteering to cook the evening meal, or fetch water, and not binding himself to the man he hated above all others.

'But…' she whispered and Erik let out a hissed curse and tossed the pack he'd been loading to the ground.

'*Damn* it, Brynhild! Do not tell me to leave you. I cannot!'

He stood there slightly breathless, staring at the ground now scattered with cooking utensils. He frowned at the mess in annoyance, his hands on his hips, refusing to look at her.

Was he mad?

She had thought this would be their last goodbye and now he was coming with them? To face a father he hated? To join with Ulf against an enemy he had no quarrel with?

Sensing the tension between them, the pony pranced a little and Erik settled her with a hushed word and a firm but gentle hand to her bridle. It was in complete contrast to how Ulf would have handled a similar situation. A reminder to Brynhild that you could always judge a person by how well they treated their animals.

'Erik,' she said quietly, reaching up to cover his hand with hers as it gripped the leather tightly. 'You owe me nothing.'

Scarred knuckles flexed against her cool

flesh and she shivered. She would miss him, that much was clear to her now, and she wondered how she would go on without him. But thinking of her own needs above his wasn't fair or right.

His hand, his nose, all the scars upon his body—each one was a reminder of how selfless Erik was. He would always sacrifice himself for others. *For her.*

But she could not allow that. Allow him to give up on his future happiness.

Not for her.

She would survive his loss. Endurance was her best attribute.

There was no hope for them. Better to end it here and now.

To set him free.

They wanted different things... *Didn't they?*

Although, at this moment, she was beginning to think she might even consider prancing around in a dress, if it meant they could stay together. But giving up her life as a shieldmaiden wasn't the answer, because it would mean giving up on Helga, too.

'I know...' He sighed quietly and a pulse on his shadowed jaw jumped.

He looked tired and unkempt, his hair long

and knotted from the number of nights he'd slept in the ponies' shelter. A rough beard had grown along his usually smooth jaw—usually he shaved it each morning with his knife, but he'd not bothered for days. The effect was devastatingly attractive, especially because she knew he looked this way because of his disappointment over her.

'So, there is no reason for you to come with us when we join with Ulf,' she reassured gently.

'But I *want* to!'

'But there is no need. Sihtric will help us. Tomorrow you can leave…you will never have to see Ulf ever again. Return to Jorvik or go wherever you wish. You do not need to help us any more.'

'I *want* to!' he said again, glaring at her with dark fury, as if she were the one being unreasonable.

'Why?' she whispered, shaken by the conviction in his eyes. 'You deserve to be free of him. I want you to be free of him…of us.'

Erik cursed. He was tired of being at war with himself. He could no longer stand it. The suffocating pain her rejection caused him was unbearable. But there was also the burning need to stay with her, to do all that he could to help. Anything. Even if it did mean joining with his father.

He wasn't Halfdan. He couldn't talk his way out of a situation with golden words and clever schemes. He had always been a man of action. The strength of his back and the sharpness of his blade were his only words. The only things he could offer a woman like Brynhild and he would give it all.

His loyalty, his sword arm, his life.

But he could never find the right words to tell her such things. To explain that even if she didn't want to be his wife, she would always have his heart.

The air became close and suffocating as he stared into her eyes and tried to think of how best to explain the reasons *why*. 'I didn't stand up for you once before and I've always regretted it...' he said, realising immediately that he was being a coward.

Brynhild sighed and looked away as if disappointed in him. 'That wasn't your fault. You were protecting me in your own way. Like how you protected that family and Halfdan,' she said, touching his burned hand that still held the reins by her head. 'Oh...' She sucked in a sharp breath, as if realising something for the first time, then shook her head, as if to clear it.

'What is it?'

'I just realised how much you thought you were protecting me back then, too. I know you said so, but I never think of myself as needing protection. But, it's just who you are, isn't it? You always put others first.' She smiled weakly, before adding firmly, 'You don't need to do that any more. Go, live your life. You deserve it.'

Erik's hand bit into the reins, clenching them tight, and the pony danced forward a step. Immediately Brynhild soothed it with a friendly stroke down its neck and their fingers brushed, causing goose pimples to shiver down his arm.

He couldn't let it end like this!

'I know you never wished to marry, Brynhild. But...you must know... I would never seek to *own* you.'

'What?' she asked, staring at him with wide eyes.

He nodded, rushing forward and praying that she would understand his garbled explanation. 'I have no family, no property, no family name to offer you. But... I know how important freedom is and I would never demand that you give me yours... However, if you allowed it—' he straightened his spine, trying his best to show some dignity, even if his words had none '—I would like to remain by your side. Fight and work with you...*love* you... Not as your neighbour, but as your partner.

'You wouldn't have to leave your mother and sister. I would stay on this mountain for the rest of my days, if that is what you wished... And I wouldn't expect you to marry me...' He sighed, suddenly losing some of his courage to a weak jest. 'But if you did...on our wedding day—you wouldn't have to wear flowers in your hair... Not if you do not want to. Although, at Valda's wedding I thought you looked very beautiful... with the ivy.'

'I...' She stared at him as if she had been struck by a bolt of lightning. 'Erik, if this is some strange extended apology...'

'No.'

'But...*why?*'

'Because I love you.'

If the mountain had fallen down around her ears, she would not have been any more surprised. Was Erik confessing that he loved her? *Loved her.*

The hurt of the past whispered doubt in her

ear like poison. 'Is it because… I was your first?'

Erik flinched, rearing back as if she had slapped him. '*Odin's teeth, woman!* No! It is because you are the *only* one for me.'

'But you wanted a wife, children…a home-maker. You cannot tell me you have changed your mind about such things!'

'I want *you*. If you love me back…then I would rather have a life with you than a life without you. I did want a family and if at some point in the future we had a child together you would make me the happiest man on Midgard. But—and listen well when I say this—the only thing I want and will ever want is for you to love me. I want you to be my family, with or without children. I have come to realise that my dream was to possess what I never had in my youth, a family. But I cannot steal or buy such a thing, even if I wanted to, and I do not want a home-maker, or a woman to breed with… I want you, *only you*, the fierce shieldmaiden Brynhild.'

'Erik, I never imagined anyone would *want* to marry me. I… I am not…as other women are,' she said weakly, wondering if this was some jest and if those hideous boys would leap out from behind the shelter and snort at her.

Which was ridiculous!

Brynhild straightened her spine and struggled to find the words. 'I am happy with who I am, but I cannot change—'

Erik glared at her. 'Do you accept me or not? Because even if you do not, I will still ride with you and fight by your side for Helga. I know in my heart that my destiny is to always be with you...if I cannot be your love, let me do this as your friend. Let me stay by your side.'

'Truly?' She took a step closer. 'You would do that for me? Stay?'

'I would.'

'Because...you *love* me?'

'Show mercy, Brynhild. Do you care for me or not?'

'Of course I do!' she replied.

He gripped her face in his hands and crushed his mouth against hers. The novice was now the master when it came to toe-curling kisses.

Pulling away reluctantly, she said, 'I do love you, Erik. I just never imagined you would feel the same way, or be willing to accept me for who I am.' She bit her lip, looking uncertain. 'I am not completely opposed to marriage or children... I just... I do not think I will be very good at it...in the traditional sense.'

'Then, we will not be traditional.'

She laughed and brushed a tender kiss against his lips. 'It appears you are my destiny after all.'

His head tilted thoughtfully. 'Tell me... What rune *did* you pick?'

'You will not believe me if I tell you.' She chuckled, her hands distractedly measuring the muscles of his biceps with a teasing squeeze. She wanted to make love to him right now, but they were surrounded by men rushing around the camp. Her mind began to whirl as she considered their options.

Erik frowned, unwilling to let it pass. 'I swear I will believe you...although I cannot promise I will not laugh.'

'Tyr.'

He looked down at his scarred hand. 'I am not one-handed like the God Tyr.'

'True.' She smiled. 'But Tyr also means warrior and sacrifice, remember? Tyr sacrificed his hand, by placing it in the jaws of Fenrir so that the gods could chain the great wolf. He knew the gods were deceiving Fenrir and that he would lose his hand because of it, but he did it anyway to protect them.'

'You think me like Tyr?'

'Better,' she said with a soft smile. 'Of course,

I always presumed it was talking about me. That I was devoted to my life as a shieldmaiden and would never marry…that a life alone would be my sacrifice.' She sighed. 'But that is not sacrifice, you taught me that. I am sorry for how I behaved…pushing you away like that. I was… afraid.'

'Of what?'

'Falling in love with you. Needing you…' she sighed, her face troubled '…needing you far more than you could ever need me.'

He laughed and she smacked his arm playfully. 'You *said* you would not laugh!'

'I am sorry,' he said, although his eyes sparkled with mirth. 'But look around you! Your family have caused men to go to war and break oaths. All for their love of you. I am a nobody, a man without a family name, I am—'

'Mine,' Brynhild said and he smiled, as she pressed her lips to his, murmuring between hot kisses. 'I love you, Erik bint al-Khusraw.'

'You remembered it?'

'Of course, it is your name.' Then she pulled away with a frown. 'Did I say it right?'

'You did. Although as I am male, it should be Erik ibn al-Khusraw. But honestly, I do not think it matters any more. I know who I am and, as you say, I am yours.'

Brynhild pulled him down into a passionate kiss, humbled that he would stay by her side and accept her for who she was.

They were both free.

Chapter Twenty-Four

'You will not be needing us for a while, will you?' asked Brynhild, a little breathless as she and Erik approached Porunn hand in hand.

Porunn's pale brow rose at the way they tightly held on to one another and then her smile widened with warmth. 'Why does this…' she said, casually sipping on her flask of mead and then pointing at their joined hands '…not surprise me?'

Brynhild frowned at her mother's odd sense of humour. 'I have no idea. *I* certainly was surprised, *by you and Tostig*,' she retorted with a raised brow of her own.

Porunn spluttered on her drink and had to cough awkwardly to clear her throat. 'That is… Well, I am not sure what *that* is. But you have made your point, Brynhild. Now, in answer to your question—no, you will not be needed. Sihtric is organising the men as we speak. We will stay here tonight and await the messenger.'

'Good, wait for us before deciding on anything. We will be back soon,' ordered Brynhild, before dragging Erik at a run towards the thick woodland at the base of the mountain.

They entered the thickest part of the forest, weaving through brambles and jumping over logs until Brynhild felt confident they were far enough away to not be seen or heard. Turning to Erik, she wrapped her arms around his neck and pressed rampant kisses across his face and neck.

Breathless from both the run and excitement, she tore open the belt of his tunic impatiently and let the leather drop to the ground, determined to see his glorious torso beneath. Erik obliged her by throwing off his tunics and tossing them aside, his hair flowing around his shoulders as he did so.

'Quickly… I need you,' she moaned, as she tried to kiss him at the same time as she took off her belt and boots. Then she laughed as she realised how ridiculous she looked, trying to hop from one foot to another while clinging on to Erik's shoulders. 'I will allow that gowns do have one advantage. They certainly make trysts in the woods far easier to manage—you just hitch up your skirts and get to it. I wonder if that's why men prefer women to wear the damn things.'

Erik smiled at her rambling. 'Let me help.'

He dropped to his knees in front of her. Took off her remaining boot and then unclipped her leg wraps. Unfurling them gently, he kissed her calf and the side of her knees once each one was revealed, slowing down the pace and building even more tension between them.

Warm dark eyes looked up at her and, biting her lip with anticipation, she undid the tie at her waist and pushed her trousers and braies a little down her hips. Immediately, his hands gripped the waistband and pulled them down. She stepped out of them briskly and kicked them aside. She was about to drag him up to her when she realised how close he was to the most intimate part of her. He took the back of her knee in his palm and gently hooked her leg over his shoulder.

'I have wanted to do this for so long,' he murmured, his warm breath causing butterflies to swarm in her belly. With gentle persuasion he opened her legs a little wider with kisses to her inner thighs.

Arousal surged through her body and she pressed her back against the tree trunk they had helpfully stopped in front of. She reached up above her head and held the branch to brace herself for the pleasure to come.

She gasped as with exquisitely slow licks he savoured the taste and feel of her. Moaning with pleasure, she wrapped both of her legs around his beautiful face and held on tightly to the branch above her head, grateful that her upper body was strong and that she could ride his clever tongue to the peak of her pleasure so freely. She cried out his name as she came, gasping and moaning as he worshipped her with his mouth.

On trembling legs, she stepped down from his shoulders. 'I think I need a lie down,' she jested, her body as light as a cloud and exhausted from his thorough attention.

'No, my love, I have you,' he reassured her, his voice husky and his eyes bright with arousal as he stood and undid the ties at his waist. Her breath hitched with renewed excitement as he cupped her bottom in his hands and lifted her feet off the ground, pressing her back against the tree trunk firmly. 'Wrap those beautiful long legs of yours around me, sweetling, and I will do the rest.'

With a blissful sigh she did as he asked, wrapping her limbs around him, clinging to his hips and shoulders as he thrust forward between her legs. He slid easily through her wetness and she rolled against him, delighting in the feel of his hard length inside her. Never would she have dreamt of trying this position with any other man, fearing that they might drop her. But Erik was powerful and lacked the capacity for false bravado. If he felt confident in taking her weight in his arms, then she would happily let him.

His thrusts were slow and deep, pushing her harder against the tree trunk, as his hips rocked rhythmically in and out of her, his groans of pleasure matching her sighs. She loved the feel of her weightless feet bouncing against the back of his thighs as he pumped into her with ever-increasing speed.

Another climax began to build once more and she gripped his shoulders and waist tightly with her limbs as she tried to match him thrust for thrust. Baring her teeth, she threw back her head and growled as she fell into another intense spiral of pleasure. Her fingers pinched into his broad shoulders tightly as waves of bright and exquisite joy rushed through her.

When he reached his own pleasure, he withdrew from her body quickly, his ragged breath hot against her neck as he spilled his seed. They stayed locked in each other's embrace until their breathing eased and then Brynhild dropped her legs and stood on wobbly feet.

Erik looked overwhelmed and elated for a moment as he stared at her and then with a happy laugh he dropped on to the forest floor, exhausted. Laughing, she joined him, her body also spent. Sitting on the forest floor beside him, she rested her head on his chest as he draped his arm around her shoulders.

'Erik, I know you want children and although I am not completely against the idea, I will need some time to…see it…for myself. It is not something I ever thought would happen for me. Do you understand?'

He nodded and brushed a soft kiss against her lips. 'I understand. I love you, Brynhild. You are my everything. My family, heart and future…whatever that may be. If for whatever reason we are not destined to have children, then I accept it gladly. I love you and I always will. You are what I need.'

Brynhild smiled at him. 'I love you, too, Erik, and I always will. You have made me the happiest woman to walk Midgard.'

'You swear it?' he asked, a mischievous smile on his face.

Brynhild tilted her head curiously. 'I swear it.'

Erik reached up and plucked something from her hair. When he showed it to her, she chuckled, 'It must have fallen from the tree.'

In his hand was a sprig of pale yellow-green ivy flowers, one of the few flowers to grow at this time of year.

'Are we married, then?'

Erik smiled, twirling the flower in his hand. 'In my mind we are.'

Brynhild sighed happily. 'Mine, too.' Promising herself to Erik was surprisingly freeing. There were no more questions or worries between them, no more uncertainty.

'Good.' Erik grinned at her, pure joy on his face, and her heart beat a little faster. Proud and glad to make him happy, especially after everything he had already suffered in his life.

'We should get back,' Brynhild said, regretfully. 'I am truly sorry about joining with Ulf. I will understand if you cannot do it. I will still love you and when Helga is free...'

'My place is by your side,' he said, kissing her nose. 'Now, come, *Wife*!' He smacked her bottom lightly with his palm and she jumped with a mixture of surprise and arousal.

'Remember, I can still flatten you on your back at any given time,' she warned.

Erik's smile broadened. 'Is that a promise?'

'Of course.' She laughed at the pleased look upon his face. She began to rise, taking his forearm in her grip and helping to lift him up at the same time. When her footing slipped in the damp earth, Erik held her tight until she was steady once more.

It reminded her of her feelings back in Jorvik. They were like a set of perfectly balanced trading scales—no matter the weight placed upon them, they would always adjust and carry the load of the other when needed. She was no longer alone with her burdens, she had Erik to help carry the load.

Bound together by love and friendship, Brynhild knew she would never be lonely again.

Love was no longer a duty. It was a blessing.

Epilogue

If only things had worked out better for her sister.

Brynhild had never been happier in her life. She and Erik had confessed their love for one another, and she knew in her heart that there was nothing that, together, they could not overcome. He loved her for who she was. A fierce shieldmaiden. And now Erik was a part of her and her family.

'Stop teasing me, you beast!' She laughed as she began to dress. They were about to head back to camp, but something in the corner of her eye stopped her.

'Brynhild!' called a soft feminine voice from behind them.

Erik and Brynhild stood motionless, staring at each other with shock and disbelief. Then Brynhild turned slowly to face the intruder.

'Helga?'

A sob escaped Helga's throat and she ran into Brynhild's open arms. Brynhild held her tight, hoping that this wasn't a dream. 'He let you go?' she asked, shocked.

'I ran away,' gasped Helga between tears.

'You clever girl!' Brynhild said, embracing her tighter with searing pride. She looked at Erik above her pale head and smiled. He smiled back—her joy was also his.

But then Helga pushed away from her arms, gripping them with surprising strength. 'We have to help him!'

Brynhild frowned. 'Who?'

'Rhys!'

'Are you mad? The man held you hostage! Why would you want to help such a monster?'

'He isn't a monster!' Helga cried. Then, with tears glistening in her light blue eyes, she took a deep breath and raised a defiant chin, and with a strength Brynhild had never seen before from her little sister, she said, 'I love him!'

* * * * *

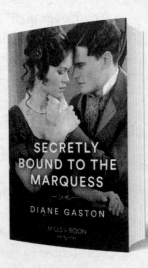

COMING SOON!

We really hope you enjoyed reading this book. If you're looking for more romance, be sure to head to the shops when new books are available on

Thursday 27th October

To see which titles are coming soon, please visit

millsandboon.co.uk/nextmonth

MILLS & BOON ®

Coming next month

THE LADY'S YULETIDE WISH
Marguerite Kaye

Then Eugene saw her. Petite, with a wild tumble of curly black hair pinned up in a top knot, clad in a dark dress with a white apron tied over the voluminous skirt. He told himself that it was merely the resemblance to a nurse's uniform that made him think it could be *her*, but his instant reaction was too visceral for him to be mistaken. He would never forget that one, fleeting memorable night.

He remembered the silky, springy texture of her hair when it tumbled loose over her shoulders. He remembered the olive tone of her skin, the voluptuous curves of her body, the full breasts, the flare of her hips. He remembered the roughness of her calloused hands on his skin. The tangle of their limbs, slick with sweat. The scent of their lovemaking mingling with the all-pervading smell of battlefield mud. The soft, muffled cry she made when she climaxed.

He remembered the flickering oil lamp in the makeshift wooden hut. The coarse sheets and inadequate blanket on the small bed. The open trunk, half packed with her belongings. He could vividly recall his last glimpse of her sitting up in the bed, the sheet clutched around her, as he picked up his clothing from the floor in the grey light of dawn. And that last, lingering kiss goodbye.

All this flashed through his mind in those seconds as he stood rooted to the spot, both entranced and shocked.

He had never thought to see her again, though their passionate night still haunted his dreams, nine months later. What the hell was she doing here? He had barely formulated the question when she turned. Heart-shaped face. Huge brown eyes under fierce brows. Full mouth which formed into an 'oh' of shock when she saw him. She stood perfectly still, absurdly rooted to the spot just as he was, the colour draining from her cheeks, before returning, colouring them bright red, as she hurried towards him, pushing him out of the door and back into the entranceway.

'Hello, Isabella,' he said, as if there was any doubt.

Continue reading
THE LADY'S YULETIDE WISH
Marguerite Kaye

Available next month
www.millsandboon.co.uk

MILLS & BOON

THE HEART OF ROMANCE

A ROMANCE FOR EVERY READER

MODERN

Prepare to be swept off your feet by sophisticated, sexy and seductive heroes, in some of the world's most glamourous and romantic locations, where power and passion collide.

HISTORICAL

Escape with historical heroes from time gone by. Whether your passion is for wicked Regency Rakes, muscled Vikings or rugged Highlanders, awaken the romance of the past.

MEDICAL

Set your pulse racing with dedicated, delectable doctors in the high-pressure world of medicine, where emotions run high and passion, comfort and love are the best medicine.

True Love

Celebrate true love with tender stories of heartfelt romance, from the rush of falling in love to the joy a new baby can bring, and a focus on the emotional heart of a relationship.

Desire

Indulge in secrets and scandal, intense drama and plenty of sizzling hot action with powerful and passionate heroes who have it all: wealth, status, good looks…everything but the right woman.

HEROES

Experience all the excitement of a gripping thriller, with an intense romance at its heart. Resourceful, true-to-life women and strong, fearless men face danger and desire - a killer combination!

To see which titles are coming soon, please visit

millsandboon.co.uk/nextmonth